Praise for Jill Shalvis

White Heat

"Shalvis firmly establishes herself as a writer of fast-paced, edgy but realistic romantic suspense, with believable and likable supporting characters and fiercely evocative descriptive passages." —*Booklist*

"Definitely a must read!" —The Best Reviews

"A unique and passionate story filled with adventure, danger, and emotion." —Romance Reviews Today

and other novels

"Irresistible heroes . . . downright flammable . . . so bleeping sexy, you'll break into a sweat."
—Stephanie Bond, author of *Whole Lotta Trouble*

"A lighthearted romantic romp. . . . Sit back, relax and just enjoy the heated tale." —*Midwest Book Review*

"Jill Shalvis delivers the goods." —*Affaire de Coeur*

"Fast, fanciful, and funny. Get ready for laughs, passion, and toe-curling romance." —*Rendezvous*

"Jill Shalvis is a breath of fresh air on a hot, humid night."
—The Readers' Connection

"Heartwarming, humorous, passionate, and sometimes profound." —Romance Reviews Today

SEEING RED

JILL SHALVIS

A SIGNET ECLIPSE BOOK

SIGNET ECLIPSE
Published by New American Library, a division of
Penguin Group (USA) Inc., 375 Hudson Street,
New York, New York 10014, USA
Penguin Group (Canada), 10 Alcorn Avenue, Toronto,
Ontario M4V 3B2, Canada (a division of Pearson Penguin Canada Inc.)
Penguin Books Ltd., 80 Strand, London WC2R 0RL, England
Penguin Ireland, 25 St. Stephen's Green, Dublin 2,
Ireland (a division of Penguin Books Ltd.)
Penguin Group (Australia), 250 Camberwell Road, Camberwell, Victoria 3124,
Australia (a division of Pearson Australia Group Pty. Ltd.)
Penguin Books India Pvt. Ltd., 11 Community Centre, Panchsheel Park,
New Delhi - 110 017, India
Penguin Group (NZ), cnr Airborne and Rosedale Roads, Albany,
Auckland 1310, New Zealand (a division of Pearson New Zealand Ltd.)
Penguin Books (South Africa) (Pty.) Ltd., 24 Sturdee Avenue,
Rosebank, Johannesburg 2196, South Africa

Penguin Books Ltd., Registered Offices:
80 Strand, London WC2R 0RL, England

First published by Signet Eclipse, an imprint of New American Library,
a division of Penguin Group (USA) Inc.

First Printing, May 2005
10 9 8 7 6 5 4 3 2 1

To Laura Cifelli,
editor extraordinaire

PROLOGUE

Twelve Years Ago . . .

There was nothing good about running laps, except for maybe the view of the guys in nylon shorts ahead of her. Actually, she liked the ocean air in her hair and face as much as the cute butts, but today Summer Abrams's thoughts were occupied elsewhere altogether. She was fantasizing about Kilimanjaro, Rio, the Amazon . . . all the places her bohemian father had taken her on his research travels over the years. Summer lived for those trips. "Only three weeks until we're out of school," she said with breathless glee.

Joe didn't say anything, so Summer looked around for him. He'd lagged behind, camera swinging awkwardly off his back with each plodding step. He always had his camera, but especially now that he was working on his final project and wanted the freedom to take a picture when it suited him. He was her best friend in the whole world and she slowed down to match his pace, inhaling deeply the tangy air from the Pacific Ocean only half a block away. She could smell day-old fish from the pier, kosher hot dogs from one of the lunch stands, and coconut-scented board wax. The last was from her own hands as she'd gone out surfing at the crack of dawn.

Much as she loved to travel, she also loved it right here. In her mind, Ocean Beach didn't deserve the reputation of being the redheaded stepchild of the San Diego beaches. Sure it had far more leather-skinned old-timers, starving students, and unemployed transients than say La Jolla, but it also had more character. For Summer, O.B. was everything, and life was good.

Change was coming, though. As a senior, Joe would be graduating soon, and then heading off to San Diego State College. Not Summer. She still had two years left in high school, which she hated to think about. She wanted to start her life too!

But no one deserved the ticket out of Dodge more than Joe Walker. At the moment he was attempting to take a picture of her and trying keep up at the same time, huffing and puffing like a locomotive in the clinging late May heat— the punishment for not taking his required regular physical education classes as a sophomore and junior. "You've been neglecting your cardio again," she said. "I bet you're not even carrying those energizing crystals I gave you."

"I'm fine," he panted, clearly not. He outweighed her by seventy-five pounds, none of it muscle.

"Admit it, you'd rather be eating a doughnut."

This got her first genuine smile from him since PE class had begun thirty minutes ago. His perpetually scruffy light-brown hair was plastered to his head, his face beet red and dripping sweat into his show-all eyes.

He had the biggest heart of anyone she'd ever met, and a fading bruise on his chunky cheek. A burst of deep worry worked through her at the thought of the things he suffered at home, things she'd never fully understand. Though her parents were so in love they often excluded her by accident, she'd never been treated with anything but kindness. "Let's walk."

"I'm fine, Red." He swiped his face on the front of his T-shirt.

"Hey, look. Fat Boy's gonna have a heart attack."

This from one of the four football players who'd just caught up to them. Forced to run in their pads by their coach, they slowed down to pass, three of them eyeballing Summer with leering grins.

Ignoring them, Summer smiled only at the fourth boy. He was Danny, the school's star quarterback. Tall, dark, and yummy, he was the cutest guy in the school, and she wanted him to take her to her prom so badly she could taste it. She'd been wearing her lucky charm bracelet all week in hopes that it would work its magic.

"Hi Summer," he said in a reverent tone, taking an elbow in the ribs for doing so. He gave an elbow back. "How are you doing?"

She felt a dopey grin split her face. "Good."

"Oh, jeez. Move." One of the others shoved Danny out of his way.

If Danny was the cutest guy in Ocean Beach, then Mitch was their village idiot. Still jogging backward, he sent a bunch of wet disgusting kissy noises toward Summer while two of his fellow idiots hooted and hollered. "What do you say, Flower Power Girl? You and me. Tonight. Ditch Fat Boy here and let me show you what a real guy does with his hands. And trust me, it won't be taking pics—unless you want me to."

"Shut up, Mitch," Joe said.

Summer glanced at him, silently begging him to let it go. But he never let anything go. Instead he wore his heart—

and temper—out on his sleeve for the world to stomp on. The last time he'd confronted Mitch and gang, he'd gotten a black eye and fat lip out of the deal. Little damage compared to what Joe's father could do on a drunken rampage, but still.

"Come on, Summer." Mitch had a nasty smile that made her skin crawl. "How about a little show'n'tell? I'll show you mine, you show me yours. And I don't mean your fancy little crystals either." He laughed uproariously over this until Joe growled and lunged forward, hands fisted, camera banging awkwardly around his neck.

"Joe, no," Summer cried, and hauled him back by the shirt.

"Joe, no," Mitch taunted, but Danny finally grabbed his friend and shoved him along, flashing a glance back at Summer with an apology in his eyes.

She smiled her thanks.

He smiled back.

It made her knees wobble, and for a moment as they kept running, she just stared after him, sending *ask-me-to-the-prom* thoughts his way. Then she turned to Joe.

He'd left the track.

"Joe? Where're you going?"

He didn't slow, and given the speed he'd taken on, he'd finally gotten his second wind.

"Joe, stop!" she called out to him. "We'll lose ten points if we ditch the rest of class!" She hesitated, because the ten point loss would put her into the B range and she prized her As, but this was Joe, and the misery weighing his shoulders down tore at her. "Damn it."

He raced down the little side street behind the school as if he'd turned into a marathon sprinter, and having never seen him move so fast, Summer followed.

If Joe realized she was following him he gave no clue, just continued to haul ass as if his life depended on it. The muggy heat seeped up through the asphalt into her running shoes as they slapped on the ground with each step. They were at the heart of O.B. now, passing the liquor store where they bought their sodas, the five-and-dime where she purchased lip gloss and magazines when she had money, and then her favorite burger joint, next to the new trendy restaurant with the neo-scripted name flashing on its front. "Joe? Wanna get a drink?"

He turned onto Newport Avenue.

"Or not," she muttered as they passed a tattoo parlor offering custom tattooing in the "San Diego tradition," whatever that meant, before the street ended at the beach. Joe turned onto a tiny little side street Summer knew well because her mother and aunt owned one of the old warehouses here, where they kept the stock they hadn't yet put into Creative Interiors, their downtown beach furnishings and design store.

She and Joe often sneaked into the cool basement on a hot day just like this one. If they had any money, they'd buy a frozen yogurt first, then come here to talk for hours. More recently she'd met Danny here for more than just a frozen yogurt.

The place was a tall, old, secret haven, and she knew when Joe ran around to the back of the warehouse that he'd remembered that her father often sneaked away and came here as well.

Tim Abrams coveted his privacy, Summer thought with a fond smile. Her father loved to climb up into the open loft above, where he'd gaze out the small window overlooking the city and the Pacific Ocean as he wrote. Here, he always claimed, he could cleanse his aura, and lose himself in his stories.

But right now it was Joe, and *his* need to lose himself that worried Summer. She followed him through the back door, down the long, steep steps to the basement, watching as he navigated around the large wood beams and stacks upon stacks of boxes of stock.

He flung himself to the small mat they often sat on. Arm over his eyes, he lay silent except for his ragged breathing.

The only light came from a small bulb over their heads. A hazy cloud of dust hovered in the still air. "Joe?"

"I want to be alone."

Her father's new orange tabby kitten appeared and wound her warm body around Summer's ankles, bumping her head against Joe's hand. Socks had one green eye, one brown, and four white paws, hence her name. She never gave up until the human she'd targeted paid attention to her. Face still covered, Joe caved, stroking the kitten beneath her chin until a loud rumbling purr filled the room.

Summer's wobbly legs needed a break so she sat at Joe's hip, hugging her knees. "If you wanted to be alone, why did you come here?"

He didn't answer and she sighed. She could feel his misery, and she ached for him. "I'm sorry, Joe."

"For?"

For your mother being dead. For having a horrible, cruel father. For hating school. For being different. "For whatever's bugging you."

He let out a rude snort. "Go away, Summer."

That he used her real name instead of his nickname for her, Red, scared her. "Look, jogging is stupid, okay? I'm only good at it because—"

"It's not the jogging."

"Mitch's a big jerk. He's just acting that way because I wouldn't go out with him—"

Joe dropped his arm from his face and stared at the ceiling. "This isn't about you for once. Imagine that."

Shocked, she shut her mouth.

"Mew."

Summer ignored the kitten and absorbed the pain of Joe's words. He'd never, ever, said anything hurtful to her in all their years of friendship. They lived next door to each other. They walked to and from school together. They studied, they listened to music, and late at night, when his father came looking for blood, usually Joe's, she waited up to watch him climb out his window and into hers, where she'd pretend not to see the suffering in his eyes because he hated her pity. She'd swallow the urge to hug him tight, instead lighting a soothing incense and tossing him her extra pillow and blanket. Then he'd silently curl up on her beanbag chair to get some safe sleep.

Now she stared at her closest friend in the world, the person she trusted above all else, a ball of hurt in her chest because he was shutting her out, snapping at her when all she was doing was trying to help. "Joe—"

"I said go away." He reached into his pocket and thrust her amber crystal back at her.

She stared down at it. She'd given it to him for its gentle and nurturing nature, but he hadn't allowed it to work. Worse, he'd never sent her away before, never, and stunned, she stood up. "When you're not so grumpy, you know where to find me."

"Yeah. With Danny."

"There's nothing—" But she broke off, because the truth was she had a huge, gut-tightening, heart-melting crush on Danny. She did. She wanted to write his name in her notebook all day long, with little hearts circling it. She wanted to gobble him up.

But that was different from her love for Joe, so very different. "Joe—"

"Don't deny it."

Embarrassed, she backed away from him. "I'll be waiting for you."

"Uh huh."

She had no idea why he was taking this out on her. It was cruel and unfair, but she knew he wasn't either of those things.

"Summer?"

She whipped around at the sound of Danny's voice. Still wearing his football gear, he stood at the bottom of the stairs, unable to see Joe lying on the floor because of the supporting wood beam and piles of boxes. Grinning, he held up a condom. "I followed you, though I lost you at the last turn. Figured you'd come here. Look what I have. We won't have to stop this time."

Joe jerked upright, eyed what Danny held between his fingers, and shot Summer a look filled with so much all in one glance that she nearly fell over with it. Before she could open her mouth, he'd vaulted to his feet, the camera banging against his side as he leapt at Danny, the back of his T-shirt still drenched with sweat.

Danny cried out with surprise, and both boys toppled to the floor, rolling as they fought. Terrified, Summer moved in, thinking that Danny, the leaner, tougher, and much more athletic of the two, would kill Joe. "Stop it!" The camera shattered into pieces at her feet. "Oh my God, *stop*! Danny, no—"

But Joe held his own, landing a punch to Danny's stomach. He pulled his fist back again but Summer grabbed his arm. "No! Joe, please, stop!"

He didn't want to, she could feel a shocking violence rolling off him in waves, and she knew she had to tell him the truth. "I like him. Okay? I like him a lot. Are you listening?" she sobbed. "*I* brought him here last time, *I* was the one who wished we'd had the condom."

He went utterly still with shock, and because she held his arm, was helpless to the solid, powerful blow Danny dealt him, right in the jaw. Summer threw herself over Joe's body so that Danny couldn't hit him again, but the protective gesture was not only too little too late, but also unnecessary because Danny sagged back and clutched his stomach. "What the fuck is his problem?"

But Summer couldn't answer, she was staring in horror at the top of the stairs. *"Oh my God."*

Both boys whipped around. Their eyes widened in shock.

From around the edges of the poorly hinged door drifted long fingers of smoke, writhing in the air like flying deadly snakes.

The warehouse above them had caught fire.

Chapter 1

Joe Walker couldn't believe his bad luck. He lay flat on his belly in an inch of cold, mucky water, surrounded by grime and soot and the thick stench of smoke, all of which was slowly permeating through his coveralls, his skin, and the mask he wore to protect his lungs. Just another day at the spa.

Or a day in the life of a fire marshal who worked for MAST, the Metro Arson Strike Team out of San Diego.

The fire had occurred only hours before. Now he turned on his camera, clicked the shutter, checked the digital display to make sure he had what he wanted, and blew a speck of dirt off the lens.

Firefighting was a dirty business. But inspecting the damage, searching for burn patterns, putting together the story of what had happened and ruling for natural causes or arson, was dirtier.

Even so, he'd never expected to be *here* again, in the very basement of the warehouse that had so irrevocably changed his life twelve years ago. It was just past the crack of dawn—he stifled a yawn as he glanced at his watch—far too early to think about the past.

Damn he hated getting up before the sun, but given that the majority of arson occurred at night, early mornings were a common fact of his life. A common fact that never failed to annoy Cindy.

"Being the lover of a firefighter was supposed to be exciting," she'd murmured as he'd crawled out of her bed at four a.m.—an hour ago now. "Not utterly exhausting."

He opened his mouth to correct her—he'd gone from firefighter to fire marshal two years ago—but she'd run a hand down his torso, her eyes going molten as she did.

That she found him so desirable still stunned him. He'd never told her that he'd been the fat loser all through school, or that he couldn't have gotten laid if he'd begged, a phenomenon that had lasted until the sheer physical labor of firefighting had gnawed away at his baby fat.

"Come back here." Her soft voice had floated on the predawn air as he'd stumbled through her bedroom trying to find his clothes.

"I can't."

"Of course you can." She opened her legs, danced her fingers between them.

His tongue had nearly fallen out but he buckled his belt and added his gun and pager to it. "Cindy. I have to go."

"Fine." She turned over, exposing a mouth-watering ass as she stretched for a pillow, which she then aimed at his head. "But don't even think about coming tonight. Figuratively or literally."

He'd caught the pillow an inch from his face and sighed as he'd grabbed his shoes on the way out. After dating her for the past two months, he knew he had to give her a break. Nearly half of their overnights had been interrupted.

He didn't know how to tell her that the stats weren't

going to get better. Fine as her body was, and as much as he enjoyed it, he lived and breathed his work.

Except today. He couldn't believe he was back. *Here.* Drawn now by something beneath the shelving unit, he put both his past and Cindy out of his mind and inched in a little closer.

There were no windows in the basement to let in the early sun. The electricity had been blown in the fire, which might or might not explain why the overhead sprinklers hadn't gone off. There was nothing but the narrow beam from his flashlight guiding him as he followed a curious burn pattern underneath the large, heavy, unbudgeable metal shelving unit. He fired off a few more pictures, then swung the camera around his neck to lie against his back while he studied a particularly interesting find with his light.

"Anything?" his partner asked from behind him, still standing straight up, and probably nice and dry to boot.

"Yeah, I've got—" Joe broke off as his flashlight suddenly highlighted two glowing eyes only inches from his outstretched hand. Accompanying those feral eyes came an unwelcoming hiss. *Shit.* Jerking upright, he smashed his head into the metal shelf above him.

"What the hell is that?" asked Kenny from his helpful perch five feet back.

Joe waited until the stars faded from his vision, but his heart still raced, pounding his ribs as he eyed whatever was currently eyeing him right back. "I'm not sure."

After the historic bushfires in the entire San Diego area two years ago, which had drawn rabbits, raccoons, deer, and even mountain cats into the suburbs, the gleaming, sorely pissed off gaze could belong to anything.

And nothing he wanted to be this close to.

"Well, don't get bit," Kenny said.

"Thanks." Joe watched the animal as it watched him. Neither of them moving. "Helpful advice."

"I try."

Joe shifted his flashlight over the cornered animal, but it didn't help because the shallow water covering the floor made a crazy reflection. "I can't see."

"Who needs to see, it's growling like a wild possum on a bad PMS trip. Get the hell out of its way."

"I think it's hurt." And Joe had spent enough years growing up as the underdog to be unwilling to just leave it. "Do you think you could come closer than the two miles you're standing back, and give me a hand?"

"I have a healthy fear of rabid, hissing animals."

"We were just hanging off the roof staring a thirty foot fall in the face as we studied the loft and you didn't blink, but a little animal scares you?"

"I didn't get enough love as a child. Are you sure it's little?"

Joe eyed the decidedly not-so-little silhouette hunched over and miserable. "It's shaking like a leaf, does that count?" But since he couldn't see its teeth, he still didn't move. "Come distract it so I can back out of here."

Into Joe's peripheral vision came Kenny's two boots *not* caked in muck like Joe's. Kenny's boots rarely got dirty. In fact, Kenny rarely got dirty. It was just one of the strange little mysteries of life.

"I'm going to scare it out from the back," Kenny said. "So watch yourself."

"Wait." Joe began to scoot out from beneath the shelving unit, his life flashing before the eyes he didn't want to have scratched out. "Okay now," he said, dirty water dripping off him.

Kenny banged his flashlight against the metal, and with a screeching howl, the hissing thing zipped out from beneath the unit and into the inky blackness of the basement.

Both Joe and Kenny whipped around, shining their twin beams across the wet, dank floor to the far corner, on the large, orange . . . cat. She had white paws and a deep scratch down one side of her face, which held one green eye, and one brown.

"A cat." Kenny shook his head, a few drops of dirty water marring his glasses. He removed them and wiped the lens with a handkerchief he pulled from his pocket. "A *damn* cat."

Filthy, wet, and overheated, Joe stripped out of the top part of his coveralls, letting the sleeves and torso hang off his hips. He wore a sweat drenched T-shirt beneath, but he left that on as he stepped closer in disbelief. *"Socks?"*

Unhappy and wet, the cat shook first one paw and then another, glaring at him the whole time.

Hunkering down, Joe outstretched his fingers. "Here, Socks."

Above them the building rumbled ominously. He knew there was still an entire firefighter crew out there clearing hot spots and checking the soundness of the structure. Everyone knew he and Kenny were down here.

The ground shook again.

Kenny and Joe stared at each other. Kenny pushed up his glasses and gestured to the stairs. "Let's hit it."

"Yeah, but we'll be back later."

"Why, what did you find?"

"A rainbowlike sheen to the water beneath the unit."

They both knew that could indicate an accelerant, such as gasoline or paint thinner. Since there was nothing in the basement but boxes of stock for a furnishings shop, the appearance of such a chemical was automatically suspicious.

Or was that simply because Joe had personally been in this very spot for another fire entirely? One that had ended in a terrible, tragic death?

Either way, he and Kenny would know everything there was to know by the end of their investigation. If it had been arson, they'd uncover it. Conviction, however, was another story entirely. That was because arson was a sneaky bastard of a crime, usually done quietly in the dead of the night, a solo act more fervent than masturbation. The evidence never lied, but being able to actually prove motive and cause, not to mention tying a suspect to the scene of the crime, had often proved frustrating.

Over the years, Joe had learned the hard way that the key to the job was detachment and an unflappable composure. But this case would test both because he had memories to battle here as well, memories strong enough to begin a low throbbing at the base of his skull.

Socks had been just a kitten on that long ago day when everything had gone so terribly wrong, costing Tim Abrams his life, costing Summer Abrams the rest of her adolescence, costing Joe the only bright spot in his life at the time.

But whether this cat at his feet was Socks or not, Joe couldn't leave her down here, hurt and terrified. "Here kitty, kitty."

"I wouldn't," Kenny warned as Joe reached for her, and sure enough, the cat turned into a wild thing in Joe's arms, hissing and spitting, using both paws to swipe down his chest, making him hiss as well. He didn't look down to see if the damn feline had yanked out his heart or if it only felt like it, because at that moment the building shuddered wildly.

Both their radios squawked to life. "Walker, Simmons. *Get out*," came a booming voice in stereo. "Do you copy? Roof is going to collapse. *Get out now.*"

"Copy," Kenny yelled as dust rained over them. He snatched up their evidence-collecting bag and Joe's flashlight. "Let's beat it."

Joe still had his arms full of pissed-off feline. Chest burning from the scratches, he shook his head when Kenny turned toward the stairs that led up through the burned shell of the warehouse. "Not that way."

"It's our exit, Walk. Time to get off this train."

"There's a back door, and if it wasn't destroyed in the fire, it's a faster way out."

"If we die down here, I'm taking that cat to hell with me," Kenny vowed, following so close on Joe's tail he could feel him breathing down his neck.

"We're not dying, not today." The dust and dirt falling on them turned to a cakey mud on Joe's drenched body as they ran down a narrow hallway to a second set of stairs, leading up.

The set he and Summer had always used when they didn't want to be seen.

"You weren't here when they fought the fire last night," Kenny said breathlessly as they began to climb the rickety wood steps. "And we haven't seen the blueprints yet. How did you know—"

"Been here before. Keep moving—"

From behind them came another foreboding tremble, and everything around them began to shake as if they were in an earthquake.

Not an earthquake, Joe knew, just a warehouse that had taken more punishment than it could withstand. He hoped to God everyone was off the roof because this sucker really was going to collapse.

It wouldn't be the first time. Horrifying visions rushed him. Summer screaming for her father, as she raced up the other set of stairs to the main floor, yanking open the door before he could stop her, allowing the smoke and fire to overcome her . . . He'd torn up after her, through the licking, hot flames, just as the roof collapsed through the center. He'd stood there in the blinding smoke and dust, frantically yelling for her before finding her trapped in the rubble, unconscious and bleeding. He'd dragged her outside, next to where Danny had escaped to without trying to help.

The fire department had come that day, and so had an ambulance, but it'd been too late to save Tim Abrams from the collapsed loft. It'd taken Summer two days to awaken from her head injury, and after a two-week hospital stay, during which time she'd missed her father's funeral, she'd left town for the summer to join a river guide company in Colorado.

Joe hadn't seen her again, she'd made sure of it. She'd taken her high school equivalency test that fall, graduating two years early, hiring on at a different expedition company after that. She hadn't entered San Diego State with him as planned. In fact, they hadn't exchanged a single word since that terrible, stupid fight in the basement.

Now he and Kenny charged up the last few steps, shoved open the door to the outside, and stepped into the early morning salty sunshine. In the parking lot in front of them were two fire engines and an assortment of fire personnel, all visibly relieved to see them.

"Everyone accounted for?" Joe asked their Chief, who nodded just as a huge, thundering crash had them all whipping around in time to see a section of the main roof cave in, shaking the ground beneath their feet.

"Jesus," Kenny muttered, and removed his glasses with a shaking hand, leaving him standing there with a perfectly clear imprint of the lens on his filthy face.

The rest of the building stood firm, though looking a bit like an accordion on one side. All around them firefighters were still checking the perimeter and the hot spots. A cop was helping to keep looky-lous at a distance and out of harm's way, and on a summer's morning near O.B. there were many of them, in a variety of dress. Joggers, construction workers, students, bums, rich patrons of the galleys nearby . . .

In the midst of all the chaos, Joe strode over to his city-issued truck, opened the driver's door and set the cat on the seat. "Don't tear up anything."

Socks gave him her back and stuck her tail in the air.

Damn thing didn't remember him, a reminder that when it came to his past, not many did. He slammed the truck door and put his hand to the front of his T-shirt, which not only came away muddy, but sticky with the blood now flowing freely from his deep scratches. "Nice," he said to Socks through the window, and wiped his hand on the thighs of his coveralls before flipping through his clipboard.

"You looking for the owner info?" Kenny asked, coming up behind him. His face was already clean. Joe had no idea how he did that. "Two sisters," Kenny said, consulting a sheet of paper. "You going to call, or should I?"

"I'll do it." Joe glanced at the names, though he already knew what he'd see. Tina Wilson and Camille Abrams— Summer's aunt and mother.

"Chief says he spoke to both in the middle of the night

when the fire was still raging. They mentioned they have a vagrant who sometimes sleeps here. The old guy's been known to leave odd things, or to try to start a campfire. Camille Abrams was reportedly pretty shook up, and didn't stay long. But I'm surprised she hasn't made another appearance in the light of day."

Joe knew exactly why Camille had been shaken up, and why she hadn't made another appearance. She'd lost her husband here. With a heavy heart, he took his cell phone out of his pocket and dialed the number listed. She answered on the first ring. "Mrs. Abrams, this is—"

"Is this about the warehouse?" She sounded anxious. "Did you find my cat? She was there with me last night and then vanished, and finally I had to leave without her, but I've been worried sick—"

"I have Socks."

"Oh, thank God. How'd you know her name?"

"I'm Joe Walker, Mrs. Abrams. Do you remember me?"

"Joe Walker . . ."

"I lived next door to you growing up."

Silence.

He could have asked her if she remembered him sneaking into Summer's window to escape his father's fists. On the worst nights, Camille had brought him homemade healing tea and toast with cinnamon and extra butter. His first experience with basic kindness from a woman, and his first comfort food.

"Joe Walker?" she repeated softly.

"I'm a fire marshal now," he told her. "I'm at your warehouse. With Socks." If she gave any indication she found this as unsettling as he did, she gave nothing away. "The cat's safe in my rig, though she appears to have a cut on her face. Your building—"

"I'll have to get her to the vet."

"Yes. Your warehouse—"

"I know. It burned again." Her voice quivered, giving her away. So she did remember. "No one died this time."

"No, ma'am," he said gently, wishing he'd taken a seat to make this call because his legs felt a little wobbly. Whether from his own close call or the memories, he had no idea.

"Thank you, Joe."

He hadn't done much, but he wished he could. "Mrs. Abrams—"

She clicked off.

He stared down at the phone. "Yeah, and how are you? Me? Oh, I'm good. And Summer? *Jesus.*" The ball of memories lodged in his throat, he shook his head. "You fool."

"So, fool. Who's Summer?" Kenny handed over a first-aid kit, presumably for the scratches burning a slow path of fire down his chest.

"No one."

Kenny eyed him thoughtfully. He was nine years older than Joe's thirty, and he believed those years gave him license to know everything. They'd been partners for two years, and had grown close as brothers. Bickering brothers. That suited Joe fine, as he'd never had a smooth relationship in his life, starting with Summer. He rubbed his chest, not sure if it was the scratches or his heart that ached like a son of a bitch.

"You okay?" Kenny finally asked.

"Yeah. Why?"

"You look pale. Want to sit?"

"Do *you*?"

"I'm not pale."

"I'm fine."

"Okay," Kenny said, sounding unconvinced.

"I *am*."

"Whatever you say."

A car pulled into the parking lot. A bright blue VW Bug with the windows down and U2 blaring out of the speakers. When the engine turned off, silence descended everywhere but within Joe, because he knew.

His heart took off again, just as Summer got out of her car. He'd heard about her career leading rafting, hiking, and biking treks all over the world for some big expedition company, but he hadn't heard she was back. Why would he? He no longer lived next door to her mother's house, and she'd never sought him out.

She stood there by the Bug, eyes covered in mirrored shades, head turned toward the warehouse. Twelve years ago she'd been a beanpole, long and too thin, with waist-length auburn hair Joe had thought looked like pure fire.

Now she wore some sort of gauzy sundress that clung to her body, still long and lean, but graced with the curves of a full grown woman. Her hair was reined in. Sort of. It was piled on top of her head in a careless, precarious knot with strands escaping to brush over her bronzed shoulders. The eyes he knew to be a soft, dreamy jade were hidden, but seemed to take everything in with disbelief, and even from his distance of twenty-five feet, he could see her breath catch.

Was she remembering the last time she'd been here? The smoke and flames and sirens wailing in the distance, in tune to her own screams?

She turned and unerringly caught his eye, and her sorrow shimmied through him so that he nearly staggered. He actually took a step toward her, with some idea of trying to comfort her, but a polite smile crossed her lips.

And if he'd thought Socks's scratches had dug deep, it was nothing to this.

She didn't recognize him.

Jesus, what a day. It wasn't often he felt eighteen again, leaving him stupid, pathetic, and yearning for a doughnut, but she'd done it to him in a blink.

"Who's that?" Kenny wanted to know.

"Summer."

"Summer, the No One?"

"In the flesh."

At his flat tone, Kenny looked at him. "You know her."

"She's related to the owners."

"But you *know* her."

"We grew up next door to each other," Joe said.

"Ah. She's the one you were in love with. The one who loved you back but only as a friend."

Joe shot him a long sideways look and shook his head. "Thanks for the recap."

Kenny placed a hand on his shoulder. "No problem, buddy."

Having clearly decided the two of them were the closest authority figures, Summer shut her car door and started toward them, marching into Joe's world the way she'd once marched out of it; like a wild, magnificent, deadly twister, leaving awe and destruction in her wake. Her hips swung, the soft material of her sundress molding to her thighs and legs, her breasts.

Joe let out a grim smile as his heart skipped a beat, then turned his back, the burning scratches providing a welcome distraction. "I don't want to do this. Not now."

"I'll see what she needs," Kenny said.

Joe nodded gratefully, and Kenny moved to head her off at the pass.

Joe got into the MAST truck, and while stripping out of the coveralls, glanced at an equally miserable cat.

Socks hissed.

Joe sighed. "Yeah. I know just how you feel."

Chapter 2

Life was short, so grab it by the balls and run.

This was Summer Abrams's motto. As a result, she'd scaled mountains, traversed canyons, and kayaked down rapids not meant for humans.

She'd survived it all, and more.

But standing right here in the spot where her world had once fallen apart just may kill her. At the sight of the charred building, the confusing circle of fire vehicles, fire-fighters and cops milling around, her breathing quickened. Number one warning sign of a pending panic attack. She couldn't control it, being here brought her back.

She could only imagine how her mother must have felt standing in this very spot. Once upon a time, Camille and Tim Abrams had been everything to each other, sharing an all-inclusive love that had begun when they'd been still in school. Their bond hadn't required a child, but Summer had come along anyway, when Camille had been only eighteen. She and Tim had accepted their fate, arranged a quickie marriage on a beach in Mexico, and for the next sixteen years, life had been bliss for them, pure bliss.

Until the first warehouse fire.

Summer knew her mother still missed her father, so

much so that she'd never really invested herself emotionally again. There'd been men, but nothing deep, nothing
emotional, a phenomenon that included the relationship she
had with her own daughter.

Summer knew she couldn't have prevented what had
happened that long ago day, no one could have, but she still
felt responsible. If only she and Joe had gone inside the
warehouse sooner, if they'd only smelled the smoke earlier,
if only . . .

So many *if onlys*.

Her chest tightened with anxiety. *Second warning sign.*
She breathed through it because she would absolutely not
have a panic attack now. She hadn't had one in years. Of
course she hadn't come back to this very spot either, but she
could do this.

To prove it, she smiled with remarkable calm at the firefighter approaching her. He was covered in a fine layer of
dust so that she couldn't tell if his hair was blond or gray
but oddly enough his face was perfectly clean. He wore
black-rimmed glasses that magnified his light blue eyes and
friendly smile. She let go of the lucky crystal in her pocket
and held out her hand. "I'm Summer Abrams, the daughter
of one of the owners of this property."

"Kenny Simmons, fire marshal, from the Metro Arson
Strike Team." He pushed up his glasses. "I'm sorry for the
loss."

"It's a total goner then?"

"Most likely. We'll know in a little bit."

Her stomach sank to join her heart at her toes. She felt
sick for her mother and her aunt. Unable to tear her gaze
from where the roof had collapsed, she kept seeing the original warehouse as it had stood twelve years before. Hearing
her own screams, inhaling the smoke—

That was all she had, all she could pull out of her memory. The rest was blank, like an unpainted canvas. She'd lost it all when she'd been hit by the falling debris, then trapped there. She didn't remember getting out, she remembered nothing beyond that first lick of fear at the top of the stairs.

She put a hand to her chest, as if she could pump her own air into her deflated lungs, but she couldn't. Damn it, this always happened when she thought about the fire, or was enclosed in a crowded space. There were too many people around here, standing too close—

The fire marshal's brow furrowed in concern as he moved in closer. "Do you need to sit down?"

"No, really. I'm good." She straightened her shoulders and sent him the I'm-in-charge smile, the same one that allowed her to run crews on some of the fastest rivers and steepest mountains in the world with unquestionable authority.

What she wouldn't give to be on a trip right now, out in the wilderness, with only a handful of people around. In her element. In control. Where life was lived in the moment, with no time for thoughts of the past, and no need for thoughts of the future.

Life was too short for either. "My mother said you found her cat."

"We did. Feisty thing, too. She's over there, in that truck. I'll go get her—"

"Oh, no, that's okay, I can do it." Needing to keep moving, needing to get away from here, she waved her thanks over her shoulder and walked toward the truck to which he'd pointed. The driver's door was open, so she came around and peeked in, and *hello,* found another fire official. This one sat behind the wheel, shirtless, his coveralls shoved low on his hips, holes torn in each knee, a tube of antiseptic in one hand and a fistful of Band-Aids in the other, eyeing Socks with a healthy mistrust.

. From her perch on the passenger seat, Socks eyed him back.

Then the man craned his neck toward Summer and said the oddest thing. "Are you okay?" he asked in such an intimately low voice suggesting such intimacy and familiarity, that she blinked. "Sure," she said, and shrugged.

He just watched her. She couldn't help but watch him back. He was filthy, but he had an extremely nice chest. Sinewy, tanned, with a spattering of hair from pec to pec that wasn't too light, wasn't too thick, but juuuust right. The Goldilocks in her wanted to smile. After all, she loved men, all shapes and sizes, but this man . . . yum.

Unfortunately, all that extremely decent male flesh also sported a series of deep, nasty-looking scratches that appeared to be Socks's doing. "Ouch," she said in sympathy.

His light, light brown eyes, with the impossibly long, dark lashes met hers with . . . amused cynicism?

She went still. Wait. *Wait.* She knew that slashing scar above his eyebrow. She knew that dimple on the right side of his mouth. She knew that wry, slow smile, it had always made her day. "Oh my God. *No.*"

He just kept looking at her.

.She took closer stock. Shaggy sun-kissed brown hair, still apparently untamable in thick waves framing his face. Light stubble over his lean jaw—*lean* jaw. *That's* what was so different, besides the years that had turned him from boy to man.

He'd lost his softness, every single bit of it, coming out with a rangy, leanly muscled build that spoke of long days in physical labor. He looked liked he'd lived each of the twelve years that had passed, every single one of them, well and hard. There were fine laugh lines fanning out from his eyes, and laugh lines around his mouth too. The thought made her heart leap. He'd smiled, laughed, and often. *Oh I'm so glad,* she thought, and felt the grin split her face. "Joe Walker."

"So you do remember."

"Of course I do." She laughed, because just looking at him made her feel young and carefree, but the smile faded away when he didn't do the same. "I can't believe it's you."

"In the flesh." Twisting around, he reached for a dark blue T-shirt hanging over the back of the passenger seat.

"Don't you want to treat the scratches first?" she asked.

"Later."

"But—" She thought of the herbal cream she always carried for blisters, cuts, and any other nasty surprises she encountered on a regular basis out on a trek, and reached for the little purse hanging off her shoulder. "I have—"

"I'm good." He pulled the shirt over his head, the muscles in his biceps flexing, his hard, ridged belly revealing a nice six-pack as he sat up straighter to pull the material down to cover his torso. A firefighter patch now covered his pec, making him look official. Grown up. And then it hit her. He looked right at home here. He'd lost the haunted, hollow look that had plagued him all his childhood, and had found something for himself, a place he belonged.

So had she. Far away from here. Unfortunately, her basis for that distance had been a single tragic event, not a strong enough foundation, she'd discovered. She'd lived free as a bird, yes, and had loved it, but a very small part of her knew she'd missed something by walking away from everyone and anyone who'd ever cared about her.

She just didn't know what exactly.

And yet standing here, looking at the warehouse, seeing Joe, it was like a high-speed internet connection to the single most traumatic event of her life, and without warning, her vision wavered. Oh, damn. The third and final warning.

"Summer?"

She blinked into Joe's eyes. He had her wrist in a firm grip.

"Here." He stood, then pressed her to the driver's seat. "Sit."

"I'm okay." She went for a smile but couldn't quite stick the landing as she continued to suck air into her lungs too fast. "It's just . . . hard to be here." She waved a hand in front of her face to fan it and gulped air like water.

"Yeah," he said, watching her carefully. "And it's going to get worse. You probably shouldn't hang around for longer than necessary."

"No." *Keep breathing, Summer.* It took a few minutes to even it out, to gain control. Humiliating.

His mouth was grim as he waited, his eyes blazing with emotion. This was hard on him too, incredibly so, and yet she could still hardly believe it was him sitting there. "You look good, Joe."

He laughed.

"What's so funny?"

"Absolutely nothing."

It was a shock that she couldn't read him, not at all. "You used to wear your emotions on your sleeve."

"Yeah, well, that never really worked out for me."

She nodded and stood on legs she told herself were steady now. "Look, I'm sorry. I know I left things badly. I never said good-bye. I—"

"It doesn't matter."

He sounded as weary as she felt. Just yesterday she'd

been in San Francisco, planning and organizing a hiking trip through the Sierras for a large group of business-women. Then her mother had called at two in the morning. An oddity in itself because in all these years Camille had been extremely cognizant of the fact that Summer didn't like to come back to Ocean Beach, and had never asked her to.

As a result, Summer'd had an amazing freedom to do as she pleased. And what had pleased her was to roam, far and wide.

But her mother needed her now, an event shocking enough that Summer had hopped in her car and driven seven straight hours to get here. She'd had no sleep and it was catching up with her. But looking into Joe's eyes she could see that he'd had a long night too. And probably an even longer morning. "I'm sorry," she said again. After a hesitation, she reached past him for Socks. "Here, kitty, kitty."

"Watch out, she's still skittish."

"I'll be careful." Her shoulder brushed his. Beneath his shirt, he was warm and hard with strength, but that wasn't what struck her with an almost unbearable familiarity as she found herself in such close proximity to him. No, his scent did that because he smelled the same, and it took everything she had not to throw herself at him for a desper-ately needed hug.

But he sucked in a breath and stepped back.

To avoid her touch.

She stared at him, the hurt sneaking in and squeezing her heart. She wrapped her hands around the fat, scared cat, who came compliantly, even happily, pressing her furry face into the crook of Summer's neck affectionately. "Mew."

She hugged Socks close, feeling unusually awkward and out of her element. *He didn't want her here. Didn't want to see her.* "Did you fight the fire?" she asked.

"No, I'm a fire marshal."

"So . . . you're investigating?"

"Yes."

That was somehow both unsettling and comforting. "It was an accident last time. A terrible accident."

His face softened. "I know."

"Is it this time?"

"I'll find out."

He sounded so sure, so confident. So unlike the Joe she remembered. His radio squawked, and he reached for it, talking into it with a shocking, easy authority.

He bewildered her, this the man who felt both familiar and so much like a stranger. There was a lot to say to him, and yet nothing to say at all. Cuddling Socks, she turned away, giving him privacy, and taking a moment for herself as well.

The knowledge that the warehouse was probably a total loss dragged at her, fatiguing her all the more. She wondered if her mother and Aunt Tina would rebuild for a second time, and glanced back at Joe.

He was still talking into his radio, and didn't appear to notice she'd left.

So she kept walking, surrounded by people and still somehow more alone than she'd felt in years. Utterly, completely alone.

Chapter 3

"Fifteen minutes until the staff meeting, Walker."

Buried in paperwork at his desk inside the San Diego Fire Department's central headquarters downtown, Joe looked up at his micromanaging, anal chief. "I'll be there."

With a curt nod, Chief Michaels moved on, stern frown still in place, ready to terrorize the next underling.

Joe let out a breath, not intimidated—no one intimidated him anymore—but frustrated. It'd been a hell of a week, and not just because of the blast from his past a few days ago, though that certainly hadn't helped, especially in the thick of the night when the dark dreams sometimes came back, when he dreamed he was still hopeless, helpless, when the only bright spot in his life had been Summer.

But even that he could shove aside in the light of day. He'd been doing so for years.

It'd been seeing her again.

Facing who he'd once been.

The Chief poked his head back into Joe's office. "Don't forget, you're presenting on prevention."

Joe didn't jump, didn't do anything but cut his eyes to the clock. He had thirteen and a half minutes left. "I'll be there," he repeated, and when he was alone, got up and flipped over the WELCOME sign to STAY OUT! before shutting the door firmly.

Then he went back to brooding over the stacks on his desk, held in place by three of his cameras. He moved his favorite carefully aside, the new and so-expensive-it-still-made-him-queasy digital, and pulled out one of the fourteen sets of blueprints he had to approve for the building department. Behind them was another stack of new building sites to inspect. Everyone in the entire county seemed to be building or rebuilding this year, and as a result, his scheduled workload had tripled.

This did not a happy Cindy make.

She'd been hot under the collar for days, which had meant no sleepovers for him. And now she'd given him an ultimatum. Cut back the hours or stick a fork in her, she was done.

He had to admit, she wasn't asking for anything unreasonable, but cutting back just wasn't going to happen, not at this time of year.

Adding to his troubles, it'd been three days since the warehouse fire, and he hadn't yet satisfied himself that they were done with the scene. The suspected accelerant had turned out to be gasoline, which both Camille and Tina had told him in separate phone interviews they didn't keep around. The mysterious vagrant hadn't materialized, though they'd found evidence that someone had been there as recently as a week ago in the way of a boot print—size eleven and a half with diagonal tread. Interestingly enough, the print had held a trace of gasoline. Maybe the vagrant had attempted to light himself a campfire. No one knew.

Kenny thought they should rule undisclosed accidental fire caused by neglectful drifter, but Joe didn't want to let it go. Only he wasn't sure if that was because he felt tied up with the past, or if his instincts were truly screaming.

Kenny's theory—which he'd been happy to share just this morning on a downtown high-rise fire inspection, where they'd been meticulously going through plans and checking fire escape routes—was that it was both. That because of the way Joe had grown up, he tended to keep people at bay, never sharing the real Joe Walker.

Joe had retaliated by pointing out that he'd shared plenty, using Kenny as an example, at which his partner had rolled his eyes. "Like I'm going to keep you warm at night. You need a woman, a good one for the long haul."

"This from the guy who changes women like shirts."

"That's only because I haven't found the right one yet, but I plan to." Kenny smiled at the challenge. "Can you say the same?"

"Yes." He scowled at Kenny's scoff. "And it's not my fault I keep getting dumped."

"Yes, it is. You don't open up enough. How many times have I told you spill your beans, open the floodgates. Women get off on that stuff."

"I've been dating Cindy for two months."

"Because she thinks you're hot and you're pathetic enough to be bowled over by that. But sooner or later she'll realize you're not talking enough and you'll get dumped again. Come on, Joe, you're not the fat kid anymore. You can let someone inside. Have a real emotional attachment."

Joe had grumbled then and he grumbled now. So he didn't let people in, so what? It wasn't just how he'd grown up. He knew that a person took their experiences and made their own path. He didn't have to be an alcoholic asshole who beat on kids to feel like a man.

But if he knew that, he also knew he didn't have it in him

to really connect on a heart and soul level. Doing so would make him feel too open, too vulnerable.

Besides, he was perfectly happy this way.

He was, damn it.

His door opened, which meant someone was blatantly ignoring his STAY OUT warning. He lifted his head, prepared to growl.

And Summer flashed him a smile. "Friendly sign you have there."

"If it was any friendlier it wouldn't work."

"It didn't work this time." She leaned back against his office door as it clicked shut.

He tossed his pen aside and struggled to get it together in the face of this beautiful, smiling, warm woman who ridiculously reminded him of a time he'd rather not think about. "What do you want?"

"Hmmm," she said, and stepped forward. She wore a colorful flowery skirt low on her hips that didn't quite meet the hem of the layered tank tops, one white, one red. The strip of abdomen exposed was smooth, flat, and tanned. A gold hoop flashed at her belly button, which for some idiotic reason, made his mouth water.

For the second time this week he felt eighteen, horny, and pathetic.

And in need of a doughnut.

"Interesting and dangerous," she said softly, drawing his eyes back to hers. "Asking me what I want."

It suddenly felt hot in the room. Was it hot in the room? He resisted the urge to tug at his collar. "I think it's a simple enough question," he managed evenly.

"Sure. But to be honest, I want a lot of things." She eyed him for a long time, then slowly sat in a chair. She crossed her mile-long legs, which left one sandal dangling playfully off her big toe. "*Three* cameras now?" She laughed and fingered a strap. "I still think of you when I see one of these."

Was she *trying* to destroy him? Her hair was loose around her shoulders today, and still could catch the light like wildfire. She had something glossy on her lips but no other makeup. There was a Band-Aid on a knuckle and a silver ring on her thumb but not her ring finger, and she sat there like some complicated mix of mischievous girl and sexy, earthy woman.

His brain didn't know what to do, but his body seemed to. And yet it felt odd to look at her, the one bright spot in his shitty childhood, the only reason he'd ever made it through high school, the first woman who'd ever held a piece of his heart.

And then broken it.

Jesus. If that wasn't a mood wrecker, then the fact that she was looking good enough to lap up like a bowl of cream should do it. Lusting after her was apparently never going to change, which made his gut clench hard. "Just tell me why you're here."

"Is seeing me that bad?"

"I have a meeting in ten minutes, and my chief is breathing down my neck about it."

"Oh, I'm sorry." She stood up. "Do you still do those breathing exercises I once showed you for releasing stress? Because maybe I can—"

"Summer."

She let out a soft laugh. "Right." She nodded, looking as if she felt a little foolish. "We're not exactly still in each other's back pocket, are we?" She backed to the door, that incredibly arousing belly ring glinting. But that wasn't what got to him.

Her deeply troubled expression did.

Damn it. Damn *her*. "Summer—"

"Look, I get it. You're busy." Her smile didn't reach her eyes. "I didn't mean to intrude." She reached for the door handle.

"Stop. Red—"

At the use of her old nickname, she glanced back, startled.

"I have a minute," he admitted.

"Or ten." She smiled but it faded quickly. "Okay, listen, I'm sorry for the interruption, but it's my mom. She's not doing well. The fire really got to her, you know?"

"I can imagine."

"She asked me for help." She sounded bowled over by that. "Me." She lifted her hands. "I'm going to handle all the paperwork for her."

"There's going to be a lot," he warned.

"Yeah."

There was something deeply disconcerting in her tone. He alone knew the phantoms she must face being back in O.B., and he wondered how long she'd be able to handle being here at all. "You're unhappy to be back."

He hadn't meant to say anything personal, and she looked just as surprised as he that he had. "I guess I am," she admitted, and paced the length of the room. "I'd rather be on a mountain. On a river. Anywhere else, really."

"Why?"

She lifted a shoulder but didn't meet his eyes now that they were talking about her. "I don't know. It's closed in here. Crowded. It's not the same."

Well, there was a news bulletin.

She turned and faced him. "Uncle Bill wants to get my mother and Tina into the warehouse to see the damage but they're still being held out."

"I can get them in but after they look around, the scene will be sealed again. It's a safety issue."

She sank back to the chair. "And?"

"And . . . what?"

"There's an investigation."

"There usually is."

"Yes, but do you think it's arson?"

"Don't know yet."

"Why not?"

"These things take time," he said. "You know we found an accelerant."

"Gasoline. Which is crazy."

"Exactly. That's what makes it suspicious."

That was clearly not the answer she'd expected. Again she got to her feet. "What reason would there be for arson?"

"Insurance fraud, revenge, blackmail—" He broke off at her wide-eyed look of horror.

"You think that my mom and aunt—"

"No, I don't think," he said. "I don't think anything until the evidence tells me what happened. There could be any number of possibilities, accidental or otherwise. Employees, acquaintances, the vagrant . . . " She still looked horrified. "Summer, it's nothing yet. Okay?"

"Okay."

She turned to look at the plaques and pictures he had scattered around, stopping at the corner wall behind the door to look at one in particular. It was a shot of him and his squad, drenched, filthy, and dirty, arms slung around each other as they celebrated the end of the horrifying and tragic San Diego County fires two years ago.

"You asked me why I'm not happy to be here," she said, staring at the picture. "But you are. You're happy here."

When he didn't say anything, didn't know what to say, she turned and looked at him. "I always wanted you to be."

He absorbed that for a moment, but before he could respond, the door to his office opened again. Cindy, dressed to kill in a siren red business suit, still wearing her name tag from her position at an executive headhunter agency in town, came in and smiled at him, clearly not seeing Summer behind the door. "Since you don't have time to come to me, I've come to you," she said. "I've brought the lunch special. It's called Sex On Your Desk." She shut the door behind her, put her fingers to the buttons on her blazer, then executed a comical double take when she saw Summer standing there. "Oops."

Summer lifted her hands. "Oh, no, that's okay. I, um . . ." She glanced at Joe with an indescribable look on her face. "Gotta go."

Joe himself sat rooted, morbidly fascinated by the differences between the two women, one so fully made-up and blatantly sexual, the other's appeal more natural, somehow more genuine. Both women were looking at him curiously, probably wondering why he'd gone speechless, and he thought that tonight, for once, he'd have a new nightmare.

Summer moved first, around Cindy and toward the door. Ah, hell. "Red."

Her hand on the doorknob, she glanced back at him.

What could he say? And he couldn't help but wonder, is this how she'd felt that long ago day, standing between him and Danny? Did she appreciate the irony? "I'll contact you as soon as I have any answers on the fire," he promised.

"Yeah. Thanks." She offered a small smile and glanced at Cindy.

"I'm Cindy Swenson by the way," Cindy said, thrusting

out her hand to Summer. "And I interrupted your business meeting. I'm sorry."

"No problem."

"Cindy, this is Summer Abrams," Joe said. "We're . . ."

Summer locked her eyes on his.

"Old friends." Which felt like both an understatement and an overstatement at the same time. "From school."

"Oh, that's so sweet," Cindy said to Summer. "I'm so sorry for my abrupt appearance, but Joe and I don't get much time together, as he lives and breathes his work." She flashed him the look that for two months had been giving him an instant hard-on, but now acted like a shriveling agent.

Summer reached for the door again. "Okay, well, I'll just let you two get to your, um . . ." She gestured to his desk. *"Lunch."*

He grimaced. "Red—"

But she was gone.

When the door shut, Cindy perched a hip on the corner of his desk and waggled her brows. "Ready to *eat*?"

"Can't. I have a meeting— Whoa!" He lurched back up and put his hands over hers when she started to undo the buttons of her blouse. "The door— My Chief—" She kept stripping. "Cindy, I mean it."

She trailed her hand down his abdomen, and then even farther, cupping him between his thighs. "Mmm, look what I found."

He grabbed her busy hands. "Cindy, I've got to go. *You've* got to go."

He spent the last two minutes before his meeting walking her out to her car and seeing her off before racing into the conference room with thirty seconds to spare. Chief Michaels eyed him curiously but apparently had the willpower not to point out the oddity of two beautiful women visiting his usually woman-challenged fire marshal within five minutes of each other.

"Hey, gigolo," Kenny said with a grin, possessing no such willpower at all.

Chapter 4

Ocean Beach really hadn't changed much, at least not to Summer's eyes. It still had a bohemian feel to it with its complex mix of poor college students, wanderlust-stricken surfers, and derelicts living on the streets, as well as a whole new socio-group: the young, wealthy urbanites.

The sand was still hot, the water a frothy blue as it pounded the shore. The air smelled like salt and fast food. Once upon a time, this had been home, but now Summer felt like one of the tourists she'd always resented.

After she'd left all those years ago, her mother had dealt with her grief by selling their house a few blocks inland and buying a tiny condo downtown. She'd filled it with her handpicked collectibles, healing supplies, and homemade teas, but to Summer the place seemed too far from the water, too small and closed in, and after the first awkward, sleepless night, she'd made an excuse about needing to be on the beach and had gone to one of her Aunt Tina's properties, a small cottage on the bluffs overlooking the ocean.

The decision seemed to disturb Camille, and Summer had spent the past few days trying to make up for it. They'd gone to breakfast each day, where Summer had tried to draw her mom out, but all efforts had hit a solid block wall.

Summer could just leave it alone as she tended to do with all things awkward and uncomfortable, but she didn't want to. Damn it, she was here, she wanted to fit in, wanted to be a part of the family. Wanted to be close again.

On the fourth morning, Summer once again got into her VW Bug and took I-5 toward the bay to meet her mom. Shaped like a hook and protected by the peninsula of Coronado, the San Diego Bay formed a natural deepwater harbor around which the second largest city in California had grown. Summer headed directly into the heart of it, into the famous Gaslamp Quarter, once notorious for its nefarious activities such as prostitution, gambling, and drinking. Years ago the entire area had been given a welcomed revival. Historical buildings had all been renovated in grand Victorian style, carved into the original architecture, leaving a wealth of hotels, shops, galleries, and trendy clubs and restaurants, all illuminated by the prominent, graceful gas lamps lining the pavements.

Determined, Summer pulled into one such Victorian, where Creative Interiors was housed, and parked in the lot behind it.

Camille was just getting out of her car, with a sleeping Socks in her arms. Her mom would be forty-seven this year, but if Summer hadn't known, she'd have guessed no more than thirty-five. The woman simply never aged. Lean and toned from her morning jogs, she wore clothing extremely well, including the vintage bohemian-style dress she had on right now. She had porcelain skin, long wavy hair the color of roasted chestnuts, and a way of talking that made you listen. "Morning," she said with a welcoming smile. "How are you?"

Summer returned the smile. "Good."

"So what's up? I need to open the store."

"I know." Tread carefully here. "Mom, I've been thinking. The insurance paperwork isn't that difficult, and I could really use something else to do while I'm here." Such as get close to you again. "How about a job?"

Camille stared at her as if she'd suggested getting a third eye. "Why?"

"Well I'm going to be here a while, so—"

"But honey, *why* will you be here a while?"

Summer blinked. "Because I told you I would."

"I don't expect you to drop everything for me."

"I'm not."

"But you've never stayed more than a few days." Camille sounded baffled.

"I know," Summer said quietly. "But I want to do this. For you." Just as she wanted, *needed,* to reforge a bond that had never been the same since her father's death.

Camille made a noncommittal sound as she nuzzled the cat and then began walking. Her crystal earrings made a tinkering sound that floated on the air.

Summer followed. "I really do want to help," she said softly, longing to see a real smile cross her mom's lips. "You're opening a second shop this week, right? And it's a big deal. I'm sure everyone's crazed, worrying about the loss of stock from the warehouse fire, and getting the new store ready. Surely you could use an extra set of hands."

"Hmm."

That hmm was the sound of Camille thinking, and no one, not even God himself could rush her through a decision. There'd only been one person who'd ever been able to break through that stubbornness, and that had been Tim Abrams.

Other men had tried since Summer's father had died.

Camille had enjoyed them each for a time, and then on some schedule only she had access to, she'd set them free.

Summer admired the spirit but not as it applied to *their* relationship. "Mom, five days ago you called me in the middle of the night in tears." Clingy. Scared. "You wanted my help. You wanted me here." And that had meant so much, Summer had dropped everything and rushed here.

And yet she hadn't seen a hint of that soft, clingy Camille since she'd arrived. "You wanted me here," she repeated, softly, reaching for her mom's hand, squeezing the cold fingers. "Now let me do something."

"You've done plenty. You brought Socks back. You went and talked to the fire marshal."

"Joe."

"I invited him to our grand opening of Creative Interiors II tomorrow night. He's been very kind. I'm going to send him a box of my teas. I think he could use some peace and tranquility."

Summer didn't want to think about Joe, needing tranquility or otherwise, because thinking about him at all confused her. The memories of her youth were all tied up with memories of him. He'd been her best friend, her rock. Her everything. Granted, their relationship had been decidedly asexual, but she honestly believed that *that's* what had made it so strong and binding.

But then, like everything else in connection to O.B., she'd let it go. She'd let it all go, and life had gone on without her. Twelve years, gone, like a breath of air, and now Joe was no longer that scruffy kid, but a full grown man who disturbed her in ways she couldn't really grasp.

No, she didn't want to think about him fitting into his quiet intensity, having sex on his desk with a beautiful woman who clearly had claimed him as her own.

Did the two of them talk into the wee hours of the morning? Did she say his name softly when he moaned with fear in his sleep from the old nightmares? Did she know he was addicted to Dr Pepper but hated Coke?

Undoubtedly she did, and that made Summer feel like brooding when she had no right to do so.

But the fact was, nothing here was the same. Not Joe, not her mom, nothing.

And actually, she could live with that, she could. She just wanted to find her place. "Mom."

Camille stopped and sighed, softening on the spot. "Honey, listen. You came when I called you. That means everything to me."

"And I'm still right here. Ready to be needed some more."

"But for how long? I mean I just don't see you staying, Summer. I don't."

Why that hurt when it had always been the utter truth, she had no idea. Camille had never complained, or even let on that she'd have liked more than that from Summer. She'd said nothing at all, and in return, Summer had taken that as tacit permission to stay gone.

But now she wondered at all she'd missed. At what her absence had meant to Camille. Maybe her mom thought she didn't care, that she'd left and had never looked back.

"How long do you really think you'll stay?" Camille asked.

An honest question. Summer struggled with an honest answer. "For as long as it takes to get this fire thing over with."

"That could take weeks."

"That's okay. I want to do this." *Please want me to do this.*

Camille was quiet for a long moment. "All right, then. Let's go in and see what we have for you to do."

Creative Interiors had once been a premiere boat shop. The building had been built in 1926, and remodeled in the fifties when the original owners had sold it off. Directly across the street was another furnishing shop owned by their most fierce competition, Ally's Treasures. Ally herself was well named, Camille had always claimed, because she was like an alley cat, always sneaking in to see Creative Interiors's stock, checking out their prices, often returning to her shop to price slash.

But in reality, a little competition hadn't hurt either store. Uncle Bill had recently repainted the outside of their building a shiny cream with a navy trim. He'd made a colorful hanging sign that read CREATIVE INTERIORS: FOR FUN BEACH LIVING!

The inside opened to one large showroom with two small alcoves off to each side. In the back were the offices, employee break room, and extra storage. The walls were the color of melted butter, with soft wood trim and a rough texture. Decorated like an expensive yacht, it was filled with furniture, photos, and all sorts of other knickknacks such as Bill's handmade ceramic lighthouses and a set of Tim's old, savored travel books. There were also pretty, soft sofas covered in pillows with throws over the backs of them, with lamps providing lighting, and rugs on the wood floors that were easy to maintain by their employees.

As for the employees, Tina and Camille had kept it mostly in the family. Tina had three children from her first marriage. Chloe, her oldest, worked here, usually with major attitude. Chloe's younger twin sisters, Diana and Madeline, were high school divas forced to work at the store whenever they were grounded, which was constantly.

Once upon a time, Summer had been close to them but they'd been young children when she'd left. Too much time had passed now, and, for whatever reasons, there was little love lost between the cousins. Actually, Summer knew the exact reason they kept their distance.

They'd felt like she'd abandoned them. And she had.

There were also a few employees who didn't share the Abrams blood. Stella and Gregg were an easygoing, likeable couple in their thirties. They helped clerk the store and inventory stock. The newest hire was Braden Cahill. The tall, dark, and silent type, he was a twenty-something out-of-towner whom no one knew much about except that he was extremely easy on the eyes and could work a computer.

As Camille, Socks, and Summer let themselves into the store, a long set of working chimes went off. Diana and Madeline, standing at the front counter, lifted their heads in unison.

Camille waved at them, then turned to Summer. "I'm heading to my office. Think about this, okay? And if you really want, I'll find you something to do." Then she took Socks and let herself in the back.

Left alone, Summer smiled at her cousins. Diana was tall and lanky, and wore her eye makeup so heavy that Summer always marveled that she could even open her eyes. She wore a peach halter top and matching skirt, a little diamanté heart tattoo on her shoulder blade, and a scowl on her glossed mouth. Madeline had the same coltish physique but wore faded hip-hugging jeans, a snug, stretchy light-blue baby T, and next to no makeup.

Before Summer could greet either of them, Tina rushed out from the back. Like the rest of them, she was tall and lean, and though she was in her early forties, she tended to favor items from the Victoria's Secret catalogue. Today she wore a silky camisole top with a matching skirt and sandals, ribbons laced up her calves. She had four silver hoops on one ear, matching the silver beginning to streak her deep red hair that tumbled in thick waves to her shoulders. She had the sparkling green eyes of a pixie and the smile of a saint as she came close for a warm hug. "Darling Summer," she said. "It's about time you show your pretty face. I thought maybe you'd leave without coming by."

The reproach was gentle, and easily swallowed. "I'm not leaving yet."

Tina didn't comment on that, just hugged her again. "The girls are thrilled."

Madeline didn't verbalize any such thing, but then again, Madeline rarely verbalized at all. She just rolled her eyes.

Diana didn't say a word either, just kept coolly reading her *Cosmo* magazine.

Oh yeah, they were thrilled. "Grounded?" Summer asked them.

Blowing a huge bubble as she kept reading, Diana lifted her middle finger. Madeline actually let loose of a small smile, and shrugged.

Chloe came out the back and took over the room with sheer personality presence. She'd been nine when Summer had left. She'd recently turned twenty-one, and in celebration of that happy event had dyed the ends of her blond hair green, matching it with a green lip gloss. According to Camille, Chloe had a habit of changing the color of her hair with the seasons, saying whatever popped into her head, and dumping men before they dumped her, which actually happened to be a family trait in general. At the moment, Chloe was on a summer break from classes, working full time in the shop for lack of a better offer, but as she herself put it, a girl had to eat.

Having been old enough to really remember Summer, Chloe held a bigger grudge from being dumped. She didn't hug Summer, but she did offer a cool smile filled with trouble. "So. The prodigal daughter finally returns."

"I was here at Christmas," Summer reminded her.

"For what, like two minutes?"

"Two days."

"Ah. So long. Well, I hope you're here to work."

"She's on vacation," Tina said.

"Hey. *I'm* on vacation, but *I'm* working," Chloe said.

"Because, darling, you owe me a lot of money." Tina smiled and fondly patted her daughter's cheek.

"I'm *not* on vacation," Summer said, getting tired of explaining that. "I want to work while I'm here. I want to be with all of you."

Madeline snorted.

Diana laughed.

And Chloe joined them.

"It's true," Summer said.

"We'll see how long that lasts."

Diana popped another bubble and laid her magazine out for them to see. "Look, my horoscope says it's a good day to land myself a guy."

"What does mine say?" Chloe asked, shoving Madeline aside so she could get closer.

"That you're a born bitch, but since it comes naturally to you, you should embrace it, not fight it."

Chloe smiled. "Excellent. What does Summer's say?"

Madeline pushed close again and flipped the page to search it out. Diana read it out loud. "It says, and I quote, *follow your heart.* Hmm. Where will that lead you, I wonder? Not here, its never been here."

"Things change," Summer said, trying not to be insulted.

"And I'm staying until the warehouse fire report is filed. That could be a few weeks."

"Weeks? Good," Chloe said with selfish glee. "I just happen to have some work I'll happily share. You can start by folding the new tablecloths and napkins. I suck at it."

"You definitely do," Tina agreed, her crystal earrings a perfect match to Camille's. "But we all have our faults. Now girls, I mean this in the most loving way possible, but get your sweet asses to work."

Summer braced for an argument, because for as long as she could remember, Tina's relationships with her daughters had resembled a roller-coaster track. Up and down, and then back up again, never a calm moment, rarely common ground, and yet there was always emotion: huge, passionate, wild emotion.

And also for as long as Summer could remember, she'd envied their relationships with all her heart. Not that Camille wasn't wonderful, and always kind, but there hadn't been huge emotion, passion, or much of anything in a very long time. "I can fold."

"Really?" Chloe beamed at her. "I just got officially happy to see you."

Tina just shook her head. "Summer darling, you're too sweet." She shot Chloe a look that said *take notes*.

Chloe gave her a mock saccharine smile back, complete with salute and Tina laughed. "Oh, go on with you. Go be free and let me be."

"Gladly." Chloe scooted close to Summer as Tina drifted off. "Hey."

"Hey yourself."

"See that guy over there?"

There was only one guy in the place. The *GQ*-handsome one who'd just moved behind the counter. He'd slouched

on a stool, and was working on a laptop. Summer knew he
was the infamous Braden, the new bookkeeper. "I see him."

"Good. Now *stop* seeing him."

"Why?"

"He's mine." At Summer's long, appraising look, she
caved. "Okay, maybe not yet, but I intend for him to be. So
hands and mouth off."

"It's hard to take you seriously with green hair."

"I mean it, Summer."

Summer eyed Braden again. He wore loose black cargo
pants and a black collarless shirt on his slightly too-lean
body, and an expression that said back off. And though he
was scowling at his computer, his long dark hair in his eyes,
he *was* pretty. In a caged tiger sort of way. "Consider my
hands off. But—"

"No. No warnings from you," Chloe said with an
adamant shake of her green-tipped hair. "You do as you
want. You do *who* you want. You always have. Hell, you
graduated from high school two years early, then skipped
college to roam the planet. Do you know how cool that is?
Now it's my turn to do what I want, so go away before he
sees how gorgeous and curvy and irresistible you are. Go
save my hide and fold the new kitchen linens. They're that
way." She gestured to the first alcove, decorated like a
beach kitchen, complete with sand on the floor.

Summer didn't go. "I'm irresistible?"

"Oh, please. Like you don't know it. Now go."

"Chloe?"

"What?"

"Just so you know, *all* the women in our family are irresistible." She smiled. "Even your bossy, cranky hide."

That got a smile. "Just remember, he's still mine."

Summer lifted her hands in surrender and moved

through the store. Not exactly a warm family greeting, but she'd take it. She'd come because she'd been asked. She'd committed to staying because once she'd gotten here she'd been overcome by a desire to fit in.

But she clearly didn't, not really, a thought that made her feel just a little lost. She stopped at the back wall, distracted by a long row of interesting photographs from the turn of the last century. Her mother loved such pictures, and had been collecting for years. Summer felt drawn to them too, though she'd never given it much thought as she'd rarely stayed in one place long enough to unpack her clothes, much less pictures. This particular series had been taken at the seashore, depicting the interesting bathing suits and the quaint lifestyle of the time, but it was more than that that made them a set. It was the people, and the warmth and affection and love pouring out of the frames. They were connected, deeply, and it seemed so simple. Sweet.

She stared at the frames as a yearning went through her. She wanted a simple but deep connection, she wanted that with all her heart. She'd had it once, she just had no idea how to get it back, and that she felt so lost right here at "home" disconcerted and confused her.

She heard the footsteps then, just behind her. Work boots, but with a light, sure gait. Looking up, she met a pair of unbearably familiar whiskey-colored eyes and her heart skipped a beat.

If Joe's heart skipped as well, he hid it. His hair fell in waves over his forehead, brushing the collar of his slightly wrinkled white dress shirt, which was shoved up to his elbows and had some official patch on the pec. It wasn't tucked into his soft, faded Levi's, which sported a frayed hole over one knee. Looking just a little edgy, a little dangerous, he had one hand in his pocket, the other holding a clipboard, which he tapped against his thigh as his eyes checked off the details of his surroundings. Always alert.

There was something about his mouth that suggested the slightest of smiles when his gaze landed on hers, but then again it could have been a grimace at having to see her again.

"Hey," she said.

"Hey yourself."

Startled at the old familiar greeting, and at the ease in which they'd slipped into it, they stared at each other. And for a single beat, Summer didn't feel lost at all. "What are you doing here?"

He shoved his free hand through his wavy hair, making some of it stick up. Instead of making him look rumpled, it somehow seemed . . . endearing. "I have some interviews," he said.

"For the investigation?"

"Yes."

She glanced at the unmistakable bulge of the gun at his hip beneath the drape of his shirt. Wondered at all it implied, at all he'd seen and done since they'd been kids. "With my mom?" she asked.

"Yes."

"What do you need to know?"

"Quite a bit, actually."

She sighed. "You're being obtuse."

"I don't mean to be."

Damn, he'd gotten good at not giving anything away. Apparently the long years of fighting fires and then investigating them had taught him a lot about control. He seemed so rough and ready standing there, so absolutely unflappable, body relaxed, eyes watchful, with a confusing mix of temper and passion humming just beneath the surface. She felt almost helplessly sucked in by that—utterly, morbidly, erotically sucked in.

She wondered if he ever felt as out of place as she did right now, then remembered that if he did, he had his girlfriend to go to. Cindy.

Had they had sex on his desk that day after she'd left?

"Is Camille in her office?" he asked.

"Yes." That brought her back. "But she's feeling fragile. Be gentle, okay?"

"And here I was hoping to use my torture rack."

His eyes had cooled, his smile gone. She'd insulted him. "This has been hard for her, that's all."

He slapped his clipboard against his thigh again. His only sign of agitation. "Do you remember me as being particularly insensitive or cruel?"

"No, of course not."

"So have I changed *that* much?"

Now *that* was a tough one. It would have been impossible for her to describe what seeing him did to her. His eyes were the same, and so, she suspected, were his heart and soul. Such incredible memories were stirred up by just his face, and yet new things were stirred up too. He'd put on height over the years, as well as lost those inches. Summer was five ten, but she had to tip her head back a little to see into his eyes. That gave her an entirely inappropriate shiver of appreciation, as did the sheer physical presence of him. "Some things have definitely changed," she murmured.

"Right. The outer package." And that clearly vexed rather than flattered. "That's fairly obvious, Red. And it's the second time you've mentioned it. I guess that's what's important to you."

"That was never important to me." But she flushed at his long stare, and she had to admit as she remembered the dazzling but empty-hearted Danny, that once upon a time, Joe had had every reason to believe that appearances *were* what was important to her.

How the hell had she gotten off on the wrong foot with absolutely everyone? "All I meant," she said, "was that if anything's different—on the *inside*—it's how carefully controlled you are. That's *very* different, Joe."

"Maybe I only show my feelings to the people I'm close to."

Touché. "Because what right do I have to know anything about you at all, is that it?"

He said nothing.

Another new trait.

She turned back to the seascapes on the wall. There was a young couple, smiling, arms flung around each other. So happy, so carefree. She'd always thought of herself as happy and carefree, too, but she felt neither at the moment.

There'd been ties over the years, with coworkers, clients. Other men. She'd enjoyed every one of them, and had amazing memories, but none compared to the tie she'd once had, and then given away, with this man. "Do you ever think about it?" she murmured, still staring at the joyful couple who'd lived one hundred years ago. "About us?"

He was silent for so long she tipped her head up and looked into his face. His lean jaw hadn't been shaved today, maybe not yesterday either. His mouth, wide and firm, was unsmiling. And yet in those light eyes flickered a few memories as he gave her a long, considering look. "Sometimes."

"I do too," she admitted, but not the rest. That the old Joe had drawn her because he represented everything that had been wonderful about her childhood. That the new Joe, with his laugh lines and knowing eyes, with his matured low voice and confidence in his own skin, with his badge and gun, drew her too, yet in a very different manner. The decidedly unexpected sexual tension—at least on her side—was new enough to shock her into silence.

He turned from the pictures and slid his eyes to hers, revealing nothing of his own thoughts. "It was all a long time ago."

And people moved on. She knew that. She'd moved on first, in fact, but she'd never regretted anything more. "I wanted to see you on the few trips I made here. I . . . didn't know how."

"If it was that hard for you, you did the right thing."

She smiled past her regrets, determined not to spill her guts just because once she would have. "You're probably right."

"Yeah." He lifted the clipboard. "I have to go find your mother." He paused. "I'll be easy on her, I promise."

A reassurance. A kind one, and grateful, she put her hand on his arm. Under her fingers, his muscles tensed. She stared up at him, registering, without meaning to, that beneath his shirt his body was muscular and hard.

Once she'd been out on a winter snowshoe trek in Alaska. She'd stood too close to the campfire trying to get warm and had singed her fingertips. They felt singed now, too, though she didn't pull back. "Thanks," she whispered.

He stared down at her hand on him, then back into her eyes. "This is new."

So he felt it too. "Yes."

"It's not going anywhere."

"Joe—"

"It's not." Slowly, with only a speculative and quietly unnerving look, he walked away.

Okay, she got it. She'd given up their deep, abiding friendship without looking back, and she was paying the price for that. She was no longer a priority of his. He had his work. And Cindy. Let's not forget Cindy, with the hungry eyes and sharklike smile. "You're crazy," she whispered to herself at the strange stab of jealousy, and yet she watched him go, a yearning rushing through her so strong she had to bite her lip rather than call him back and give herself away.

With a sigh, she went to find the linens she'd promised to fold. The small alcove was decorated like a formal sitting room/dining room. Surprising her, Camille was already there, going through a small stack of new afghans.

Summer pulled one from the box, a soft chenille in golds and auburns and purples like a sunset, and attempted to fold it as effortlessly as her mother. "Joe's here. He wants to talk to you."

"Yes. Tina's going first."

Summer set the afghan over the back of a light blue chair and smoothed the edges. "I think he suspects arson."

Camille's hands went still for a beat. Then she picked up the afghan Summer had just folded, redid it, and draped it over an oak blanket stand. "Doesn't go with the blue."

"Yes, but I'm talking about the fire."

"Well, I'm talking about your horrible sense of color scheming."

Frustration bubbled from deep within Summer. "Mom. Why do you do that? Hide what you feel from me?"

Camille looked genuinely surprised. "Do I?"

"Yes. Always. Tina and her daughters don't hide a thing from each other."

In fact, from the main room came the sound of Chloe and Tina yelling over a phone message, making Camille smile wryly. "They certainly don't."

"Please tell me what you're thinking about," Summer said. *Let me in.*

"All right." Camille clasped her fingers together. "I'm thinking about things that I don't normally think about. The first warehouse fire. Your dad." She stared down at her hands and sighed. "Tim was my life."

Summer's heart tripped, and she moved closer. "It's only normal to think about him, since the warehouse burned again."

"The first time was an accident." Camille grabbed another afghan and began folding. "They ruled it an accident."

"Yes." Her throat ached. "It was a terrible, tragic accident. But then, it was a long time ago."

Camille tossed the afghan onto a high-legged end table, messily folded. Her only sign of distress. "With you here, it feels like yesterday."

Summer didn't know how to respond to that. The last thing she wanted to do was cause her mom more pain. Leaving would help the both of them, but leaving was what had caused this distance in the first place, and besides, she'd promised not to go. She might be confused, lonely, hurting . . . but she still had her word.

"I know Joe suspects arson," Camille said. "But there was nothing in that warehouse couldn't be replaced. There's no one else on any of the papers except Tina and me. No one but us would gain from an insurance payoff."

"It doesn't have to be insurance fraud. Maybe you made someone mad. A boyfriend?"

Camille adamantly shook her head. "No."

"The vagrant?"

"No. He's a very nice man. Just homeless. He's very careful."

"Another family member then? Diana? Madeline? Just kidding," she said when Camille eyed her acerbically. "I'm just thinking a little juvy hall wouldn't hurt their attitude."

Camille actually let out a laugh. Socks came into the room and wound himself around her ankles. She scooped him up and buried her face in his neck. "It's not arson."

"I'm sure you're right," Summer said slowly, not wanting to argue.

Camille closed her eyes. "And at least this time, thank God, no one—"

She didn't finish her sentence. She didn't have to. Because they both knew.

At least this time, no one had died.

Chapter 5

For three days, Joe worked around the clock. He had inspections, plan development meetings at town hall, fires to investigate and reports to write, and now he sat at dinner with Cindy, nodding as she talked about her day, forcing himself to sit straight up for fear he'd fall asleep and land face-first into his meal.

The fact was, he'd wanted to stay home, maybe barbeque, definitely rest his weary body. But Cindy had wanted to take advantage of his rare night off, so here they sat, at an expensive steak house with a waiter hovering and Joe with a headache brewing.

"It's a great neighborhood to raise kids," Cindy was saying while he cut into his steak and unintentionally tuned her out. He figured if he could just get to bed early, he'd wake up refreshed and get to his reports. Yeah, that was it. He'd—

"Joe? Are you listening to me?"

He would be if she'd just rest her tongue for even a second. The thought made him feel like a jerk. It wasn't her fault he was exhausted, heading into a coma. "I'm sorry." He tried to put his mind back into her one-sided conversation, but while he watched her lips move, thoughts of work invaded.

The city was trying to rush him through one of the inspections for a large commercial complex, and yet the plans hadn't matched the actual work done. Now he had several city officials riding his ass for slowing them down. And then there were several fires disturbing him, not the least of which was the Creative Interiors warehouse fire.

They'd released the scene two days ago. There'd been no other evidence found to go with the gasoline and boot print, except for a half-burned cigarette butt. They'd not put out an official ruling but the general consensus between MAST and the insurance company was that it would probably be undisclosed accidental fire—

"Babe, please. You're not even *pretending* to hear me now."

Caught off guard, he blinked at Cindy. "I'm sorry," he said again, and scooped up a bite of baked potato, instructing himself to tune in. "I really am. Can you say that again?"

She reached over and squeezed his hand. "You're going to make me think I'm boring."

"I'm just tired."

"Which is my point. My La Jolla town house is bigger than your place, which goes without saying since you live on a sailboat in a marina in Mission Bay."

Uh oh.

She shot him a smile. "And I have plenty of extra closet space for you."

Joe tossed back his entire glass of water and thought *please don't do this now.*

But Cindy turned out to be a lousy mind reader. "I mean

I really do understand the allure of living on the water, but it's just not big enough for both of us . . ."

"Cindy—"

"And I have to admit, I have a secret fantasy about having a house in the suburbs. Something simple, with a nice yard for the kids." She let out a bubbly laugh while he stared at her. "And a white picket fence. It's got to have one of those."

The succulent steak he'd eaten caught in his throat.

"I know it's silly," she said. "But you know I grew up in Manhattan, in a third floor walk-up. No yard, no place to call my own. Nothing like my dream house."

Joe had grown up in her so-called dream house, but he'd only found nightmares there. A white picket fence was on his *Never Have* list.

"Our kids will love it."

Kids. He nearly choked. He didn't know the first thing about raising a kid, and with his father's blood running through his veins, that was just as well.

"Joe? You're looking pale. Like you've seen a ghost."

Yeah, the ghost of his future. "Cindy," he said again, gently now, because he was going to hurt her and he hadn't meant to ever do that.

Her smile faded. "Is this about moving in together?"

"We've only been dating a little over a month—"

"Two months. *Two* months, Joe. And that's plenty of time."

"Maybe if we'd been seeing each other regularly."

"Your job doesn't let you do anything regularly."

"That's true. And because of it, out of those two months we've really only been together a handful of times."

She stared at him for a long, long moment. "I see. You're not ready. I should have known, you've never even told me about you. You've never really opened up."

The same old refrain. Kenny would be happy to hear it. "I'm sorry, Cindy. I'm . . ." He spread his hands helplessly. "Just not ready."

"Okay." She folded her hands and paused, looking incredibly hurt. "Will you ever be?"

Don't. God, don't. "Cindy—"

His pager went off and he had no idea if it was relief that washed through him, or shame that he needed the out. He glanced down at the display, saw the emergency code, and grimaced as he set down his fork. "I'm sorry."

"You're always sorry."

Yes. Yes he was. He was just one sorry son of a bitch.

"Don't listen to it," she begged him. "Don't leave now."

"You know I have to." He stood and opened his wallet, taking out the money to cover their meals while she just stared at him, boring holes into his body with her resentment. With a sigh, he bent over her and brushed his mouth over her temple. "I really am sorry," he murmured.

"Please just answer me." Her voice trembled and he felt like the lowest bottom-feeder as she grabbed his wrist. "Will you ever be ready for this? For me?"

They were in a restaurant, surrounded by a crowd. He didn't want to do this to her, not now, not here. But she wouldn't let go of him.

"Do you even want that white picket fence, Joe? Just tell me that."

He swiped the pad of his thumb over the tear that had slipped down her cheek. "No," he said quietly. "I don't."

At that, she pulled away from his touch. "Good-bye, Joe."

And then she walked away before he could.

*   *   *

The emergency page was a fire. It always was. By the time Joe arrived at the single-story residential structure, the damage had been done. Flames leapt fifty feet into the black, opaque sky. More sirens sounded in the distance. A backup engine arriving to help protect the houses on either side. There were two ambulances there already, but Joe could tell from the screams as he got out of his truck, someone wasn't going to make it to the hospital.

His stomach sank.

The on-site fire captain, Jake Rawlins, was an old, close friend. He came over to Joe while still yelling commands to his squad through his radio. "Carter and Martinez, pull back from the east side! Too hot! *Too hot!*" He watched as the truck engineer obeyed his orders, pulling the ladder away from the house, protecting the two firefighters on the end of it. Long streams of water from the hoses on the ground hit the hot flames.

"What do you have?" Joe asked.

"Hottest on the east side. Kitchen."

"Who was inside?"

"A woman and her three young children. One didn't make it out."

"Christ." Joe could still hear the mother screaming, hoarser now with her inconsolable grief.

"The father's MIA," Rawlins said. "They're in the middle of a nasty divorce. He was spotted outside the kitchen window about three hours ago. The cops were called but when they got here, he was gone. They're looking for him now."

Joe knew all about asshole fathers. Too much. With a heavy sigh, he began taking notes. It was another half hour before the firefighters beat the flames down. During that time, Joe took pictures of the fire, the surrounding houses, the people watching. Later he'd study them all for clues but for now he just worked to record everything. He interviewed the witnesses, and all the neighbors.

Kenny showed up and joined the fray. "I got called out in the middle of an incredibly hot first date. And you?"

"Cindy's pissed."

"Shocker."

"She told me to keep walking."

"She'll want you back."

"No." Joe shook her head. "Not this time. It's not going to work out."

"Yet another shocker. Let me guess. You got the 'you don't open up to me' complaint."

"Actually, she was willing to overlook that if I moved in with her."

"And you said 'oh goodie, where's my key,' right?"

"You're funny." He tossed Kenny a flashlight and they went into the house. As always, the work distracted Joe, he lost himself in it.

The kitchen had been hit hard. The countertops, floor, ceiling, and walls were down to blackened studs, and yet right across the room, the Formica and steel table and chairs stood perfectly in place, though the plastic coverings on the chairs had melted, and the cushions had burned.

Joe spent the first few minutes taking more pictures, recording the scene to preserve it for their report. Then he began to investigate for evidence of the origin/cause. He went through everything with a fine-tooth comb before his attention was caught beneath the sink. Before tonight there'd been a cupboard there but now only the shell remained. As he moved closer, a sudden, piercing, heart-wrenching scream filled the air outside. Lifting his head, he met Kenny's eyes from across the room.

"They found the kid's remains," his partner said quietly, his eyes shiny with emotion.

Joe let out a long, shaky breath and nodded. "Look." He pointed with a gloved finger to the charred remains of a rag, balled up beneath the sink. Shining his flashlight for better illumination, he slowly pulled out the rag. The stench of paint thinner had his nostrils flaring. "Bingo," he said softly.

"Maybe the mother had been removing her fingernail polish," Kenny said, coming closer, playing devil's advocate, as was their routine.

"Maybe." Joe flashed the beam of light on the gallon-sized container of paint thinner, hidden behind the plumbing. It was charred on the outside, but opened and tipped over. "Because using a full gallon of paint thinner is so much easier than a small bottle of fingernail polish remover."

The woman kept on screaming, the sounds ripping a hole in Joe's chest. He flashed his beam of light on the carefully placed childproof lock on the inside wall of the cabinet, which would have kept her kids out. He took in everything else beneath the sink, all child-safe products such as a bottle of bubbles and kiddie soap.

Not another chemical, not so much as a cleaning agent, nothing. No, he would not buy that she'd have hoisted a heavy can to remove her fingernail polish. And he didn't buy she'd have kept it under the sink either. Joe thought of the missing father and his gut twisted with memories of his own cruel father. He met Kenny's gaze with his own grim one. "We've got some good evidence here."

Which, with the mother's heartbreaking sobs in the distance, brought no satisfaction at all.

* * *

The building for the new Creative Interiors II sat on a square block of other shops and galleries in the center of Ocean Beach. It was a Tudor-style cottage, two story, with wide open rooms and windows with views of the Pacific Ocean only a street away. Perfect party house, and Summer knew tonight there'd be quite a gathering. It was the opening bash, and if there was one thing Camille and Tina could do and do well, that was throw a party.

Just the idea of it, with tons of people sequestered in close quarters, gave her a tight feeling in her chest.

She tried not to think about it as she worked with Stella and Greg to hang streamers and fill balloons with helium. Stella was a soft-spoken, petite blonde, adorable and sweet, and completely unassuming. Gregg was even more quiet, if that was possible. Summer often wondered if the two of them ever got boisterous or wild. Camille said she'd seem them at parties and after hours socializing, and that they did, but Summer couldn't picture it.

She stopped decorating to look out the windows at the sunset. But off in the distance, in the purple sky, rose a long plume of dark smoke.

A fire.

Everything within her gripped in sympathy, in horror, and she wondered who the flames were affecting. Wondered, too, if Joe was there, with his quiet intense eyes, trying to find the cause.

"Miss being outside?"

She turned and looked at Bill. He and Tina had gotten married after her first one had failed, and they'd been together for fourteen years. He wasn't crazy about the furnishings business, always grumbling about how much time it took Tina away from him, but he'd never failed to be there when his support was required.

Like tonight. He hated crowds, and here he was in his
suit and tie. A wrinkled ill-fitting suit and tie, but he'd tried.
He wasn't quite as tall as she, and was used to being tow-
ered over by the women in his life. He had a mop of wild
gray hair that always made her think of Albert Einstein, a
poet's sorrow-filled blue eyes, and the stained, callused
hands of a ceramic artist.

And a big glass of what was undoubtedly spiked punch
in his hands.

"Yes, I'm missing being outside," she said with a smile
for the first person in O.B. who hadn't looked at her with
wariness, frustration, or open hostility. She wondered if he
still took Prozac like water to even out his moods. Or
maybe he really was fond of her. "I miss it a lot."

"How's your mom?"

"Unnerved about the fire."

He sighed, sending his hair into movement like wild cotton in the wind. Gray cotton. "An unfortunate coincidence,
that was." He looked around at the interior of the new shop,
at the fresh, bright paint he'd put on the walls himself, and
all the beachy stock within them. One entire wall was devoted to his handmade lighthouses. "Nice, huh?" he asked.

"It's great."

"Yeah. Great."

But they both sighed unhappily. "With all the free food
and drink around on every surface, no one'll ever want to
leave," he grumbled. "This thing'll go all night."

"The trick is to get out of here before the crowd shows
up," she said.

Just the thought made her feel better, until she remembered Camille had picked her up and brought her here. At
the time it'd seemed like a good idea, a way to spend an

extra few minutes together, but now she realized the folly of that. She was stuck without a ride.

Bill looked at his watch. "If you're going to escape, you'd better hurry. People are going to arrive."

Too late. A couple walked in, followed by a handful of others. Then Diana and Madeline called her over to help finish the balloons and put out the boat-shaped party favors.

Around them the place began to hum with conversation and laughter. Summer concentrated on breathing and hanging balloons. It wasn't too crowded yet, she assured herself. Not crowded at all. Just because her toes had been stepped on twice already and she couldn't see the front door . . .

"Here. Pour." Diana handed her the champagne and a tray of glasses. "And look alive," she said, then turned to grab Madeline.

"Oh, no," Summer said when they headed toward the closest exit. "You two are supposed to do this. *I'm* the one leaving—"

Madeline pointed to the door.

"Yeah, I see. Alley cat at ten o'clock," Diana noted.

A tall, dark-haired woman dressed in a beaded vintage dress entered and took a long gaze around her.

"The suspense was probably killing her," Diana said.

Madeline nodded grimly.

"Look at her scoping out the stock," Diana said. "So rude."

Summer watched the tall brunette sniff at the hors d'oeuvres with a curling lip.

"Freak," Diana muttered.

Madeline nodded again, popping her gum in her jaw.

"Yeah, well." Summer didn't care about Ally. She cared about being able to breathe, which she suddenly couldn't do in here. She looked at the door. "I've got to run."

Diana smiled as she took over pouring the champagne. "Of course you do."

"What does that mean?"

"It means you always run. That's what I heard your mom say to my mom once. She was crying when she said it."

Summer's chest caved in as if she'd been sucker punched. "Maybe no one ever told you it's not nice to repeat things people say."

Diana lifted a shoulder. "Maybe not."

Summer stared at her, then let out a careful breath. "You know what? The hell with this." She moved away from her and Madeline, and toward the front door. People were swarming now, pressing close. Her breathing quickened again. *Damn it.* She pushed her way through and was nearly there when her wrist was snagged.

"Oh, no, you don't," said Aunt Tina.

Summer stared at her aunt's stubborn face, her chest cinching down. The bell over the door tinkled noisily. Two more people entered, laughing and talking. Summer swallowed hard as the room, so large only moments ago, began to close in on her. "I've really got to—"

"Stay. Eat. Talk. Be merry." Tina thrust a flute of champagne into her hand and smiled. "Just look at your mom, darling. She looks so happy tonight, doesn't she?"

Somehow Summer forced herself to turn and look. Indeed Camille was smiling as she greeted some of their guests. She wore a beautiful flowing gown in a pale silver that seemed to make her skin glow. She caught Summer's eye and waved.

Waved. Summer's throat tightened a little as she waved back. Impossibly, the crowd grew again, pouring in now, pressing against her to get by. With the front door open, she caught a whiff of the smoke from the fire she'd seen earlier. Spots appeared in her vision.

Too close. Too tight.

"Well, would you look at that," Tina murmured.

Kenny was handing her mother a flute of champagne. He wore khaki trousers and a crisp, white button-down. If he was armed, the gun was hidden. The tall, handsome fire marshal pushed up his glasses and smiled at Camille, who smiled back. An open, sweet smile.

Summer hadn't seen many of those. Probably because she hadn't been around to see them.

You always run.

Summer closed her eyes. "I really have to go."

"He's awfully handsome," Tina said. "I think he's attracted to her."

Summer opened her eyes. Camille had put her hand on Kenny's arm, leaning in to listen to him.

"She does seem happy," Summer allowed.

"Yes." Tina hugged Summer. "And darling, you being here is part of the reason."

"Then why does she keep trying to get me to leave?"

"It's what she expects from you." Tina tugged lightly on a strand of Summer's hair. "So prove her wrong. Now go on, go join the fray." She nudged Summer forward to mingle. "And for God's sake, smile!"

There had to be a hundred people here already. Surely that was against the code. In fact, Kenny should be kicking people out. Summer craned her neck to find him but he just kept talking to her mother . . .

Damn it. She tossed back her champagne and waited for the kick. Nothing but her chest tightening further. All around her was talking and laughter, and yet suddenly there wasn't enough air for her lungs. Each new person sucked even more oxygen from the room. She knew that it was just in her head but that didn't make it any less real. The walls continued to close in, until she couldn't draw a full breath at all, but she was good at pretending nothing was wrong. She even managed to keep a smile on her face despite the line of sweat trickling down her spine as she pressed her back to a wall and wished for another drink.

Braden walked past her without a word, then stopped and turned back. "You okay?"

"I need a drink."

He shot her an odd look but grabbed a flute of champagne from a tray and handed it over.

She gulped it down, but her throat remained parched. "Thanks."

"Sure." He wore his usual black, though his standard cynical smile was gone. "You might want to wait a few before your next one."

"I already need another one."

"Yeah." He scrubbed a hand over his mouth and looked longingly at a tray of champagne. "I hear that."

Madeline, and what looked like an entire gaggle of her friends, passed by giggling and teetering and smelling like cigarettes as they eyed the champagne. When she caught Summer watching her, she stuck out her tongue and moved on.

"So, is it being home again?" Braden asked. "Or the crowds?"

When Summer's gaze whipped to his, he lifted a brow. "A shot in the dark."

"A good one." She set down the empty flute. "And for the record, it's both." She took a deeper look and saw the stress in his eyes even though he'd done a damn good job at keeping it to himself. He was just as unhappy at this party as she was. "How about you?"

"I'm perfectly fine."

He was lying, but who was she to press? Besides, at that moment, she caught Chloe's baleful stare from across the room. Oops. She was talking to Chloe's property, wasn't she. She lifted her hands and wriggled her fingers, showing her territorial cousin she was still hands off.

But when she turned back to Braden, he was gone. Without him standing in front of her, buffering her view of everyone milling around her, her breathing hitched again. It seemed as if the amount of people had doubled in the past few minutes. Tripled. Her chest hurt, the spots were back, and she again staggered for the door. Fairy lights decorated the entire front façade, and the helium balloons she'd tied to the canopy were floating in the light breeze. She saw all this in her peripheral vision as she finally burst out.

And crashed directly into a hard chest.

Joe's hands came up to grip her shoulders, probably because she'd just about knocked him flat on his ass. He stood there holding her upright, a faint five o'clock shadow shading his jaw, hair weeks past needing a haircut, smelling like soap and man. An involuntary pained sound escaped her and she slapped a hand to her mouth to keep the next one in.

Hands still on her shoulders, he bent and peered into her face. "What's the matter, Red?"

Oh, God. His eyes. The haunting sadness was back in the swirling whiskey depths tonight, and it reached her. He'd always been able to reach her with a look. "N-n-nothing."

He lifted her chin with a finger. "Don't add lying to your sins. You okay?"

His voice was low, and somehow devastatingly sexy.

And the way he asked her what was wrong, as if he really cared, as if maybe, at least for a moment, he'd forgotten to hold back with her. Her throat simply closed up, and all she could do was shake her head. No. No, she wasn't okay. She might never be again.

His hand, big and warm, came up, tracing her hairline with a long finger, pushing her hair behind her ear. The gesture was an old one, and she nearly lost it right then. She was holding on by a string here, and if anyone could break her, he could. But she knew that while *she* needed a connection tonight, any connection, he did not. At least not from her.

Pushing free, she ran across the street, heading for the beach. She needed the cool night air, the clarity the pounding surf would give her, the wide open space.

"Red?"

She kept going. It wasn't the smartest thing she'd ever done, racing away from one of the very people she wanted to prove herself to, but the minute her feet hit the sand she kicked off her sandals and kept running, hard and fast, not looking back, trying desperately not to look back.

Chapter 6

Joe stared after Summer, not so far gone in his own miserable evening that he hadn't seen the shine of tears in her eyes, or the hitch of panic in her breathing.

It was none of his business. She was none of his business. And so telling himself, he took another step toward the front door of Creative Interiors II, then stopped. "Ah, hell." Turning around, he caught a fleeting glance of her racing into the night as if the devil himself were on her heels. She wore a soft white sundress over her tanned skin, the material gleaming beneath the moonlight as she kicked up her heels, never slowing.

Not his problem.

And yet he didn't go inside. He stood there talking himself out of making yet another mistake in a long series of such mistakes he was getting so proficient at making.

"Idiot," he muttered, and crossed the street to the beach. He stepped onto the sand, kicked off his shoes. "First a jerk, now an idiot."

He'd kept up with his physical training even though technically he was no longer fighting fires. He ran in the mornings, several miles a day when he could manage the time, and hated every sweaty, struggling minute of it. But he had to really kick it in gear to match Summer's long-legged even stride.

The dark beach was deserted except for the occasional other crazy person out running. After about a mile, she slowed, thank God, and then came to a sudden halt, breathing like a misused racehorse, head down, feet in the water as a wave lapped her toes.

Joe came to a halt besides her and let the cool water hit his feet as well while he bent over and tried to catch his breath.

"You're a better runner than you used to be," she said.

He had to laugh between gulping gasps for air. "That's what happens when you drop seventy-five pounds."

She tilted her head and looked at him in the moonlight. The waves crashed onto the shore but other than that, the night felt quiet. Like the calm before a storm.

"I never thought of you as overweight," she murmured.

"If that's true, you were the only one who didn't."

"I liked you just as you were."

"Really?" Still breathing humiliatingly hard, he picked up a smooth stone and chucked it into the pounding surf. "You had a funny way of showing it, cutting off years of friendship without a word, without so much as a 'fuck you, Joe.' "

She squeezed her eyes shut tight at that. "Does it help to hear me say I regret it?"

"Not really."

She pressed her fingers to her eyes. "I should have had more than two glasses of champagne." Then she sighed and looked at him. "*Why* doesn't it help to hear it?"

"It was a lifetime ago." He'd gotten over it. Mostly. "We were just kids."

"Yeah. Kids." She wriggled her toes, including the one

with a tiny little crystal ring on it that looked incredibly sexy.

"You moved on," he said. "And then so did I."

She nodded at that, sadly, and though he didn't understand why, he felt an urge to draw her into his arms. He wanted to stroke away her pain. He wanted to do more than that too, but that would be the mother of all mistakes because with her, one touch would never be enough. "What happened at the opening?"

"Nothing."

"Nothing made you cry?"

The waves were white and frothy by moonlight, and she didn't take her eyes off them. "I wasn't crying."

"You looked like you were having a panic attack."

"Don't be silly."

"Did someone hurt you?"

"No."

"Did someone say something to you?"

"No."

He began to wish *he'd* had two glasses of champagne. "Red. Are you going to tell me what happened?"

"It's nothing. It's me." She threw up her hands in the way she'd always had of talking with them. "I . . . don't fit in here."

"What do you mean?"

"I've been gone too long." The light wind whipped her hair around them. The ends hit his chest and arm. He used to fantasize about having her hair brush over him, but in his dreams she'd always been naked.

"I don't have a place here," she said.

"You have a place wherever you make it for yourself." When she only stared at him, confused, she broke the heart he hadn't realized she could still touch. "You used to be good at that," he said. "Being happy anywhere, doing anything."

She picked up a rock, threw it. "I guess being back is harder than I thought."

"Because you never dealt with it."

She chucked another pebble, her back to him now. "It."

"The fire. Your dad's death."

He saw her flinch. Her shoulders were ramrod straight. "It's hard to deal with an event you can't remember," she said softly.

He felt the surprise reverberate through him, and he pulled her around to face him. Her eyes were shadowed, troubled, and there he saw the shocking truth. "You really don't remember the fire?"

"I remember being in the basement with you and Danny, and seeing the smoke. Then running up the stairs. That's it."

He'd always figured what had happened after that had to be her biggest nightmare, but had also figured she'd put enough time behind her to soften the horror. But that she'd never remembered, and had never really faced it because of that, hadn't occurred to him. "Red—"

"I don't want to talk about it." She gave him a weak smile. "Not tonight."

He opened his mouth, but she set a finger to his lips. "I don't want to talk about it," she repeated. "When I can see you had a rough one too."

He thought of the fire scene he'd just left and tensed. "Yeah."

"Can you tell me about it?"

No. Hell, no, but on the night air, over the sound of the waves, the screams came back to him. The sight of the body bag being carried out, the shape in it so small. So defenseless. He closed his eyes.

"Was it the fire I smelled earlier?"

"Probably."

"What happened?"

"A bad residential fire. A little kid—" His throat closed. He shook his head.

"Oh, Joe." She had a charm bracelet on her wrist, probably for good luck. She'd always believed in that stuff. It jangled when she skimmed her fingers over his. "I'm so sorry," she whispered, and squeezed his hand.

"I think it was arson," he managed to say. Christ, he shouldn't be telling her this. "I think his father killed him."

Only she would know how that would get to him above all else, and with a soft sound, she stepped even closer. A breeze shuddered over them, and a strand of her hair slid over his jaw now, clinging to the stubble. He left it there.

"Do you ever think about him?" she asked quietly. "Your father?"

"No." But lying to her had never been possible, and he let out a long breath. "Not that often."

"My mother wrote me when he died last year. Did you two ever . . . get close?"

By the time his father had stopped drinking and had come along looking for forgiveness, Joe had been graduating from college and hadn't been able to find any forgiveness within him. "No."

He thought he'd said the word forcibly. With confidence. Without a hint of the doubts that sometimes plagued him. But Summer's eyes searched his and read his deepest, most darkest thoughts, the way no one else ever had. *Ever.*

"He didn't deserve your forgiveness," she said fiercely, holding his hand tight as she brought it up to her heart, cushioned between the soft warmth of her breasts. "When I think about all those times you came into my window, bruised, bleeding—"

"Red, don't."

"He didn't deserve your forgiveness," she said again, and keeping their fingers entwined over her heart, looked up at the stars. "Sometimes, when I'm out on a trek, in the wilderness with just a handful of people, it's easy to forget all the cruelty in this world. But you . . . you grew up with it. You have to see it all the time in your job. How do you do it?"

He shrugged. "Most people are basically good. The ones that aren't, I can help put away. I just keep that in front of me I guess."

She slowly shook her head. "I've been spoiled out there."

"Speaking of that wilderness, when are you going back to it?"

"I told you. I'm staying to help, until all the work for the fire is done."

"And given your mood here tonight, it's going so well."

"I know." She let out a low laugh. "It's just that I feel so tense, all the time. So uptight. So . . . unlike me."

"What, no special crystals? No special breathing exercises?"

She played with her bracelet. "I don't think they work anymore."

She looked so devastated over that, he searched his brain for a way to help her. "You used to hike to relieve stress. Straight up Palomar Mountain, remember? I hated doing that with you almost as much as I hated jogging."

With a low laugh, she let go of his hand and bent to pick up a rock. "Actually, I was thinking of another stress reliever entirely."

He watched as she chucked it hard. "Like what?"

"Like the kind that involves the oblivion of a good orgasm."

In the dark her self-deprecating smile didn't shoot to his heart, but straight between his thighs.

"Don't worry," she said quickly. "I'm not propositioning you. I met Cindy, I know you're taken." Her next rock took a trip halfway to China.

"She dumped me," he heard himself say.

She looked at him for a long moment. "Before or after the lunch special?"

"I really wish you hadn't heard that part." He shook his head, surprised to find himself embarrassed. "We, uh, didn't. Not that day, anyway."

She let out a little smile. "A shame for you."

"Red." He grimaced. "I don't want to talk about this."

"Okay." She looked at her toes, then back into his eyes. "I'm sorry if you got hurt."

"I didn't."

"Getting dumped is never painless."

He shrugged.

For a long moment, she was quiet, reflective. Then she asked the million dollar question. "Did you ever wonder what it would be like between us?"

He looked into her warm, dreamy eyes and felt everything within him react. "This is a bad idea."

"What? We're just talking."

"Yeah, about what it'd be like between us."

"All I'm getting at is how can one really great night without strings be a bad idea?"

"Red." Christ. He was only human here. "We have a past. That makes it impossible to do the no strings thing."

"Hey, I can make a no strings night work with just about

anyone." Her smile turned self-mocking. "It's a special talent of mine."

He'd held the same talent. In fact, in a true ironic twist, the last person he'd had any deep, emotional ties to had been her. Knowing that, there was no way for him to make just talking to her casual, much less a physical intimacy.

If they slept together, she'd do him in for sure.

"You know what I want?" she asked softly.

His body leapt in spite of himself. Yeah, he was pretty clear on what she wanted. To escape, to forget. She'd just never wanted it from *him* before. "The oblivion of a good orgasm."

She closed her eyes, hiding. She was good at that, too. "Besides an orgasm. I want to go home, Joe."

"That's easy enough."

"I need a ride."

No. Don't offer. *Don't say a word.* "I'll take you," his mouth said, clearly disconnected from his brain.

She smiled at him, the kind that used to grab him by the throat and squeeze until he couldn't breathe. Then she nudged his shoulder with hers, an old gesture that brought him back years.

He nudged her back, and with a laugh, staggered toward the water, laughing, losing her balance. He grabbed her wrist and pulled her upright, knocking her right into his body.

Bracing herself with a hand to his chest, her fingers curling into him, her grin slowly faded. "You know what gets me?"

"Um . . ." His mind raced. "The ridiculous price of gasoline?"

"No."

"The amount of crumbs at the bottom of a box of cereal?"

"Silly." She smiled, but it was a sad one. "What gets me is that you sound the same." Her fingers tested the strength of him, from pec to pec. "But you sure don't feel the same."

Her touch made him want to roll over like a puppy and expose his underside. He stepped back so that her hand fell free. "We'd better go." He turned toward the way they'd come, flinching when he felt her hand on his arm.

She just danced her fingers to his shoulder, down his spine, slowly but not tentatively, tearing away his defenses as only she could. "Don't," he managed.

Her other hand joined the fray.

God, don't. "Red—"

"You feel good, Joe. Warm. Strong."

Not strong enough to resist this, but he gave it a valiant effort. He had to, or lose it, because with her, only with her he felt far too vulnerable.

Take that, Kenny, he thought. *I did it. I found the woman I could actually let in.*

Only I can't really do it because she can't be trusted to stay in.

Chapter 7

"Take me home, Joe," Summer whispered, and stroked her hands up his back.

Taking her home would be bad, Joe thought. *Very* bad. But she kept touching him and suddenly he couldn't remember *why*.

Because she's leaving.

Because she'll hurt you.

Oh yeah, now he remembered. Turning to face her, he encircled her wrists with his hands.

She merely leaned into his chest, their hands squished between them, and looked at his mouth.

A low, rough groan tore from deep in his throat.

Reaching up, she kissed his jaw.

He hissed out a harsh breath and tugged her hands behind her back, pinned low on her spine. It seemed like a good idea at the time, but that meant she was helpless, pressed against him. He could feel her breasts, her belly, the outline of her thighs, and before he could pull away she arched into his hard-on with a little hum of pleasure.

And just like that, he was a goner. Dipping his head, he did what once had been his greatest fantasy. He covered her mouth with his and dove headfirst into a kiss that rocked his world, curled his toes, and drained the blood right out of his head.

When they had to break apart or suffocate, he stared at her, unable to catch his breath. Had he thought her helpless? She smiled up against him, her mouth still wet from his, with so much promise in her eyes he would have followed her to the damn moon, which meant *he* was the helpless one here. *Send out a life vest, he was going down.* He let go of her but she merely slid her arms around his neck and nibbled at his throat. When he groaned again, she sank her fingers into his hair, changed the angle of his head to suit her, and took his mouth.

Damn it, he was *not* going to do this, but then she murmured to him, stroking him with her hands, her tongue, her body, and he began to drown after all. *"Red."*

"You're shaking," she said with surprise.

"I know." He was the biggest fool on the planet, a fool who *had* to touch her. He ran a fingertip over her jaw, down her throat. Over her collarbone.

"Kiss me again," she whispered, and outlined his lower lip with her tongue.

That was all it took. Some big, bad, tough guy he was. He sank into what she offered, giving it back, until they were *both* shaking. His hands and mouth couldn't get enough of her.

"Mmm." Eyes closed, she let out a long, catchy sigh. She had her hands beneath his shirt, touching skin to skin. "You kiss so amazing. Where did you learn to kiss like that?"

His fingers dug into her hips, squeezing. He didn't want to talk, he wanted—

She sank her teeth into his lower lip and tugged. His knees nearly buckled and the next kiss lasted even longer.

The urge to drag her down to the sand shocked him back into awareness. He was breathing like a lunatic, and had one hand gripping her ass, the other cupping her breast. Even as his senses began to clear, his thumb stroked over the hardened tip of her nipple, once, twice.

She gasped and her head fell back, exposing the beautiful, tempting line of her throat. He leaned in to taste her there and she let out a sexy little moan. "See how easy it is to forget all your troubles?" she gasped.

His mouth open on her, he went still. He'd been about to inhale her whole, but he closed his lips and set his forehead to hers. Forget his troubles? She *was* his troubles!

"Home." She kissed one corner of his mouth, then the other. "Take me home, Joe."

Incredibly bad idea, but they moved in silence along the soft, giving sand, with the waves occasionally sloshing over their feet as they went, thankfully not running this time, and when he stopped at the sleek black classic Camaro parked near Creative Interiors II, she laughed. "This used to be your fantasy car! When did you get it?"

He shrugged off the vague embarrassment. "A few years back."

"You ever make out in it?"

"Red."

She laughed at the look on his face. "Well, I hope you have. That's why you always wanted it, remember?"

"I wanted it," he corrected, having to laugh at her, at himself, "because of the power of the beast."

"Ah, yes, the size of the engine." Her eyes flashed warm and affectionate. "What is it with men and the size of their . . . toys?"

"Ha-ha. Just get in."

She put her hand over his and tried to take his keys.

"Hell, no," he said.

"Come on."

"Do you think I've forgotten who taught you to drive, and that you suck at it?"

"I'll have you know I no longer plow into mailboxes."

He lifted the keys up over his head. She was tall, but not quite tall enough, and he decided he was a sick, sick man to enjoy how she tried to climb up his body to get the keys. "You had two glasses of champagne."

"Far too long ago," she replied.

"Maybe next time," he said, knowing there wouldn't be one because he was going to get smart and stay far away from her. Any minute now. He waited until she buckled up before he hit the gas. The car leapt to life, and she whooped with glee as they took off.

She'd always been able to do that, find the joy in the moment. He'd never been nearly as good at it, but he felt a surge of joy now, for no reason other than the car was running like a sweet thing, the wind blew fresh sea air in his face, and . . . and Summer was smiling at him.

She'd kissed him. He'd kissed her. Amazing, she'd murmured, and he had to agree. He felt her glance at him, but pretended not to notice, pretended not to be hard as a rock as well, wondering what the hell he'd been thinking to be taking her home. She was bad for him, bad for his mental health.

He was absolutely not going inside her place. No way. Maybe he should chain himself to the seat just in case he forgot that fact.

She gave him directions and he pulled onto a street lined with small, narrow cottages sitting on the bluffs above the ocean. "Why aren't you staying with your mom?"

"I did that first night, but Chloe's friend was staying

here, and she left for Maine for the summer, and I thought I might enjoy the location . . ." She trailed off with a lift of one shoulder.

"And . . ."

"And what?"

"And the real reason you're staying here instead of with your mom?"

"I don't know." Her gaze skittered away. "I think my family's just waiting for me to leave."

"Maybe because you have a history of doing exactly that."

"But not this time."

"They'll come around." When he turned off the engine the night was quiet and dark, and they might have been alone in the world. He gripped onto the steering wheel as if it were his lifeline, anchoring him to a reality that was slowing slipping away.

"Thank you," she said.

"I didn't do anything."

Wasn't going to do anything.

"Come inside."

Yes. *Yes.* "No."

"Why not?"

Her hair glimmered in the night. Her eyes were bright and clear and full of the things they could be doing to each other. She'd pulled her legs beneath her but he could still remember how perfectly long and smooth and tanned they were, and at the thought of how they'd feel wrapped around him, he nearly drooled like a knuckle-dragging Neanderthal. He held onto the steering wheel for all he was worth. "Because."

"Good reason."

"Okay, how about because you're feeling vulnerable, and so am I."

"Because of Cindy?"

"Not because of Cindy, no."

"Because of the fire?"

Because of you. "Look, it's been a long night all around. A rough one." He scrubbed a hand over his face and when he dropped it, she had sympathy and compassion welling in her eyes and he had to close his. "It'd be better if you stopped looking at me."

"Better for who?"

"For me."

She didn't stop looking at him.

"You should go in," he said a little desperately.

"It's such a beautiful night." She leaned back, tipping her face up to the night sky, apparently in no hurry to go anywhere. The white sundress glowed in the night air, her expression open and caring. "We could just talk."

He couldn't take his eyes off her. Maybe a bag over her head would help.

"We used to talk for hours," she said. "Remember?"

Yeah, he remembered. He remembered lying with her in the warehouse eating, laughing. Being. But he wasn't that kid anymore.

"Did you go to San Diego State on your scholarship as planned?"

"Red—"

"Play along, Joe. Talk to me. Unload."

"Why?"

She laughed. "Such a guy. Come on, it won't hurt."

He sighed. "Yes, I went to State."

"Did you love it?"

He shrugged. "I worked a lot. Studied a lot. It's all a blur now." He sighed into her expectant face. "Yeah, I loved it."

"Now you," she said.

"Now I what?"

"Now you ask *me* a question."

Do you really use orgasms as a stress relief? "Were you happy out there, doing your thing?"

She smiled. "I was." The smile slowly faded. "And I figured I could be that happy here, too, but I can't seem to quite manage it. I think it's because all these years ago, I left wrong. It's like I have to fix that before I can go on." She met his gaze. "I was young and stupid to leave here the way I did. I honestly didn't realize what I had, with my mom, with you. That relationship of ours . . . the truth is, I've never been able to replicate it."

Going there was a bad idea. "Red—"

"I hate that I hurt you, Joe." She put her hand on his. "Come inside with me. Please? Let me make it up to you."

Her soft, sensuous voice slid right through him, cut down his defenses as effectively as her sad smile did. "Why?" he asked. "Because we're both lonely?"

"Yes, because we're both lonely. A good orgasm banishes loneliness, I promise you."

"How about pain? Does a good orgasm banish pain too?"

Her eyes lit, and her soft laugh echoed around him. "Absolutely."

Good Lord, the woman looked like sin personified. He wanted her so badly his jeans were cutting off circulation to some critical parts, but she'd been right. He had learned quite a bit about control over the years. Slowly, with great effort, he sat back until the door handle cut into his spine. "I'm not going to be the scratch to your itch, Red."

"You're not?"

"And I most definitely don't want to be your pity fuck."

"Your pity—" Her eyes flashed. "Maybe I just wanted to be with someone tonight."

"I'm not that someone. I can't be."

"Because it's me and I once hurt you?"

"Because it's you and I can't seem to keep the distance you require."

She stared at him for a long moment. "Let me make sure I understand. You *do* want me."

Only more than my next breath. "Yes."

"But you're afraid it won't be just sex? Honestly, Joe, that's just . . ." She lifted her hands helplessly.

"Yeah," he said grimly. "Words fail, don't they?" With more strength than he knew he had, he got out of the car, moved around to the passenger door and opened it for her. She brushed past him, then turned back. "It doesn't have to end like this tonight."

"But what about tomorrow night? Or the night after that?"

"Just so happens I'm free those nights too," she said.

She was going to kill him. "Red."

"Right." She stepped back. "You're not."

"Not for this. I'm sorry."

"No. No, that's okay."

Calling himself a fool, he leaned back against his car, folded his arms over his chest and waited for her to get inside.

Halfway to her door, she glanced back. "You're going to be in your bed tonight, cursing yourself for being alone when you could have been with me."

"That is the absolute truth."

She just stared at him for a long beat, then unlocked and

opened the front door. She turned the light on inside, illuminating herself like a fish in a fishbowl.

He drank her up, all those long limbs and shiny hair. She leaned back against the doorjamb, much in the same nonchalance he was.

A face-off. He wouldn't go anywhere until she was inside, but she didn't seem to be in any hurry. "Lock the door," he said, hoping she would before he forgot himself and went after her.

Her lips twisted in a wry smile. "Sweet dreams."

"I doubt they'll be sweet."

"That's your own fault. I hope you're aching and yearning and in need of a cold shower."

"Should I wish you sweet dreams back, Summer?"

She shut the door on that.

Her light went off.

He let out a slow breath, not sure whether he hated her, or still loved her.

Chapter 8

Summer slept restlessly. She got up before the crack of dawn and grabbed her hiking gear. There was an early staff meeting at Creative Interiors II, right before the big opening day, but she still had several hours before that, so she drove northeast to Palomar to hike among the towering conifers and oaks.

When she'd finished, she felt better equipped for the day, and smiled as she showered and changed before heading to the new shop. She had the VW's windows down so that the gorgeous morning could show off its bright sunshine and already warm breeze. She breathed it all in and promised herself another long hike tomorrow.

She pulled into the parking lot of the store at the same time as Chloe. Her cousin got out of her car and looked Summer up and down. "Where did you run off to last night?"

Summer looked right back. Chloe's green-tipped hair shimmered in the morning light, matching her eye-popping green miniskirt and tank top. "You look like a lucky charm."

"Nice subject change. What happened, you get hot monkey sex?"

"Hot monkey sex?" Summer laughed. "Who gets hot monkey sex?"

Chloe put her hands on her hips. "Did you or did you not do it with your fire marshal?"

"Since when is he *my* fire marshal?"

"Do you ever answer a damn question?"

"No. But I didn't get hot monkey sex." But she'd wanted to. God, she'd wanted to. One touch of Joe's yummy mouth to hers and she'd nearly imploded. He'd been hard and sexy, and she loved how his wary eyes softened when he kissed. He put everything into it, too, knowing when to linger, when to go slow, how to drive her crazy with just a nuzzle of that mouth and a touch of his tongue. "We're just old friends," she said. "You know that."

"He's a hottie. Don't tell me you didn't notice."

"He's changed a lot." And she still couldn't believe he'd let her walk away last night. A rejection, and damn, that had hurt. It'd been a long time since a man had turned her down. Actually, a man had never turned her down. Joe was her first. The thought made her feel melancholy, and she eyed the bakery across the street. "The doughnuts smell good."

"You don't eat doughnuts."

She did if she was stressed enough.

"You know how the moms feel about junk food," Chloe said.

"Are you telling me you never have junk?"

"I'm telling you I do what every self-respecting daughter of a health nut does. I sneak them. So if you're going, I'll take an old-fashioned glazed. Two." She smoothed down her short, short skirt. "I'm going in to see if I can catch Braden's attention."

Summer eyed Chloe's wild outfit before she headed across the street. "That shouldn't be a problem."

When she got back a few minutes later, Bill was in the lot, buried under the hood of Tina's car.

"The woman never checks her oil," he said with exasperation. He wore baggy painter pants, splattered with clay from the last decade, and a Dead Head T-shirt.

"Doughnut?" Summer opened the box.

"Aren't these against Tina's and Camille's code of food ethics?"

"I won't tell if you won't."

"You know they can smell this sort of thing from a mile away, right? I got caught with McDonald's once and Tina was mad at me for a week."

"Well, if you're not interested . . . "

"Hey, I never said I wasn't interested." He grinned and took a jelly-filled.

"You doing ceramics today?" she asked.

"For a bit. Then I've got stuff to do."

He often had "stuff to do," which was code for picking horses at Del Mar, or playing cards at one of two local gaming houses. He and Tina actually met at one of them, though they no longer played together. This was because Tina mostly lost, and Bill didn't. Tina would come by and pull from his winnings, which was the only thing that ever made his temper surface. Tina thought it was funny; the man had helped her raise her three girls without a rise in his blood pressure, but she couldn't mess with his winnings until he got up from the gaming table, or he'd lose it.

"You're going to want to hurry," he said, with a nod of his chin toward inside. "Staff meeting's going to start before they split up to handle both stores."

Summer looked at the new building. It seemed so big

and roomy in the light of day, and she couldn't figure out what had panicked her so much last night. "What's the mood like?"

"Excited. Tense, too."

"Wish me luck." She went inside and opened the box of doughnuts on the employee table. Everyone promptly ditched Camille's offering of herbal iced tea and dove into the box to grab their favorite sugar rush.

Camille refrained from the box with a worried little frown as Socks wound through her legs, purring loudly. "Too much sugar in the morning isn't good for—" She sighed when everyone practically inhaled theirs. "Well. Okay, fine. Kill your arteries."

Summer surreptitiously wiped the sugar off her fingers.

Camille noticed anyway, and just rolled her eyes. "As I was saying, make sure you all familiarize yourself with the new warehouse stock. We've just received quite an impressive shipment from Tina and Bill's spring shopping trips, so that will help with what we lost at the warehouse. More stock is stuffed in every corner of the storage rooms of each of the two stores, in my house, and also Tina's, so if people are looking for something specific, make sure you check the list."

Diana was pretending to take notes but was really reading a manila file covered *Cosmo*. Madeline was making little smiley faces on a pad of paper, completely lost to the group. Stella and Gregg sat together, silent but attentive.

"Call Braden to verify a product hasn't been sold," Camille continued. "Or to get a price."

Braden hoisted his laptop. His eyes were dark and unreadable as he looked around with a cool, brooding calm.

Chloe was staring at him dreamily as she stuffed herself

with an old-fashioned chocolate glaze. "He's hot," she mouthed to Summer.

That happened to be true, but Summer was thinking hot wouldn't necessarily feed the soul. And since when had she ever cared about feeding the soul, she had no idea.

When the meeting was over, Stella, Gregg, and the twins moved toward the door to get themselves downtown to the original Creative Interiors, but Camille stopped them. "I should mention, the fire marshals'll be stopping by both shops today for any final questions they have for their report. Please cooperate with them fully."

Chloe turned to Summer and raised a suggestive brow.

Summer ignored her but had two conflicting emotions barrel through her at the news she'd be seeing Joe today. Anticipation and trepidation.

But mostly anticipation.

Madeline scooted close and showed them Diana's magazine, opened to the horoscope page. She pointed to Chloe's, and read, "Your moons are lined up."

"So full speed ahead," Diana said to her older sister.

Chloe snagged the magazine and greedily soaked up her horoscope. "What does Summer's say?"

"That she shouldn't have gotten out of bed," Diana read.

Summer sighed but she couldn't work up any real irritation because she was still stuck on having to see Joe today. She needed more time to process the embarrassment of his rejection, and to distance herself from the fact that Chloe had been wrong—she wasn't so irresistible after all.

Damn, he'd wanted her. She'd tasted that want, she'd felt it. And still, he'd walked away.

As she'd once done to him.

Well, damn it, she hoped they were even now.

She caught up with her mom behind the counter. "Where do you want me to work today?"

"Oh." Camille looked around. In her long, flowing flowery sundress and natural makeup, she looked serene and elegant. Socks meowed at her feet and got scooped up, making him look quite pleased with himself. "You know you don't have to," Camille said.

"I want to."

"You *want* to deal with beach cushions and pictures and lighthouses and grumpy toddlers and bossy shoppers, oh my?"

Teasing sarcasm. The gesture felt like a hug, and Summer grinned. "You know it."

"It's going to be too tame for you."

Maybe she was ready for a little tame, ready to belong here. She reached for her mom's hand and squeezed it with hers twice. In the old days that had been their code for "love you." In keeping with the code, Camille would squeeze back three times, meaning "love you too."

With a distracted smile, Camille squeezed back. One squeeze.

What the hell did that mean?

Camille hesitated and then said, "Honey, I'm grateful you're here, but I just don't think you should force yourself to stay. That's all."

"I'm not. I want to do this. I want to be with you."

Camille looked down at their joined hands. "You haven't always."

The words sat in the air like two thick, black storm clouds for a beat before Camille shook her head. "I'm sorry. I didn't mean to do this now. I . . . need some more tea."

"Is that what you think?" Summer asked hoarsely, having to follow her mom back to the small employee back room. She couldn't believe it. "That I don't want to be with you?"

"I'm sorry." Camille said again and closed her eyes, a trick Summer recognized all too well as she did the same when she felt the most. "I know being here is getting to you."

"Mom." She let out a mirthless laugh. "We've got to stop tiptoeing around this. Around everything. Let's just say what we feel, okay? Yes, it's hard to be here, but I want to stay." *Now you,* she thought. *Now you tell me you want me stay, too.*

"Camille!" Tina poked her head in, waved her sister over. "This you have to see."

"What is it?"

"Guess who just executed a slow drive-by to put her nose into our opening day business?"

"Not Ally," Camille said, shocked.

"I swear it's her, wearing a big straw hat and dark glasses, the sneaky bitch."

"I'll be right there." Camille looked at Summer.

"Honey, I'm glad you're here, so glad. But it's been so long since we've done this, spent time . . . I want to give you want you need, but quite frankly, I'm not sure what that is."

"You. My mom. My family."

Camille smiled, but it seemed shaky. "Well that's easy enough then, since that's what I am." Leaning in, she kissed Summer on the cheek, then left.

Summer looked at Socks. "So what do you think of this mess?"

"Mew."

"Yeah." Camille's hesitation made sense. Summer *had* run. Only once, but she'd kept going, and though she'd been back over the years, she'd never really put her heart into it. Which meant it wasn't just Camille's fault that they weren't close, or any of them for that matter.

Summer'd had a hand in this, in driving the wedge between herself and her mother.

If only it was as easy to undo.

A large crowd showed up for the official opening of Creative Interiors II, which kept everyone on their toes.

Joe and Kenny showed up midmorning. Joe wore washed-out, faded Levi's, Kenny dark blue trousers. Each man had on their white uniform shirts with the badges on them, though only Joe's looked like it'd never met an iron it liked. He also wore aviator sunglasses, shoved to the top of his head, nearly lost in the mop of wild summer-kissed waves falling over his forehead. Kenny's blond hair was firefighter short, and he had on his Harry Potter glasses.

Each man was armed, and each looked quite official in his own way.

Summer was ringing up a customer at the time, an athletic woman in her thirties who had a younger sister Summer had gone to school with. They were talking about which hiking trails were the best to take this time of year. The morning out there had rejuvenated Summer, and she couldn't wait to get out again, right in her own backyard.

Funny, but this hadn't been her own backyard in a very long time, and yet there was something comforting about claiming it again as hers, something unsettlingly promising.

But then Joe stepped inside, with his see-all eyes and watchful ways, with his gun and the baffling new confidence, bringing the heat of the day and the heat from something else entirely, and she lost her ability to concentrate. She couldn't help it, she just stood there for a moment, her tongue glued to the roof of her mouth, every thought escaping right out of her head.

Then he turned his head and unerringly found her in one sweeping glance.

The customer touched her arm, bringing her back. "You really brought the trails to life for me, thanks so much. Is it okay to go up there alone, do you think?"

"If you can read a map."

"Oh." Her face fell. "I could get lost finding my way out of a paper bag."

"I could call you next time I go."

"Really?" She lit up, and searched her purse for a piece of paper to write down her number. "That would be so nice of you!"

Kenny moved into the back rooms. Joe didn't. Summer couldn't tear her eyes off him.

"Are you sure that wouldn't be any trouble?" the customer asked, handing Summer the paper.

"Not at all."

The customer thanked her again, petted Socks who was sprawled on the counter like a fat, stuffed animal, and left.

Joe stepped close. His gaze searched Summer's face, his own expression a little tight. "You're here."

Had he thought she'd leave because things had gotten tough? Of course he'd think that. Only *she* was the tough one now and was going to prove it. "You look kinda tired," she said, and blinked innocently. "Long night?"

"Not too bad."

"Liar."

That made his dimple flash, and he laughed, and she had to admit, she loved the sound.

Another customer walked in, the hanging bells over the door tinkering merrily. "That's me," she said, but neither of them moved. For Summer, staring up at him, she didn't know what was happening to her, to them, but it seemed to her as if time stopped.

But Joe didn't say a word, and with no choice, she dropped her gaze and began to move away.

Then he caught her wrist.

He hadn't shaved again, and those light russet eyes danced with some emotion she didn't have a name for. There was heat there, too, a carefully banked fire that stoked her own. "Red," he said. Low. Gruff.

An odd feeling swept through her chest. She would have sworn it was hope.

"Hello?" the new customer called out and waved to her. He was an elderly gentleman with a sweet, kindly smile. "I need some help picking out a birthday gift for my wife."

"Yes, of course." She looked at Joe.

He let go of her wrist, then began to walk away. His long legs ate up the distance of the shop, then suddenly he stopped. Muttered to himself. Eyes fierce and hot, he strode back and nudged her around a wall partition. Actually, not so much nudged as shoved. "What—" she started, but he put both hands on her arms, hauled her up and kissed her.

When he pulled back, he was breathing hard. "Jesus." He let go of her and rubbed a hand over his eyes. "You're screwing with my head."

Her own head was spinning, her body throbbing, and she stood there wobbling on her feet. "What was that?"

"I don't know but it's your fault." He plowed his fingers in his hair, leaving it standing straight up. "You gave me that taste last night, and now I can't stop thinking about it."

"Excuse me?" The customer was apparently looking for her. "Miss?"

Summer's knees wobbled through the sale. By the time

she'd rung up the man's purchase, Joe was busy interview-
ing Braden and Chloe, both of whom had been at the warehouse in the past month.

An interview with Summer wasn't necessary, seeing as
she hadn't been in town at the time of the fire, and that she
hadn't been in or around the property for twelve solid years.

Unneeded. Unwanted . . .

When Joe and Kenny were done with their interviews,
Joe came back into the main room and shot her one long
look that seemed to scorch her from the inside out, leaving
her achy and needy all over again.

"Meow," Socks said from the counter.

"No kidding," Summer murmured as Joe left without another word, needing a fan for her hot face.

Or a kiss.

Chapter 9

Summer waited with bated breath for Joe to show up at her cottage that night. He didn't.

Then she decided that waiting for him was ridiculous, and over the next few days dedicated herself to becoming part of her family again. She had dinner with her mother. Lunch with Tina. She dragged Chloe a quarter of the way up the mountain before Chloe cried uncle and begged off.

For Diana and Madeline, Summer lowered her expectations and took them into the wilds of the local mall, where they tried on five-hundred-dollar Nordstrom shoes for the fun of it and ate pizza at the food court.

She had another dinner with her mother, and had Camille laughing out loud at the story of Diana and Madeline arguing over a pair of heavenly velvet five-inch Manolos, of which neither could even afford the ankle buckle.

It felt wonderful.

As for Joe, he stayed away, and she knew why. He didn't want to be tempted.

Inspiration in that regard struck her midweek. She drove downtown to the Fire Department, and the MAST offices. "It's not the lunch special," she said wryly when she found him at his desk looking tired, frustrated, and sexy as hell with his hair all wild and his sleeves shoved up to his elbows. "But you'll like it."

He caught the jumbo bag of potato chips in midair. Turning it over in his hands like a prized Christmas gift, he finally tossed it back to her. "I had to give up chips. Even those half-assed baked ones that taste like sandpaper."

As he'd once practically lived off chips, she was shocked. "You're kidding."

"Nope." Joe's gaze never left the bag in her hand. She'd have sworn he started to drool as he patted his now flat belly. "And believe me, it was a huge sacrifice— Damn it, don't even think about opening—"

She ripped open the bag and came around his desk, wafting the bag beneath his nose.

"You are evil," he said, gaze still locked on the bag.

"Finally my secret is out."

"Oh my God." He grabbed her arm to hold the bag beneath his nose and inhaled deeply. "Those even *smell* fattening. Stop. I'm begging you."

"Okay, you're right," she murmured, wanting to kiss him at the look of tortured misery on his face. "I'm being cruel." But before she could move away, he tightened his grip.

Holding her gaze, he tugged slowly, inexorably, until she stood between his sprawled legs. "Give. Me. The. Bag."

"I don't want to bring you to the dark side."

"Too late."

"I won't be responsible for—"

"I have a gun," he said. "And I know how to use it."

She laughed.

He dove into the bag and came out with a fistful. At his first bite, he leaned back, closed his eyes and let out a throaty moan. Then his eyes whipped open. "You'll leave these with me."

She dropped the bag in his lap. "All yours, big boy."

Munching, he smiled. It was his first, and it was contagious. "Thanks. You give great lunch special."

"You should try my bedtime special sometime."

"Oh, no. That would be waaaay too fattening for sure." Playfully, he tugged at her hair. An old gesture.

And an entirely new meaning.

He was enjoying her company. Affection burst through her, and relief. But she didn't want to push. She'd have to do this in layers with him, so she dipped into the bag for a few chips, then moved to the door. "Don't work too hard."

"Whoa there, Tiger. Hold up."

Slowly, she turned back. His hair was still wild, his sleeves still shoved up, but he no longer looked so frustrated.

Still sexy though. Still *very* sexy.

"That's it?" he asked. "You came just to corrupt me with food?"

"What else would you like?" she asked very softly.

He let out a low breath and pushed to his feet. Stopping a hair breadth away, he shook his head. "Actually, I don't have a clue."

"That's okay." She smiled as her heart tightened just a little. "Maybe it'll come to you."

He stroked a finger over her jaw. "Maybe."

She felt like turning her cheek into his touch. Or stepping closer to his body. She forced herself to remain still. "See ya," she whispered.

His mouth quirked. His dimple made another appearance. "See ya."

*   *   *

The official news came at the end of the week. In compliance with the fire department, the warehouse fire had been ruled an accident by the insurance company.

To celebrate, Summer took Camille to lunch at an old favorite, the Blues Café, where the music was excellent, the food more excellent, and it was impossible not to relax.

When they were done, Camille hugged Summer tight. There on the warm sidewalk with the scent of the ocean all around them and the welcoming feel of her mom's arms around her, Summer thought this wasn't a bad place to be at all.

"That was a lovely good-bye lunch," Camille said when she pulled back. "Thank you."

Summer blinked. *"Good-bye?"*

"Well, we have a ruling now, right? The report is just a formality, and due any day."

Ah, she got it. With the report, she was free to go. And she couldn't wait. Really, she couldn't. But her thoughts raced as they walked along the noisy, crowded sidewalk. Before they got in the car, she grabbed her mom's hand. "Mom? I need to say something."

Camille smiled softly. "I already know."

"You do?"

"Yes. You love me."

"Yes, I do, very much, but that's not what I was going to say." She sucked in a big breath. "I'm sorry I left the way I did all those years ago, that I wasn't there for you . . . I'm sorry I disappointed you."

Camille put a hand to her heart and shook her head. "I don't want you to be sorry—"

"But I am. I'm so damned sorry, Mom."

"Oh, Summer. Do you think I don't see how hard you're trying to love it here?" She hugged Summer again. "And I love it that it matters so much to you to be with me. But you've already given me nearly three weeks. I'm sure you're dying to get out of here."

"I have a few more days."

"Honey."

"No really. I'm taking a customer and a group of her friends on a day hike tomorrow." And she was looking forward to it, she really was.

Camille smiled, though suddenly it seemed strained. "That's lovely." She cupped Summer's face. "You know we're going to be fine, you and me, when you go."

But were they? Or would they revert back to not really knowing each other at all? "I just want you to understand why I'm leaving this time. That I'm not running any more. That I'll be back, *really* back."

"I do."

But was the knowing enough? Summer didn't know that either.

Two nights later Summer was at the new Creative Interiors II, helping the last customer of the day before closing. It was her last time at the register.

She was leaving tomorrow morning.

She'd led a few hikes, she'd gone out kayaking with Chloe, and she actually almost wished she had more time to keep exploring her old haunts.

But tomorrow she'd drive to her small studio apartment in San Francisco. She had a plane ticket for two days from now, to Colorado, where she'd immerse herself in river rafting season, and not think too much about what she'd left: her mom, her family.

Joe.

He'd come by earlier, with a copy of the fire report. He

hadn't said good-bye, and neither had she. And now she faced her last evening. Alone. She knew that everyone often hung out at Tooley's Bar and Grill after work. Normally the bar scene was not her thing but tonight she thought she could use it. "What are you doing after work?" she asked Chloe.

Chloe's grin said it all. "Guess."

Summer's gaze cut to the very gorgeous but very silent Braden on the other side of the shop, behind the counter, fingers clicking at the speed of light over his laptop keyboard. "He asked you out?"

"Does it matter who asked who?"

She thought of how she'd kissed Joe on the beach and had to admit that no, it didn't matter who started the asking. "He's so quiet. Do you two ever talk?"

"Maybe I'm not looking for talk."

"Yeah." There was something greatly unfair about Chloe getting lucky while she was not, despite her best efforts. "Maybe you could jump him another time."

"Why?"

Because it's my last night. But Chloe already knew that, and Summer was getting tired of pushing herself on absolutely everyone. "No real reason."

"Well, then, not a chance."

"Right." Out of sheer desperation, Summer approached Diana and Madeline. They were planning to go to some college party, and though they were actually pleasant—and Diana gave Summer a glowing horoscope for once—they didn't invite her to come along as they vanished out the door smelling like forbidden cigarettes and trouble waiting to happen.

With no customers left, Chloe was chomping at the bit to go home and get ready for her hot date with Braden, so

Summer gave up and shooed her off as well. As she did, Stella came through from the back with her purse. "I don't see why you won't let Gregg and me close up for you on your last night in town," she said to Summer.

"That's okay." If she left now, her big evening alone would start even earlier. "I've got it covered."

"All right. *Gregg!*" she yelled down the stairs to the employee break room. "He's so particular about the routine," she said to Summer. "He likes to make sure everything is closed up just right. You should have seen him when we had our own store."

"You had a store?"

"Oh, yes. And it was beautiful," Stella said with soft pride. "But then we—"

"You're not boring Summer with our life's story, are you, Stel?" Gregg asked as he came into the room. He hooked an arm around his wife and hugged her, then smiled at Summer. "See ya on the next trip home, Cookie. A couple of years maybe?"

"Not so long this time."

"Okay."

"Really, it won't be." She managed to keep her smile in place until they left. Alone now, she sighed, then flipped the CLOSED sign on the door, moving through the store, turning off lights, straightening up things here and there. She had the radio on and was humming to Coldplay, thinking she should probably put on something more upbeat than the beautiful, lyrical songs that made her ache, when from behind her, a door creaked. Whipping around with a surprised gasp, Summer watched as the small bathroom door just behind the counter slowly opened. With a hand on her racing heart, she stared at Braden. "I thought you were already gone."

"I am." Dressed in his usual black from sleek stud in his ear to his ass-kicking boots, he walked toward the front door.

"What were you doing in there?"

He shot her a bland look over his shoulder.

"Right." But her heart still hadn't slowed. "You going out with Chloe tonight?"

He sent her another baleful glance.

"Let me guess. None of my business."

"You're quick." He reached for the door.

"It's just that I'm sort of fond of the spoiled brat," she said. "So be kind, okay?"

When he looked at her again, surprised, she smiled at him. He offered her a half smile in return, more than she'd ever seen out of him, and shook his head. "Don't stay long," he said.

"Why not?"

"It's your last night."

Right. And she had so many other options open to her.

When he was gone, Summer continued closing up. Tina had a thing for candles, and there were some burning throughout the shop for ambiance. She blew out each of the votives as she went, then hesitated because the dark seemed so complete.

Odd, because when she was out on a camping trip, in charge of the trek, with no city lights around for miles and miles, she was never afraid of the dark.

But here, now, alone in the store with most of the lights off, she felt jumpy. Out of sorts. Maybe because this was her last time alone in the shop for a good long while. In a few days she'd be taking a group of twelve down the Colorado River where teapots and end tables and lamps would be a distant memory.

She moved into the back of the store to shut off those lights as well. There was another door here that led downstairs to a small room they used for employee breaks. Gregg had left it open and the light on, which made her frown. So much for routine.

She stared down the long, deep, *dark* steps. She really wasn't afraid of much, but dark, tight places and spiders topped the list. Still, this had to be done. She had to go down there and turn them off. "Just do it," she said out loud, as if that would help.

The stairs creaked as she slowly made her way. So did a beam overhead. She nearly jumped out of her skin, and then laughed at herself. "Scaredy-cat."

The little TV and stereo were off. The table was cleared and clean. But what really caught her attention was the huge bean bag chair. She'd once had one just like it, it'd sat in her room at the house she'd grown up in. Many mornings she'd woken up to find Joe asleep in it.

She toed the thing, decided it was as comfortable as the original, and sank onto it. Leaning back, she studied the TV. She couldn't reach the remote, and didn't feel like moving. She hadn't realized how tired she was, and let her eyes drift shut.

She thought about what she'd done here, trying to find herself. Find her way back to the ties she'd once had. Had she made progress? She wasn't sure. The old Summer would have packed it up days ago, hell *weeks* ago, but she'd lingered because that's not who she wanted to be.

And yet she didn't have a clear picture of who she *did* want to be . . .

She jerked awake, confused, not sure how long she'd been out. A sharp, putrid scent penetrated her brain.

Smoke.

She choked on the thick, clinging cloud of it and could hardly see. No. *No, this wasn't happening.*

Coughing, she pulled her shirt up over her mouth. The smoke had settled over her like a blanket, smothering. She had to get out. She knew that much. Staggering upright, she flew up the stairs, or tried to, but her feet wouldn't seem to cooperate. Confused, she felt like she moved in slow motion, everything fuzzy and gray so that suddenly she wasn't sure if this was real, or if she was simply reliving an old nightmare.

There'd been stairs then, too, she remembered in growing panic. Downstairs while her father—

Don't open the door.

She'd made that mistake twelve years ago, not setting her hands on the door first, just ripping it open. Back then the smoke and flames had overcome her. She'd stood there, hearing her father's screams, a horrifying, hoarse sound of unthinkable pain, and blindly she'd run straight ahead.

Behind her Joe had called out, tried to catch her.

But she'd just run faster—

And then blackness. Oh God, such all-consuming blackness and despair. She remembered nothing more, nothing until she'd woken up in the hospital two days later.

Now she squeezed her eyes shut, her body fighting the images before she opened them again. The smoke still surrounded her.

This nightmare was real.

The door was hot beneath her pounding fists. It was her only exit but she couldn't get out, which made her feel intensely claustrophobic. Coughing uncontrollably now, she sank to her knees on the wrong side of the door, torn between sheer terror and fury.

Her stomach felt loose and hollow, and her body shook

even as she began to sweat. With her breath lodged in her throat, she set her forehead to her knees and did her best to pretend she was anywhere else. On the pier eating cotton candy and a hot dog. On a mountain bike in Scotland.

In Joe's arms.

Then her cell phone rang, startling her out of the living terror. Gasping, sobbing with relief, she searched deep in her pockets in her full silky skirt, but by the time she located it, the caller had given up. She saw on the display it had been her mother. *"Mom."* She began to hit buttons but had the presence of mind to pound out 9-1-1 instead.

Somehow she gave the dispatcher the information, then sat there huddled against the door, choking on the smoke and panic and memories, running out of air, hoping they made it to her in time.

Joe's pager went off at eight o'clock that night. He reached for it, thinking if Cindy hadn't ditched him two weeks ago, she'd surely have done so now. Just about every evening since had been interrupted for one emergency or another.

He called dispatch, and when he got the address downtown in the Gaslamp Quarter he forgot about everything as his heart kicked into high gear. *Creative Interiors II.* He raced there, breaking a few laws and possibly the speed of light to stare in dread at the flames hurdling out of the building and into the night sky. There were fire trucks, an ambulance, a few squad cars, and curious onlookers as the fire raged its war. Beneath their feet lay a sea of water hoses while firefighters battled to get the blaze under control, also protecting the buildings on either side. He rushed forward but Kenny came out of nowhere to block his way.

"You're not suited up," Kenny said, holding onto him

with shocking strength. "They'll get the fire out. They'll get her."

He stared at Kenny. "They'll get who?"

Kenny looked at him from anguished eyes. The kind of look you give someone when they have really, really bad news.

Joe's stomach sank to his toes. "No." Still restrained, he whipped his head back to the building. Flames pushed and shoved their way through the opening where the front glass door had been. From the windows. From the roof. The entire thing was ablaze.

And Summer was in there.

"She fell asleep downstairs," Kenny said. "And woke to smoke. She had a cell phone in her pocket and was able to call for help. They're going to get her out, Joe. They are. It's Jake Rawlins in there, you know how good he is."

"Is she injured?" he said hoarsely.

"Don't know yet."

The flames were hot and out of control, and he knew no one would be coming out the front door. *Don't be hurt. Please, God, don't let her be hurt.*

Kenny used his free hand to turn up the volume on the radio at his hip. As he did, one of the side windows blew out, and two firefighters appeared in the opening, one of them Jake, with a third person held between them.

Summer.

Joe twisted free from Kenny and rushed forward, meeting them as they cleared the building.

Someone put an oxygen mask on Summer, another wrapped a blanket around her shoulders. They were all drenched, having been nailed by the water hoses aiming in the window.

Joe nodded his gratitude to Jake and the others, and

crouched in front of Summer, reaching for her hands. He'd told himself for days now, ever since she'd shown up at his office with that bittersweet offer of chips, that they had no place in each other's lives anymore. The physical attraction had been a fluke, nothing more. The yearning to know her again . . . that couldn't be explained away as easily but he wasn't interested in following through. He'd told himself this until he was blue in the face, all the way through the second bag of chips he'd bought himself at the grocery store.

And then the third. He'd almost started to believe it.

Until right this second, looking at her. *"Red."*

"Isn't it funny?" she asked, her voice so hoarse it was unrecognizable. "The one thing I'm most afraid of, and I keep ending up in the middle of it."

"Don't talk." He rocked back on his heels and studied her carefully. The night was lit up like day so it wasn't difficult. "Are you hurt?"

"No, I—"

"Shh." He passed a hand over his eyes and took a deep breath. She was alive. Alive was good. He pushed the hair from her face. "I think you just shaved ten years off my life," he murmured. "What were you doing in there this late?"

She tried to clear her throat and winced. "I—"

"No, damn it. Don't." He cupped her throat as if he could take her pain. "What else hurts?"

She shot him a wry look but kept her mouth shut.

"Right. I told you not to talk." He sat back on his heels, marginally relieved by the mixture of temper and amusement in her face. "Like you've ever listened to me."

The firefighter paramedics looked her over. She'd inhaled the smoke and had a couple of good scratches on her legs from climbing through the window, but nothing that required stitches, and no burns.

Around them they'd contained the blaze but were still working on getting the flames out. Joe and Kenny's work was just beginning, but Joe found he couldn't leave her side.

"I'm fine," she said, and the firefighter paramedic at her side nodded his agreement.

The verdict was for her to go home, clean herself up, and rest.

Kenny pulled Joe aside. "You take her home. I'll stay until the site cools, secure the scene, and then we can meet back here at dawn."

"What about Camille and Tina?"

"They're being called now."

Joe glanced down at Summer's bowed head. She needed to get away now. She'd held up so far, she'd stayed strong, but he saw her fingers shake as she drew the blanket tight.

"I can drive myself home," she said, reading his mind.

"No." No way in hell. He looked at Kenny. "I'll take her." Once again he crouched in front of her. This time when he took her hand in his, he was alarmed to find it cold as ice. Her entire body was trembling now. Delayed shock. "Red?"

Her eyes were huge in her face. "Do you think I left a candle burning?" She fisted her hand in his shirt. "Oh my God, is that what started the fire?"

"Shh, not now. Come on."

"I did this."

"Baby, come on. I'm taking you home."

She lifted her head and leveled him with those sea green crystal clear eyes, red rimmed and tortured by the smoke.

He pulled her up, tucked her against his side, figuring it a bad, bad sign that she didn't resist.

At his car, she stopped. "You said I could drive next time."

"One more next time."

"I'm leaving tomorrow," she said, her voice craggy.

"Yeah." He didn't want to think about it.

"You coming inside tonight, Joe?"

He stared down at her bent head, her hair in his nose and so full of smoke he nearly choked. *Try to resist this one, Walker.* "Yeah, I'm coming inside tonight."

She set her head on his shoulder, and didn't open her eyes as he walked her around the car. She didn't move anything more than her feet, as if doing so was too much of an effort for her poor, exhausted body. "You called me baby," she whispered. "Before."

"Did not."

She let out a ghost of a smile. "Know what I think? I think I still have a shot at getting your friendship back."

"Is that what you want? Friendship?"

"Well friendship with benefits would be nice. But after having to beg all of my family to like me for the past three weeks, I can't handle another rejection, so you're safe."

Is that what she thought? That she had to beg him to like her? Couldn't she see the truth all over his face every time he so much as looked at her? "Red—"

"Did you throw out the chips I brought you?"

"No. I ate them. Every last one. And then bought more. I've had to run an extra mile every day since, damn it."

She laughed, then winced, clutching her throat.

"Don't. Don't talk. Don't do anything." He got her in the car. Eyes closed, face pale and filthy, her lips curved into a wry smile as he pulled the seat belt across her hips and fastened it for her.

"You're good at that," she said.

He took an inappropriate second to sweep the hair out of her eyes. And then another to take a gentle swipe with his thumb over her filthy cheek. And then one more to just look at her. Christ, he was bad off. "What am I good at?"

Lifting up a hand, she held his fingers to her face. "Taking care of people." She turned her mouth into his palm and kissed it, then let out a shuddery sigh. "And you know what else?"

He was absolutely certain that the look in her eyes should not make his heart soft. Or that the feel of her lips on his palm make the rest of him the very opposite of soft. "What, that you talk too much for a woman who should be resting her vocal chords?"

"No." A ghost of a smile touched her lips. "I was going to say the way you shoved to the front of all those other firefighters to get to me was really sexy."

He sighed.

"And also, you're cute when I make you squirm." She actually laughed softly. "I have more chips at home."

"Oh, goodie."

"And a heavenly ranch dip."

"You're going to kill me."

"Yeah." Her eyes were still closed. "It's really a shame I'm too messed up to take advantage of you tonight, Joe. This newfound quiet sarcasm you have going turns me on."

She thought *she* was messed up? She should jump into *his* head. "Yeah, too bad." And he put the Camaro in gear and drove her home.

Chapter 10

The engine of the Camaro lulled Summer as Joe drove. It felt good not to move, but the problem with drifting off into la-la land was that it all came back to her in vivid detail.

Waking up in the beanbag chair.

Surrounded by smoke.

Facing her nightmare.

She'd been saved by the grace of her cell phone. As long as she lived she'd never forget the long breathless wait for the sirens, which in reality had probably been only a few minutes but had seemed like an eternity.

Trapped.

And all she'd been able to think about as the smoke filled the room around her, as she'd finally been forced to lie flat on the floor for any air at all, was that she couldn't die, not like this, not like her father. She hadn't lived enough, damn it. Granted, she'd lived hard and good and well, but not *enough*.

She started in surprise when Joe scooped her up. She hadn't even realized he'd turned off the engine, or heard him come around and open the passenger door, but now here she was, in his arms, being carried toward her front door.

He felt warm and comfortably solid, and so achingly familiar she wanted to hold on tight and never let him go.

"Keys?"

She frowned and tried to think, but it was beyond her.

"Never mind." Still holding her as if she weighed nothing, he strode around the back of the small cottage and shouldered open the unlocked back door.

"How did you know?"

"You never used to lock your back door. Where's your bathroom?"

"Down the hall."

He passed through the bright sunshine yellow kitchen, down the hall and straight into the bathroom. Setting her on the counter, he flicked on the light, making her blink in the harsh brightness of it. The small pale blue room was well lived in. The lace shower curtains were flung over the top of the rod because she'd taken a bath that morning. Her towels were still on the floor, as were her favorite peach bra and matching panties. She had her things scattered over the counter: her favorite body lotion, a fistful of scrunchies in every color under the sun, her big round brush, her strawberry cream lip gloss, and an assortment of other necessities.

"First-aid kit," he said, looking baffled by it all. His eyes darted around, landing on her peach panties.

"There's some Band-Aids in the drawer."

He went hunting through the messy drawer, past a box of tampons and hair dryer without a word, but the box of condoms stopped him.

"Three," she said to his unasked questions.

He lifted his gaze to hers.

"Three are gone," she clarified. "You wanted to know, right?"

"Not really," he muttered, and shoved the box to the back with more force than was necessary.

She put her hand on his wrist and waited until his eyes swiveled back to hers. She was aching from the cuts on her legs now, her throat felt as if she'd swallowed glass, and her head . . . she was certain some little guy with a jackhammer had made himself at home between her eyes. She'd lived through a nightmare tonight and yet suddenly she felt like smiling at the brooding look in Joe's eyes. "None of the stuff in that drawer is mine," she told him. "It all belongs to the person who rents this place full time, who is Chloe's college roommate. I told you about her, remember? She went home to Maine for the summer."

To his credit, he laughed a little at himself, then it seemed to back up his throat when she pulled one foil packet from the box and tucked it into the front pocket of his jeans, her fingers brushing his gun as she did so. "Just in case," she murmured.

He went still for a breath, then busied himself finding some antiseptic to go with the Band-Aids. He straightened with both in his hands, and no longer looked remotely relaxed.

Not that he'd been relaxed to begin with, but his jaw was all bunched and the muscle in it was leaping. His eyes were like smooth glass but filled with things he'd kept to himself.

He unraveled her from the blanket and nodded to her skirt, which was stuck to her in places, with little spots of blood soaking through. "Lift it."

Instead, she held it down, feeling oddly self-conscious. "The paramedics already looked at the cuts."

"But you didn't let them put anything on them."

"And what makes you think I'm going to let you?"

He simply bunched the material of her skirt in his hands and firmly but gently shoved it up.

"Hey—"

Leaning in, he put his hands on her thighs, holding her skirt up, his face right in hers, eyes flashing, mouth grim. "I watched you get dragged out of that inferno tonight, watched you relive an old nightmare. A nightmare, by the way, you never let me help you through the first time."

"Joe—"

"Back then I had to stand by helplessly as you stayed unconscious for too long, too damn long, bleeding—" His eyes were filled with agony as he broke off. He drew a slow, purposeful breath. "Then you went away, and stayed away. Tonight I once again stood by as you were trapped in a fire, watched as you went into shock. Now finally, there's something I can do for you, so damn it, let me."

She stared at him. The silence stretched taut. His face was composed but the vibrations of emotion radiated in waves from his body as he stood there, her skirt in his hand, eyes locked on hers.

"I didn't stay away to hurt you," she finally said.

The rushing frustration seemed to drain from him, and he gently set his forehead to hers. "I know."

She curled into him. "I'm not going to run away, not ever again."

"Shh." With a gentleness that reminded her of the boy he'd once been, he treated each of her cuts, slowly, carefully, and when she bit her lower lip at the sting of the antiseptic, he made a hoarse apologetic sound and bent closer, one hand holding up her skirt, the other cradling a thigh in his palm, blowing lightly on her throbbing skin.

"Better?" he murmured. His jaw brushed her knee. He hadn't shaved, and the growth brought out a set of goose bumps along her flesh, which he stroked with his hand in a heart-melting gesture.

"Much better. God, I was so scared."

He lifted his head and searched her gaze. He didn't say anything, didn't offer empty, meaningless words, just slowly nodded.

And because of it, because it was him, she could admit the rest. "I thought I was toast."

He let out a low, rough sound and gathered her close.

"It made me so mad," she whispered, fisting her hands in his shirt. "I was going to die sitting there doing nothing more complicated than feeling sorry for myself."

"Why were you feeling sorry for yourself?"

"Because I was alone, damn it. I hate being alone."

"You're not alone now."

She lifted her head and stared into his eyes, not sure if she'd heard him right. "I smell like smoke."

"I noticed."

But he didn't object when she lifted her hands and sank them into his shaggy hair. "You need a haircut."

His hands went to her hips. "And you talk too much."

"What else is there to do?"

His eyes darkened. He nudged closer, wedging his body between her thighs.

Oh. Oh my. She tightened her fingers in his hair. "No more talking then."

"Yeah. We'll see how long that lasts."

He was right. She'd never been able to keep her mouth shut. She was going to try to do so now. In a minute. "The other night . . . you wouldn't. You didn't want to even talk to me."

"You hadn't just almost died."

"So this is what, just adrenaline?"

He sighed. "What happened to the no more talking thing?"

"Right." She pressed her face to the crook of his shoulder. "Then make me feel alive, Joe. Hurry."

A gravelly sound of understanding tore from his throat. His arms came around her, and she braced for the delicious, quick, hot, fast assault like the week before.

But he went for another tactic this time, sliding his fingers in her hair, tugging her face up, leaning in slowly, nibbling first one side of her mouth, then the other, until her lips trembled open and a moan escaped. Nudging her back into the mirror, he pressed her between that cool surface and his warm, hard body and kissed her. When his tongue touched hers, she nearly cried in relief but he kept at the unbearably leisurely pace until she wanted to scream.

She wanted *hot.* She wanted *hard* and *fast,* and her fingers bit into his biceps as she moaned, opening her legs further, doing everything she could to urge him on and still he didn't rush. She could feel him hard against her stomach, through his jeans, and she pressed closer still, melting under the palm he stroked languidly up and down her back.

She shivered and tried to deepen the connection but he held back. Impatient, she bit his lower lip. He inhaled sharply as his arms tightened on her. "I'm trying to warm you up here," he said.

"I'm warm. I'm hot. I'm burning up."

"I knew you couldn't do it."

"Do what? I'll do anything—"

"Not shut up you won't—" He caught her laughing protest with his mouth, swallowed it whole and worked on capturing her tongue, whipping it into submission with long, wet, hot strokes that had her whimpering, aching, dying . . . all while his hands kept up that maddening slow perusal of her body, up and down her back, her sides, her ribs, and finally, *finally,* palming her breasts, rubbing his thumbs over her aching nipples until she wrenched free to gasp in air.

"You feel alive now?" he asked.

"Yes, thank you." Head back, she closed her eyes to let the mindlessness of it close over her, but then he did the worst thing possible.

He stopped.

She cracked an eye to find him watching her, eyes hot, body tense. "What?"

"Don't escape. Stay with me."

"I'm right here," she said with a little laugh.

"Then keep looking at me." He nudged her with his erection. "Say my name."

She laughed again.

He did not.

Her smile faded. "You mean . . . now?"

"You said you want to connect, then connect with me." He made another pass at her nipple with his thumb and her eyes drifted shut on a sigh.

And just like that, his hand was gone.

Her eyes opened. "I'm sorry, I . . ." *Can't,* she realized. She'd experienced her fair share of lovers, both devoted and otherwise, but never in her life had she been completely swept away by a man. Sex was an escape. She never kept her eyes open. Never whispered a name.

Not even for him.

"It's me, Red," he said roughly. "*Me,* Goddamnit."

He didn't understand that only made it *more* difficult, not less. With him, she could really fall, and that terrified her because the fall would be harsh. The fall would hurt.

You couldn't climb back up from the fall.

Joe stared at her, clearly waiting for her to say something, and when she didn't, couldn't, he wrenched free and blew out a breath.

"Joe—"

"I know. You just want the oblivion of it. *I know.*" He shoved his fingers into his hair and turned in a circle. "I wanted that, too. I thought I could, but I can't." He turned away, reached for the door. "I'm sorry."

"You're going to go?" she asked in disbelief as she sat there halfway to orgasmic bliss. "Just . . . run away? Really?"

Letting go of the door handle, he came back to her, slid his hands up her hips and gripped hard. "You think *I'm* the one running?" One arm slid around her and brought her up against his body. The other cupped her breast. Her entire body quivered, and with a sigh, she sank into him, burying her face in the crook of his neck.

He went utterly still, then pulled free again, leaving her to sag back against the sink. "Let's be clear, Red. *You're* the one who runs when I touch you. *You're* the one hiding."

"No. I want you."

"You want the kick, not the intimacy."

Okay, yes, damn it, she wanted the kick. And maybe, deep down, something more. Just a little. But she needed some help here because it was harder, much harder to accept than she'd expected. And hell if she'd admit that while he stared angrily at her. Hell if she'd admit how badly she needed him when all she ever did these days was beg the people in her life to want her. She was sick of that, *sick of it.*

"So what now?" he asked wearily.

Her eyes burned and not from just the smoke. Her throat wouldn't work. She was an inch from falling apart, with no idea how to put the pieces back together, she could only shake her head. "You don't have to stay. I'm good."

Had there been warmth and tenderness in his eyes only a moment before? It was all gone now. "Yeah, you're good. You're good on your own," he said, his stance deceptively relaxed, his anger tautly controlled. "Too good, I'm thinking. But I'm not leaving you alone tonight, *I'm* not running. Do you understand? I'm hanging right here." He backed up to the door and crossed his arms over his chest, his gun on his hip, looking big, bad, pissed, and stubborn to boot.

And no less sexy for it either. Feeling like a mess such as she did, she resented that, she really did. "Stay, leave," she shrugged. "I don't care."

But she did, so very much. If he left now, she'd fall apart. "I'm taking a bath." Gingerly, she hopped down from the counter. Lifting her chin rather than whimper at the contact, she pushed off her skirt, then pulled off her shirt. She ignored his low, choked oath, though the rough sound of it made her nipples hard. Standing there in a sports bra and panties, she turned her back to him and bent over to turn on the tub.

He swore again.

It did something to her temper, turned it into a smug sort of womanly power, which only increased when she slowly added bubbles to the water. Oh yeah, if she was miserable, then she'd make sure he joined her in that misery. The scent of cocoa butter began to override the smoke she couldn't get out of her nose. Still facing away, she pulled off her bra and kicked off her panties. Then she spun around for a washcloth, making sure Joe got the full three-hundred-and-sixty-degree view before stepping into the tub.

Given the pained sound that escaped him, the way his eyes landed and skimmed over all of her, including the

belly ring, she had success. Woo hoo. She sank down beneath the water, and abruptly forgot all about being a sex
kitten because her cuts burned like fire.

He squatted next to her, mouth tight and grim. "You
okay?"

"Peachy," she said as the bubbles made their way up to
her chin.

His eyes never left hers. They were dark and scorching.
"You know you're torturing me, right?"

She lifted her arm and put a dab of bubbles on his nose.
"Yes."

He stared at her, so fierce, so serious. With bubbles on
his nose.

The phone rang, shattering the silence. Blowing out a
breath, he rose to his feet and left the bathroom.

Summer sank beneath the water to wet her hair. She sat
up, poured shampoo into her hand and worked on getting
the smell of smoke out of her hair. She dunked again and
stayed under a moment to let the shampoo rinse out.

Suddenly a hand snaked around her arm and hauled her
up. Blinking water out of her eyes, she stared into Joe's.

"What are you doing?" he demanded.

"Um, washing my hair?"

"Oh." He let go of her. "Right."

She stared at him, seeing the fierce angst on his face.
"What did you think I was trying to—"

"I don't know."

"Jesus, Joe, I'm not *that* distraught over your second rejection."

Looking taut enough to splinter into pieces, he dropped
his chin to his chest. His genuine distress tore at her, and
she touched his strong, square jaw. "I'm really okay, you
know."

"Yeah." He slowly backed away.

"Is my touch that bad?"

"Try that *good*." He stared into her eyes, his own glittering with all he felt. The unspoken promise was there. He'd catch her if she fell. He'd be there for whatever she needed, and it caught her defenseless and choked her up. Joe Walker was the real deal, as real as a man could get, and much too much for her to handle.

As if he could read her mind, he surged to his feet. "You might be able to be blasé about this," he said, his gaze sweeping over her. "But I sure as hell can't be."

"Joe."

"Your mom called. I told her I'd stay with you until dawn."

Dawn. There were a lot of hours between now and then.

"Finish your bath. Then get into bed and try to sleep."

"What about you?"

"I'll be in the living room if you need me."

His message was clear. *Don't need me.*

The scream shot through Joe like shredded shrapnel. He jerked out of sleep and right off the couch, landing face first on the floor.

With the last echoes of Summer's terrified cry echoing in his head, he leapt to his feet in the pitch black living room of her cottage. *"Red?"*

Only a gasping breath answered him. He rushed toward the sound, tripped over what felt like a cement pipe against his shins, and once again landed flat on his face. Something tumbled down after him, smacking him on the back of the head, making him see stars.

A light flickered on.

He'd tripped over the end table, upending the lamp,

which had hit him in the head. The pain spreading outward to every inch of his body, he flopped to his back and groaned. Summer stood in the doorway next to the light switch. Her face was pale, her eyes huge in her face as she held on to the doorjamb like a lifeline.

"You okay?" she asked.

"I was going to ask you that question. Before your furniture beat the crap out of me." With another groan, he rubbed the back of his head and staggered to his feet. "I was trying to rescue you."

"That's okay, the demons were all in my head."

"A nightmare?"

Eyes still filled with the remembered horror, she nodded.

Everything within him softened in sympathy and understanding. He knew the dreams, knew how haunting they could be. He started toward her, manfully not whimpering at the cracking, stinging pain in his shins and the base of his skull.

"I was back there." Her breath hitched. "I couldn't get out. I could hear my dad. Screaming—" Covering her mouth with a shaking hand, she looked away.

She wore only a soft white camisole and hot-pink bikini panties, but even in the low light of the lamp he could see the goose bumps raised on her flesh. Miles of sleek, smooth, bronzed flesh.

Down boy, he thought, and did the only thing he could. He reached for her. She met him halfway, curling into him, burying her face in the crook of his neck. Wrapping his arms around her, he absorbed her tremors and stroked a hand down her hair, down her back. "Just a dream," he murmured, and pressed his lips to her temple.

"The flames were biting at me."

There weren't words to take those memories away so he

just held her as tight as he could, stroking his hands up and down her quivering body. Later he couldn't name the moment when things shifted from him giving the comfort, to him losing control of the embrace entirely, but it might have been when he felt her lips against his throat.

And then the tip of her tongue.

"Red." He anchored his hands to a neutral position by fisting them in her hair.

She did the same to him, then lifted her head, lined up their mouths and took his. And just like that, he sank into her. He couldn't help it. There they were, with him wearing only his opened jeans and her in her barely there camisole and panties, naked flesh brushing naked flesh, mouths fused, sharing breath, sharing that soulful connection he'd never been able to find in anyone else. It felt like a homecoming.

Still kissing him, she slipped her hand into his jeans, humming with approval when she wrapped her fingers around the biggest erection he'd ever had.

He put his hands on her shoulders, skimming her straps down. Then he lifted his mouth from hers to watch as he tugged the thin material away from her. Her breasts bounced free, and her nipples hardened for him. "You take my breath," he murmured, and bent to taste her.

She gasped but kept her eyes open. Progress. He looked up at her in the lamp's glow and felt his heart swamp.

She still had her hands in his pants, and she stroked him, squeezing lightly. "Slow down," he warned. "Or I'll lose it before we start."

She didn't slow down.

To make them even, he slipped his hands into the back of her panties, playing his fingers between her thighs in the creamy heat he found there. Not enough. He dropped to his knees and put his mouth low on her softly rounded stomach, right next to the belly button ring that was going to highlight his fantasies for many nights to come. God, she was the sexiest thing he'd ever seen. And the tastiest. He nibbled his way lower.

After that he never remembered who dragged whom to the carpet, or who found the condom, or even who tore off whose clothing, but when he finally sank into her glorious body so wet and ready for him, he felt . . . engrossed. And not just physically. She captured him heart and soul, and as he leaned over her, touching her face, kissing her mouth, looking into her fathomless eyes so full of emotion for him, he hoped to God she felt the same way.

Chapter 11

As the sun came up, Joe drove from Summer's cottage back to the fire site. His eyes were gritty from lack of sleep and the already warm air didn't help.

After he and Summer had given each other rug burns to be remembered, he'd carried her to bed and had then proceeded to watch her sleep for the next few hours. It hadn't been her light snoring that kept him awake, but the woman herself.

He'd lain there with no covers—seemed she was also a bit of a blanket hog—staring up at the shadows on the ceiling, reliving the night. The fire. The fear. The adrenaline. Then Summer slowly stripping out of her clothes as the bath filled up, standing there in a stark white sports bra and panties, looking long and willowy and curvy.

And irresistible.

He'd pictured it thousands of times, her naked in his arms, her fiery hair draping his body as she sank down on him, taking him deep inside her. The reality of her doing just that had blown the fantasy out of the water.

She was leaving today.

He wasn't a complete fool. He knew enough about her to

understand that what had happened between them wouldn't get in her way.

Fine. So be it. When she was gone, he could get back to some semblance of normalcy, without wondering each day if she'd send one of her soulful smiles his way. Yep. Her leaving would free up a lot of mental time and energy.

He pulled into the parking lot of the burned-out Creative Interiors II and showed his badge to the officer who'd been there all night guarding the scene. Kenny pulled up right after him. All around were a crew of firefighters, checking for hot spots. The chief was there, too, looking tired and haggard.

It'd been a bad season so far, the lot of them were over-worked, and the hot weather hadn't helped. They had more fires than they could investigate, and as always when that happened, things slipped through the cracks. In their county alone they were working on two major arson cases, at least one of which was the work of a serial arsonist. Everyone was itchy because they'd had a dry spring, too dry, and the fears about the wildfires getting out of control again were running rampant.

The chief came over as he and Kenny were pulling out their gear. "Wrap this one up fast as you can," he said quietly, and when he walked away, Kenny looked at Joe with an arched brow.

"This is Creative Interiors's second fire in a month," Joe said. "Big coincidence to 'wrap up quickly.'"

They were sitting on the bumper of his truck getting their gear organized, which was easier for Kenny since he'd actually had his stuff organized in the first place.

"Yeah, but the warehouse appears to be accidental," Kenny said, pulling out his clean boots.

"We both know 'appears' means nothing."

"True." Kenny watched as Joe pulled out his own boots, not clean. "Is it possible you're too close to the case?"

"I'm not too close to the case." Joe stared at his dirty boots. "How the hell do you stay clean?"

"It's not that difficult. Look, just admit it. You're in love with Camille's daughter."

Joe's heart skipped a beat. "You've been watching soap operas again."

"I notice you're not denying anything here."

Was it love? Joe hadn't put a name to the bone-melting, heart-stretching emotion he'd experienced last night, he hadn't been able to.

But whatever it was that he felt for Summer, it was a whole lot more complicated than he'd ever felt for Cindy, or any woman for that matter, and he had to look away from Kenny's knowing expression.

"So it's serious," Kenny said.

A serious case of stupidity, maybe. "She's leaving. Hell, she might already be gone."

"That should suit you, the master of screwing up long-term relationships."

"Maybe Summer isn't my type."

"Since when is smart, sexy, and funny not your type?" Kenny pulled on gloves, also clean. "Face it, man, she's been your walking wet dream your entire life."

"No she's not." Joe doesn't have any clean gloves either, damn it. "She's . . . flighty. Unstable. She's . . ." Warm, compassionate, beautiful. Sexy as hell. *"Christ."*

Kenny tossed him a pair of new gloves from his own kit. "If it helps, I think I could feel the same way about her mom."

"Camille?" Joe stared at him. "Okay, that's it, no more soap operas at lunchtime for you."

Kenny's smile faded. "You have a problem with me going out with Camille after the investigation's over?"

"No, Camille would be so lucky as to have you. But Kenny, she won't keep you. Who do you think taught Summer that love is either a terrifying soul destroyer or skin-deep only?"

"They're just both skittish, is all." Kenny smiled confidently. "With the right man, they could learn to trust their hearts."

"You're scaring me, I mean it."

"You girls going to work or gab all damn day?" the chief barked at them from fifty yards away.

Kenny and Joe looked at each other, then moved into the building, dropping all their problems at the door to concentrate, as they'd done for two years now.

Inside the store was a mess. The walls were charred through to the studs and the furnishings were either melted, burnt to a crisp, or floating in the mud and debris on the ground. Joe flicked open the lens on his camera and began shooting.

The first thing that stuck out like a sore thumb were the puddles of wax throughout the store. *Candles,* he thought grimly, snapping pictures of them. "Summer thinks she might have left one lit."

Kenny made a sorrowful noise. They both knew exactly how dangerous candles were. They saw hundreds of fires caused by them every year. They waded through an inch of water and grime to find each and every puddle of wax, and recorded it.

The hot spot had been in the small employee's bathroom off the main floor, a room lined with wooden paneling and smooth parquet flooring. According to the burn pattern, here was the area of origin. There'd been a candle originally seated on the porcelain sink, now just another puddle of melted wax on the wood.

"If people knew the statistics on how many fires these votives started, would they stop buying them?" Kenny asked.

"Doubt it. People never think its going to happen to them." Oddly enough, even if the candle had tipped here, there was no additional fuel to keep it burning, nor was it beneath the burn pattern on the opposite wall.

Which meant the candle hadn't been the point of origin at all. Joe pulled out his handheld accelerant detector unit as a matter of course. The reading meter went crazy.

Joe exchanged a long look with Kenny.

"Interesting," Kenny said.

Given that it was a bathroom, there were all sorts of possibilities. Nail polish remover. Oil. Chemicals. A neglectful accident.

Or . . . malicious intent. Joe looked closer. On the wall beneath the burn pattern had hung a toilet paper holder. The paper itself was long gone, but he eyed the wall and saw it as it might have been before the fire.

Paper hanging down, dipping into a puddle of gasoline, or paint thinner, whatever accelerant had caused the reading on his meter. It would have acted as a wick, and if the roll had been full, all the better.

A match could have been lit, tossed into the puddle of gasoline.

Poof.

Above the toilet paper had been a towel rack, with at least two towels on it. More fuel. By that time, the flames had been hot, leaping straight up, catching the wood paneled walls, the wood ceiling.

A timber box waiting to explode.

All hidden by the more obvious "evidence," the conveniently left burning candles.

The flames would have leapt across the ceiling and down the other walls, and then outward. And with the store closed, and the bathroom right in the middle of the place, it had grown hotter and faster, burning out of control before anyone on the outside caught the scent.

There were any number of motives here. Revenge, excitement, insurance fraud. They both knew it. They'd both seen it all.

Kenny opened his evidence collecting box. "Better get everything. We just went from accidental to God knows what."

"Yeah." Joe swiped at his brow and set his camera aside. Together in the hot, damp, tiny space they meticulously began to sweep the entire bathroom.

"So were you up all night or what?" Kenny asked when Joe couldn't hold back his umpteenth yawn.

"I don't want to talk about it."

"Ah."

Joe scowled and sat back on his heels. "What the hell does that mean?"

"It means now I get why you're so prickly. You must not have gotten laid last night."

A lot he knew. "I'm not prickly."

"As a porcupine, but forget it. You don't want to talk about it."

"That's right, damn it." Joe shoved his flashlight into his kit. "Look, I was just trying to help her."

"Because she's nobody to you."

Joe gritted his teeth and eyed what was left in the room. After the fire, the water, and now what he and Kenny had done over the past two hours, there wasn't much.

"A mess," Kenny muttered. "And if this is connected to the warehouse fire . . ."

"Yeah. A bigger mess." Joe thought of how Summer had been in the basement, asleep, alone. Vulnerable. If she hadn't had her cell phone, if she hadn't woken up . . .

His gut clenched hard.

"What?" Kenny asked.

"She could have died."

"Yeah. Now let's use what we found here to prove whether or not it'd have been murder."

A few hours after Joe left, Summer turned over to her back in her bed. Eyes still closed, she stretched, and decided she felt delicious. Thanks to Joe.

She opened her eyes, then gasped.

"Sorry, darling," Tina said. She and Camille stood over the bed with twin worried expressions. "Didn't mean to scare you."

Summer drew a breath and shoved her hair out of her face. "You'd better have caffeine."

"Yes. And food too."

They gathered in Summer's tiny kitchen at the even tinier table.

"Tell us everything," Tina said, and pushed a croissant toward Summer.

Camille didn't say a word, just poured tea.

Socks, who'd come with them, wound around their feet, purring, waiting for falling crumbs.

Summer tucked her feet beneath her and tried to smell the tea to see which healing potion Camille was feeding her, but could smell nothing but herself and the smoke still in her skin and nose.

And Joe. She smelled Joe.

"Talk," Tina said.

"Yeah." She didn't suppose Tina meant the part where Joe had put his talented fingers and mouth on her, or how he'd drawn her out of herself, so far out that it would have terrified her if she hadn't sensed he'd been just as swept away.

Who'd have thought Joe Walker would have grown up to be such a passionate, demanding, giving, incredibly magnificent lover?

"Summer? Can you tell us?"

She shrugged off the memories of Joe and tried to figure out where to start with the fire, but the thought of saying it all out loud made her heart pound heavily. "Well . . . I was closing up, and had to go downstairs to turn off the lights. The beanbag was there, looking comfy, and . . ." *And I felt so alone.* "I sat down for a minute. I guess I fell asleep." And woke to the smothering feeling of choking on smoke. Her chest tightened.

Oh, damn.

"Oh, darling." Tina got up and stood behind her, stroking her hair, rubbing her shoulders. "I'm so sorry you had to go through this again. It's not right."

Her mother's grip on the teapot became white knuckled. "She doesn't remember the first fire."

"I remember more of it," Summer admitted.

Camille's eyes widened. "You do?"

"Some."

Camille looked as if maybe she wanted to say more but instead she pinched her lips together.

Tina didn't share her restraint. "What do you remember?"

"Opening the door. Hearing—" Overcome by the memory, she dropped her face into her hands.

Tina made a sound of sympathy and stroked Summer's hair. "Oh, darling, I'm sorry. Don't think about it anymore, okay? Let's just stick with this fire."

"It wasn't so bad, really." She swallowed the horror. "I just can't stand the smell of myself. It makes my eyes water." *Liar, liar.* She wiped her eyes on the napkin Tina handed her. "Anyway, when I woke up I was surrounded by smoke and was a little disoriented, that's all."

"Anyone would have been," Camille said very quietly, giving the outer appearance of being as tranquil as the tea she began to pour.

And yet there was worry and sheer terror in her eyes. Summer absorbed both and knew she couldn't tell them how she'd panicked, how she'd gotten lost in her old nightmare. She couldn't tell them that she'd had to dial 9-1-1 blindly because of the smoke, or that by the time the firefighters had found her, she'd given herself up for lost for the second time in her life. "At least they stopped the flames in time to save the building. That's good news."

"No, the good news is that you're alive and relatively unscathed." Tears made Tina's voice thick as she wrapped her arms around her niece from behind.

Camille began to add sugar to Summer's tea with fingers that shook so violently Summer was surprised the sugar even made it into the cup. "The insurance company is not going to be happy with us."

"They can go to hell," Tina said fervently, placing a noisy kiss on Summer's cheek. "We pay a fortune for that coverage and we've done nothing wrong."

Camille just kept adding sugar to Summer's tea.

"In fact, they'll be lucky if Summer herself doesn't sue us," Tina said.

"*What?* I'm not going to sue you," Summer said, horrified. "The whole thing is my fault. The candles—" She broke off as her mom let out a choked sound and dropped a sixth teaspoon of sugar in Summer's tea.

Tina exchanged a worried look with Summer. "Maybe we should talk about something else."

But in Summer's opinion, that was the problem. No one had ever forced Camille to face anything that bothered her. Including Summer. "I think we should get it all out." She leaned close to her mom. "I'm so sorry, Mom. God, so sorry." Her voice caught. "But I think I forgot to blow out a candle. I think I burned the place down."

"No. Oh, darling, no," Tina said fiercely. "*I* lit those candles, because I loved watching them burn."

Camille's teaspoon clattered to the table as she covered her mouth.

Socks, sensing her mistress's distress, jumped into Camille's lap and butted her head against Camille's belly.

Summer scooted closer. "Mom?"

"I'm okay."

"We all are, thank God," Tina said firmly, taking each of their hands. "Because no one got hurt. Anything we lost can be replaced."

"I know you'll still want to leave today," Camille said to Summer. "No one'll blame you for that."

Summer looked into her mom's jade eyes, usually soft and relaxed, now dark with emotion. "You'll need help through all this new investigation and insurance fiasco. I gained all that experienced with the warehouse fire. I'm too good at it now to pass the torch."

"Honey, no."

"I want to."

"You have your work."

"I'm going to call in and explain why I need more time."

She set a hand over her mother's, stilling the tenth teaspoon of sugar from going into her cup.

Camille began to stir her tea and didn't say a word.

Summer exchanged a helpless glance with Tina. "I thought maybe it was helping you, Mom, having me around."

"It is," Tina said for her sister. "It is."

Summer wanted to believe that, but she wanted a lot of things. She also wanted to find her place in a world that she used to belong to. Ironic that she could find her way through a jungle, over a mountain, down a river, and yet right here in her own hometown, she felt so lost. "I'm so sorry about the store," she whispered. "I'm *so* sorry. I wish—"

"No. No regrets," Camille said so forcefully it surprised everyone. "Trust me. Living with them is too hard." She turned over her hand and squeezed Summer's. Once, twice.

Love you.

Summer let out a half laugh, half sob, and squeezed her back three times.

Love you back.

And could only hope this was a sign of good things to come.

Chapter 12

By that afternoon, Summer was in the Gaslamp Quarter, in the back of the original Creative Interiors. She sat surrounded by opened boxes, going through some of the stock that Bill had just brought in from his and Tina's garage, secretly munching on the bag of cookies he'd sneaked her.

Tina kept coming into the room to check on her, telling her that no one expected her to work today, she should be resting, taking it easy.

Summer refrained from admitting that being alone, without any distraction such as a naked fire marshal in her bed, would drive her right into the loony bin.

Braden sat behind her in a corner chair, working on the computer, muttering to himself. Chloe kept finding reasons to come talk to Summer, and every time she did, she took sidelong—and not particularly discreet—glances at Braden.

He, on the other hand, kept working, not looking up from his screen, not doing anything, possibly not even breathing.

"So," Summer said to Braden after Chloe had left for the fifth or sixth or hundredth time. "You *do* have a thing for her."

Braden looked up. "A thing? Sounds like an infection."

She thought about what she felt for Joe, and how no matter that she wanted to be easy and light, it was so damn messy and complicated. "It can sure as hell can *feel* like an infection."

A low rusty sort of sound escaped him.

"Did you just *laugh*?" she asked, shocked.

"Don't flatter yourself."

"Tell me the truth. You missed the how-to-make-friends day in kindergarten, right?"

"So I'm not social." He shrugged a lean shoulder. "That's not a crime."

No, it wasn't. But his defensiveness was certainly interesting. "Does it have anything to do with why you don't drink anymore?"

His indulgent smile faded.

"I'm not trying to pry or anything," she said.

"Like hell."

"Okay, I'm prying."

"My past is not relevant to this job."

"You're right." But she had a feeling it was relevant to why he was so cynical and sarcastically witted. And while she instinctively liked him, her first loyalty was to Chloe, brat or not. "Just tell me. Do you really like Chloe or are you playing with her?"

"Do you really like your fire marshal, or are you playing with him?"

Summer narrowed her eyes.

Braden went back to his work.

"I like him," she said softly.

Braden looked up in surprise.

"I like him a lot."

"Well good for you."

"And? . . ."

He sighed. "And you're a pest." When Summer just waited, he let out an annoyed breath. "Jesus, you're stubborn, too. Okay, listen, I like your cousin. Happy?"

She grinned and he groaned. "Go back to work, Summer."

She did. But cataloging inventory was making her eyes cross and not taking up enough brain waves. She *did* like Joe, she always had. Liking him had never been a problem. They'd once shared a deep, abiding, mutual affection. A binding connection. But after her father's death, such connections scared her.

Since then, anything she'd felt for a man had been light. Easy. And purely physical. Sex for her was as it should be—a simple relief. Necessary as air, but no real ties required.

"You're thinking so hard *my* head is hurting," Braden said, startling her.

"Sorry."

"Actually, you're making me hungry, too," he said, and closing his laptop, left to get lunch.

Camille came in with Socks in her arms, and for a moment, Summer saw her mother as a stranger would. Tall, willowy, hair pulled back, only a minimum amount of makeup on her face, but still beautiful despite the dark circles beneath her eyes and her tight expression. "The marshals are on their way," she said to Summer. "They need to take interviews."

Her stomach both dropped and fluttered. "Me?"

"And some others, too, but you, yes. They wanted to catch you before you left."

"Oh. Did you by any chance tell them I wasn't leaving?"

"No." Camille bent to stroke Socks, her eyes were filled

with worry. "Because I thought you might still change your mind."

"Mom. No."

"This morning you had trouble even thinking about the fire."

"I'll be okay," Summer said.

"I'm sorry you have to go through this."

Again.

Her mom didn't say the word, but it hovered between them as the ghost of her father had for twelve years. "I'm fine. It's you who's having to go through all of this: property damage, insurance nightmares—"

"Summer, listen to me." Camille's sudden urgent tone scared her, so did the way she set down Socks and gripped Summer's hand. "None of that matters. If you want to leave, I understand. I mean that."

Summer searched her mother's face for the reason why she wanted Summer gone so badly, and found none. "I told you, I'm sticking," she said slowly. *Want me to stick.*

Her mother's stiff shoulders sagged almost imperceptibly.

With relief? With regret? Summer had no idea. "I wish there was something else I could do."

"Your being here is enough." Camille squeezed her hands twice. "God help the both of us."

"Mom." Summer felt scared for no reason. "It's going to be okay."

"Yes, it is. Because life goes on." Camille's smile was heartbreakingly sad. "That's what Tina always claims anyway."

"It's been twelve years," Summer said softly. "It's okay for life to go on."

Camille looked down at their linked hands. "I know people think I'm crazy to still miss him so very much."

Grief battered Summer, grabbing her by the throat. They'd never talked about this. They'd been wrong to never talk about this. "I don't think you're supposed to stop missing him. You're just supposed to be able to keep loving, even other people."

"Is there a manual for that?"

Summer choked out a laugh and leaned in for a hug that felt so right she thought she might never let go, but at the sound of a knock, Camille jumped and turned to the doorway.

Two tall, lean, tough, rangy fire marshals stood there. One neatly groomed, wearing an easy smile and those Harry Potter glasses, the other wearing a camera around his neck and looking at Summer in a way that upped her body temperature to unsafe levels.

Last night had been . . . amazing. Nice to know that when she needed a stress relief, Joe Walker could provide it. But she hoped like hell he remembered that that's all it'd been.

Camille dropped Summer's hand to become the consummate hostess, moving forward with her best "come drink tea out of my fancy china" smile. Kenny followed her, leaving Joe alone with Summer.

He stepped close enough that no one could overhear them. His face was all hard, angular planes. A handsome face, one that was only gaining character as he aged. "You hanging in?"

"Sure."

His welcome smile faded. "Truth, Red." His eyes were filled with concern, and there was a seriousness to his mouth that made her feel like throwing herself in his arms and having him pull her in tight and keep her safe.

A direct contrast to the reminder she'd just given herself about him being only a stress relief. She reminded herself that she was ill-equipped to deal with anything deeper. "I'm good. How are your shins?"

"Bruised." His eyes were warm and soft on hers. "Did you sleep okay after I left?"

"Sure. There was no one to steal the blankets."

"You know damn well *who* steals the blankets, and it isn't me." He rubbed a thumb over the dark smudges beneath her eyes. "What time are you leaving?"

"Change of plans. I'm going to stay until everything is settled again. The insurance stuff."

"As opposed to other stuff."

"Like?"

His gaze held her for a tenuous beat, then he shook his head. "Let's start with what I came here to do before we head down a road you're not ready for." He gestured to his clipboard. "Ready?"

Her heart clutched. No. No, she wasn't ready. "How about that weather, huh?" She fanned her face. "It's sure a hot one."

His eyes filled with regret. "We have to do this."

"I know." It was his job, but the thought of reliving it made sweat pool at the base of her spine. "Sure you wouldn't rather talk about my rug burns?"

The muscle in his jaw worked for a moment as he wrestled with his professionalism. It was fascinating to watch. "Maybe we can save that for a later conversation," he finally said.

"I'd really rather talk about—"

"Red. I'm sorry."

So calm. She wondered how many of the twelve years that she'd been gone had it taken him to master his control like that.

If only he could teach her to do it.

"Let's sit," he suggested.

She let him lead her to the small love seat by the refrigerator across the room from where Camille was pouring tea for Kenny.

Summer stared at Joe as he moved around the small table in front of the love seat and sat next to her, thinking she'd kissed those firm, unsmiling lips, she'd had her fingers in his too long, wavy, uncombed hair, and it was damn hard to forget that whenever she'd been in his arms, she felt alive, gloriously alive. As she watched, he swallowed, and his Adam's apple bounced. She wanted to bite it. Bite him. His hands, big and agile, held his clipboard and a pen, and she remembered what those long, tapered strong fingers could do to her nipples. What they felt like on her, inside her. Off balance, she shook her head, but couldn't clear it. "I'm losing it."

"You had a traumatic experience," he said. "Give yourself a break."

"That's not what I'm thinking about right now." She lifted her gaze and let him see what she *was* thinking about, and he swallowed again.

"Red," he said softly, with a desperation that made her sigh.

"I'm sorry." She rubbed her temples. "Go ahead. Ask away. What do you need to know? That I think I started the fire by accident, causing my mom and aunt untold amounts of anguish and money?"

"You didn't."

"Or that the insurance company is going to up their rates—" She stared at him. "What?"

"I don't think the candle started the fire."

Thank God was her first selfish thought. Then she took a good look at his expression and the grimness in it, and got a very bad feeling. "What did?"

"Before you fell asleep downstairs, were you alone in the shop?"

Her bad feeling spread. "Why?"

He tapped his pen on his clipboard and just looked at her.

"Joe, you're scaring me. Did someone do this on purpose?" God, the implications of that boggled, because everyone knew she'd been there. That someone could have . . . *"Joe."*

He looked bleak.

"Okay," she said, shaken. "See, this is where you talk."

"We found traces of an accelerant. Gasoline."

"Oh, God." She gripped the small table in front of them. "What do we do?"

"First, you relax." He said this gently, prying her rigid fingers off the table to stroke her hand, making her realize she'd begun breathing too rapidly again. "Keep breathing, okay?"

"I am." The spots would come next, she knew it.

He saw it all, her growing panic, her struggle to overcome it, she knew he did. Every little flicker of emotion crossing her face, every little tremble of her fingers as she let go of his to rub her temples again, now panicky because suddenly she couldn't control her breathing. "Oh, damn."

"I suppose this isn't a panic attack either," he said, and set aside his clipboard to scoot close and rub her back.

"Don't be silly. I'm tougher than that," she panted.

Letting out a rough sound that might have been sympathy, compassion, or sheer frustration, he held her down when she tried to rise. "You never used to have panic attacks."

"They're not all that bad."

"Come on."

"All right, they're bad. But rare. Really," she said to his disbelief. "At least until I came back here."

"Because of that first warehouse fire. When you got caught beneath that beam."

She squeezed her eyes shut. "I don't remember."

"Maybe that's why you're afraid."

"I'm not afraid."

"Now who's the liar," he chided softly. "Tight places upset you, and so does talking about the fires, two of which you've been trapped in. Now I'm asking you to talk about them, and I'm sorry, so fucking sorry. But I have to know what happened to make it right."

"I know," she whispered.

"How about we just take it slow. Together, okay?"

She nodded, and concentrated on breathing for a few minutes. Feeling like a wimp, she glanced over her shoulder to where Kenny was clearly entertaining her mother, making her smile. "It took me until this morning to get a real smile. He gets one just by walking in the door."

"Kenny gets a smile from any woman, and he could do it at a hundred paces."

"That makes it even stranger."

"She's young enough, and he's old enough. Don't worry about them."

"I won't, because I can't concentrate on anything knowing we still have to do this."

"Just keep breathing, slow and relaxed."

She shot him a sideways glance. "How about another lesson in relaxing? The one you gave me last night is wearing off."

"Red. I can't talk about this on the job."

"You'd rather talk about it tonight? On my living room floor? Okay, but I don't remember having a lot of breath for talking last night."

He kept his voice low and quiet with what looked like great effort. "Last night was a little more than just a stress relief."

She hadn't expected him to give in and discuss it, but she should have known better than to bait him because he never backed down, not from anything. "You know what? I don't want to get into this."

"Right." He let out a harsh laugh. "We only talk about things on *your* terms. Fine. Back to the fire then."

"I *really* don't want to get into that."

"I bet."

"In fact, I just remembered. I have to have my wisdom teeth pulled out, slowly, without Novocain." She surged to her feet but he was quicker and gently took her arm.

"Red."

She sat and sighed. "Yeah."

His eyes were solemn, his voice quiet. Calm. "Who did you work with yesterday?"

"You have the schedule." She pointed to the top sheet of his clipboard, where he'd pinned the schedule Tina had just given him.

"We both know the schedule changes on a whim at Creative Interiors."

"I worked with Stella and Gregg in the morning. Chloe came in later with stock from Tina's house. Braden was on his computer. Tina popped in and out. So did my mother." She and Joe both looked over at Camille.

Camille still had on the little smile from before, but Summer could see the stress behind it. "Hang on." She rose and walked over to them. "Mom? You okay?"

"Of course." Camille began adding sugar to her tea. One teaspoon, two.

Oh boy.

"We're talking about the fire," Kenny said, watching Camille load him up with enough sugar to handle a whole pot of tea. "How she called you on your cell. When you were trapped."

More sugar.

Kenny glanced worriedly at Summer.

"Um, Mom? Can I get you anything?"

"No, thank you." Yet another teaspoon. "You should all join me, it's ginseng. Good for your circulation. Helps oxygenation."

"I'm good," Kenny said, and stood. "You've been a huge help."

"Oh!" Camille wasn't able to hide her hopeful expression. "We're all done then?"

"For now. Why don't you let me drive you home?"

"Oh, I couldn't let you do that. I don't want to put you out."

"It's right on my way." Kenny offered her his hand.

Camille shocked Summer and put her hand in the tall fire marshal's, allowing him to pull her to her feet. "Are you on your motorcycle?"

Kenny shook his head. "I wouldn't have asked you if I had been."

"No." Summer would have sworn she looked . . . *disappointed?* "Of course not."

Kenny laughed. "When I have more questions, maybe tomorrow, I can come back on the bike."

"With an extra helmet?"

"With an extra helmet," he said.

"Mom, how do you even know he *has* a bike?"

Camille blushed. *Blushed.* "I don't work tomorrow," she said to Kenny.

He smiled. "At home then?"

Camille didn't say yes but neither did she say no. Summer stared at her mother in shock as Kenny led her out the door. "What was *that*?" she asked Joe. "He's flirting with her."

"I think you have that backward," Joe said, watching them go.

Summer frowned and dropped to a chair, nodding to his clipboard. "Okay, hit me."

"Why don't we—"

"Just do it, damn it."

Just do it, Joe thought. Yeah, sure. He'd just tear her apart, no sweat. He kicked a chair around and straddled it, needing the back of steel and the table between them. "Who closed the shop yesterday?"

"I did," Summer said.

"You were alone at that time?"

"Yes, I—" She paused. "No. I thought I was, and went around turning stuff off, and then Braden came out of the bathroom and startled me."

Joe stopped in the middle of writing. This was new to him. "Startled you how?"

"I thought I was alone. He apologized for scaring me, and then left." She bit her lower lip and stared at him, obviously seeing that she'd told him something new. "Look, I'm not saying that I think he had anything to do with—"

"I'm just putting the pieces together, Red. No assumptions, no jumping to conclusions."

She tried to read his notes. "Do you really think it's arson?"

"Don't know yet."

"But you know what you're leaning toward."

"Most fires are not arson, and I still have to ask these questions. What did you do after Braden left?"

She scrubbed a hand over her face. "There was a light on downstairs. Tina and my mom are pretty anal about that, so I went down there to turn it off. The room is—*was*—an employee rest area." She looked down at her clasped fingers. "And I was tired. Really tired. I found a big purple beanbag down there, looking so comfortable—" She looked at him and he knew both of them were remembering how many times he'd slept on a bag just like it, and why.

"I fell asleep," she murmured. "And when I woke up—" She paused. Her breathing changed, quickened, and she closed her eyes tight.

Ah, hell. Again he got out of his chair and crouched by hers, covering her hands with one of his. "Breathe, Red."

"I am." But she was breathing so quickly she was going to hyperventilate. "Last night I remembered something about the first warehouse fire. About—When my dad—" She gulped air and gripped his fingers hard.

"Slower. Come on now, in and out." He showed her with his own breath. "Nice and slow, see?"

"Oh, damn, it's bad." She clutched at his hands when she couldn't catch air into her lungs.

Gently he pushed her head down to her knees, staring

helplessly over her head while she relived the nightmare. Because of him. "Just keep breathing."

"I know— I'm trying— I'm mixing up the fires now. Old and new. God. I'm sorry. This is so stupid. I feel so stupid."

"Think of it this way. You're alive. How stupid is that?" Because he couldn't help himself, he stroked a hand down her slim, shaking back. "Can you tell me what you remember?"

"I remember standing there between you and Danny, and seeing the smoke. I remember running up the steps, screaming for my dad, then opening the basement door—" She closed her eyes and hugged herself tight. "The flames. I could hear him—" She couldn't possibly get herself into a tighter ball, though she tried. "That's all. There's more but I can't seem to get to it."

He gritted his teeth. "The beam came down and hit you."

She pressed her face to her knees and nodded. "I know this isn't the right fire. Go ahead and get this done. Ask me the rest of your questions."

"Red."

"Do it."

He ran through the list as gently as possible, memorizing her answers to write down later because he wasn't going to take his hands off her.

No, she hadn't used the bathroom in the hours before the fire. No, she hadn't heard anything while she was down in the basement. No, she hadn't used gasoline in the shop.

And when he was done, she leapt up. "I have to get out of here."

"Yeah." He looked away from her, remembering he was going to like it when she was gone again.

"No, I mean— I just need some air."

He met her gaze, the woman who pretended not to need any emotional attachments, and realized he wasn't ready to let her go. "How about some company?"

"I don't know, what if you feel the urge to talk about sex?"

He caught the teasing light in her eyes and felt a profound release of the tension gripping his body. She was going to be okay. "I'll try to restrain myself."

"Don't do so on my account."

He shook his head and took her hand. "Come on you. I know just the thing to cheer you up."

Chapter 13

"A frozen yogurt?" Summer laughed, and it was the belly laugh Joe remembered.

He found himself smiling at her as he handed over the strawberry yogurt cone he'd just bought her.

They'd walked past the pier and out onto the beach. The early evening sun beat down on their heads, the sand blazing beneath their feet. A nice breeze washed over them with every wave that hit the shore, the sound and light spray both soothing and calming. Around them were a variety of surfers, raucous young couples, and tourists.

Summer, in her crepe camisole top and skirt and easy grin, looked right at home, unless one knew her and could see past the slightly shaky smile. She was still hurting. Even so, she dug into her dessert with typical gusto, then twirled around on the sand like a kid, her feet splashing in the water, making her skirt cling to her calves. "You're right," she said, coming to a stop and facing him. "This definitely hits the spot."

Oh, yeah, it did, he thought as he slurped his own chocolate shake down his throat and watched her begin to shed her tension like an unwanted coat. God, for the ability to do that.

"Trade," she said, and before he could blink, she thrust her cone at him and took his shake—an old habit. She slurped at his dessert for a moment. "Not nearly as healthy as mine, but good," she said and switched back, happily resuming her cone. "Joe?"

"Hmm?"

"I have a confession." She licked her lip to get every last drop, also an old habit, though it hadn't used to make him hard.

"A confession?" he asked, his gaze locked on her wet tongue as it darted back into her mouth.

"Uh huh. And I'll tell you what it is if you give me a secret back."

"You first," he said warily.

Her eyes held his prisoner. She spoke very solemnly. "I missed the beach."

He stared at her. "That's it? Your big confession? You missed the beach?"

"Yes." Another torturous lick of her cone. "Now you."

"Oh, no. That's not good enough."

She took yet another slow noisy lick of her yogurt, which made his eyes cross. "Okay, I'll give you another," she said. "Ready?"

Expecting another statement like "I missed the beach," he relaxed. Even smiled. "Hit me."

"I missed you. More than I missed the beach."

He went still, then forced a smile. "Yeah, I noticed how much you missed me. All those letters cluttering up my mailbox."

She dug her bare toes into the sand. Her crystal toe ring sparkled. "I wanted to write you. I must have started a hundred letters. Last year I came home for Christmas, I even looked you up. I drove by your place. I didn't expect it to be a sailboat in Mission Bay. It's lovely."

"I take care of it for the owner, who's a fire chief in Los Angeles. Why didn't you stop and see me?"

"Nope, that's enough of me. Your turn now. A secret, Joe."

He stared out at the five-footers and gave her his deepest, darkest one. "I lied when I said I never thought about you."

She smiled, warm and bright, as if he'd just given her a gift.

"Want to know the truth about why I never came to see you?" she asked. "I was afraid."

"Of me?"

"Afraid we'd never find our way back to the way things were." She lifted her head and pierced him with those jade eyes he'd never been able to resist. "Can we?" she whispered.

"I never look back." He took another sip of his shake, then handed it to her. "Trade."

She did but held onto his wrist before he turned away. "Joe."

She wanted a better answer, and he wasn't sure if he was ready to share it. But he'd never been able to hold back with her. "I never look back because there's not much for me there." *Except you.* "I live for the here and now, Red. It's good. It works for me."

"Like last night. Last night worked for you."

"Last night was . . ."

"Good," she said softly.

More than, he thought, and since she'd wanted a confession, he offered a doozy. "One night wasn't enough for me."

Her smile slowly faded. "No?"

Hell, no. But then again, he'd known it wouldn't be. "I can't do this as casual as you're looking for, and survive it."

She nodded and played her toes in the sand for a moment. She still smelled like smoke. There was a cut visible on her ankle. Damn it. "Red."

"I know. You don't want to go back. You don't want to go forward. I know."

He sighed and opened his mouth. "Maybe we could start over from a new place. In the here and now."

Her head whipped up. "Really?"

He was insane. A glutton for punishment. "As friends."

Her eyes went bright with emotion and before he knew what she meant to do, she leaned in, pressing her mouth to his jaw in a kiss he was certain she thought as sweet but fired his engines like no simple little peck ever should.

"So," she said. "Friend. What do you do in the here and now for fun? I know you run."

He shuddered and made her laugh. "I don't run for fun, but for necessity. There's a huge difference."

Her gaze ran over his body. "It works."

"No." He waggled a finger in her face. "None of that."

"None of what?"

"That look."

"What, I'm just standing here," she said innocently, lifting her hands.

"Yeah, you're just standing there. Looking at me like I'm a ten-course meal and you're starving. Stop it."

"Why?"

He shifted uncomfortably.

"Why, Joe?"

"It makes me hot." *You make me hot.*

Her smile was slow, pure sin. "It's supposed to."

"Okay, clearly we need rules for this," he decided, and scrubbed his hands over his face. "Lots of rules."

"What, like friend rules?"

"Yeah. No funny looks. No—"

"Kissing?" she asked. "How about kissing?"

"Definitely no kissing. I can't handle it, Red. I mean it. I can start over. I can be your friend. I can do anything you want except fall for you again and watch you walk away when it's time."

She sipped from his shake.

"Red?"

"I hear you," she said softly.

He only hoped that was true.

Joe and Kenny met to exchange interview information. They sat in Kenny's office over fast food, their files spread out in front of them.

They were taking a good, hard look at Braden. "He's relatively new at Creative Interiors," Joe said. "No one really knows him."

"We'd better run him through the system," Kenny said, making notes. "And then go talk to him."

"And I think it's time we take harder looks at some of the others as well. Stella and Gregg. Did you know they'd failed at their own shop?"

Kenny looked up. "How long ago?"

"Fifteen years. According to Summer, this came from Stella, and Gregg wasn't happy about her telling the story."

Kenny let out a low whistle and began writing again. "Interesting."

"Very. And then there's Ally."

"From Ally's Treasures."

"Red mentioned seeing her a lot lately." Joe read his

notes. "She was at the opening party, and seen driving by the next morning as well. She has a definite grudge, though given as successful as she is, it doesn't make much sense."

"If we're talking grudges . . . Have you noticed any grudges against any one particular employee?"

"You're talking about Red." Joe's stomach clutched. "And how they all seem a bit wary of her."

"Yes."

"That's the past reaching out to bite her on the ass."

"Relevant here?" Kenny asked.

"I want to say no," Joe said slowly. "But . . ."

"Never say never."

"At least not in this business." Wearily Joe pushed to his feet. "Let's go scour the site again."

As the sun set, Joe and Kenny showed their badges to the patrol officer and entered the Creative Interior fire site.

They'd already taken all the pictures they needed of the still wet, charred building. They'd investigated the point of origin. Now they needed to finish the tedious task of going through each room to see if there were any more clues or evidence.

They split up. Kenny worked the front room and Joe took the employee break room where Summer had ended up trapped. The actual fire destruction there had been minimal, mostly just smoke and water damage, but he went through it meticulously, including the purple beanbag that gave him more than a few bad flashbacks.

He climbed the stairs as Summer must have done, stood where she'd said she'd stood when her cell phone had gone off.

Camille had called her. If no one else but Joe thought that was strange, he wouldn't back away from it. Camille

and Summer were circling their way around their mother-
daughter relationship. By Summer's own words, Camille
hadn't yet made a real stand there. Any progress, any contact, had been made by Summer herself.

And yet Camille had called at a most interesting time . . .

"You done down there?" Kenny called.

"Yeah. You find anything?"

"Nothing. But I have more questions."

"Me, too."

They moved outside, working their way around the
perimeter of the building, searching for anything out of
place. The parking lot was concrete. The Dumpster sat on a
dirt pad off the concrete lot, and there in the dirt lay a cigarette butt. They stared at it, then Joe let out a breath and
pointed just ahead.

In the dirt in front of the Dumpster was half a boot print
with diagonal tread.

Just like the one at the warehouse fire.

Standing there, heart thumping, Joe squatted down,
opened his kit and pulled out his accelerant meter.

It registered.

Kenny swore softly.

"Yeah." Whoever had been wearing this boot had
stepped in something flammable, and Joe would be willing
to bet it'd match the warehouse print, right down to the
trace of gasoline in it, tying the two fires together. Which
meant that without a doubt, the warehouse fire had no been
an accident at all.

Nor had this one.

At home, Joe fell on his bed and crashed. He slept like
the living dead until near dawn, when the dreams came.

Creative Interiors was on fire, flames leaping into the

night, burning so hot he couldn't get close. He stood back, watching in horror as the firefighters pulled Summer through the window.

Only suddenly it wasn't Summer surrounded by the flames, but *him*. His skin prickled with the heat. Sweat poured into his eyes. And then in a blink, the fire was gone and he was climbing into Summer's window. He stood by her bed, bruised and battered from his father's fists, breathing too harshly, tears that he refused to shed burning in his throat as he stared down at the only person in the world who'd ever given a shit about him.

She didn't sit up and hug him. She didn't hand him her extra pillow and cover him with the throw cover on the foot of her bed.

Nothing.

"Red," he whispered.

She didn't move.

"Red?" Reaching out, he nudged her shoulder, then turned her over.

She began to scream, writhing in agony as she burned, just as if she were that kid in that horrific house fire the other night, melting into the sheets—

With a gasp he sat straight up in bed.

His own bed.

And he was no longer a kid.

And neither was Summer.

Drenched in sweat and shaking like a leaf, he picked up his phone and dialed before he had his thoughts together.

"'Lo," came Summer's sleepy voice.

"Hey."

"Joe?" She went from sleeping to alert, as always reading him better than he could read himself. "You okay?"

"Sure." He lay back, his legs still trembling. He knew

why he'd dreamed badly. It was his suspicions about the two fires. It was that she could have died. It was the bone deep, gnawing fear. Fear for her. "Just checking on you."

She was quiet a moment. "You had a bad dream."

"No, I—"

"You did." Her voice was soft and warm and wrapped around him like a blanket. "I'm sorry."

"I'm fine," he said.

"Uh huh. And I don't have panic attacks." She snorted. "We're pathetic, you know that? I'm coming over. I'll bring something good and fattening."

"Don't even think about it." He let out a low laugh though, feeling better already. "Seriously, don't."

"But—"

"Have a good day, Red."

"Joe. Are you sure?"

Oh, yeah. If she came over this early, looking rumpled and sexy, he'd never be able to resist. "Very."

"You going to work?"

"Yeah." Work was, and always had been, his only salvation.

Chapter 14

Joe skipped his run that morning and made a stop at Mc-Donald's for breakfast on his way to work, making his fall off the diet wagon complete. It was going to be a hell of a day, facing the implications of their new evidence on the Creative Interiors fires, and he needed all the fortification he could get.

He parked and headed toward his office, not happy to see his light on, which meant someone was already waiting for him.

Indeed, Cindy sat perched on his desk in a light blue suit snug to her curves, eyeing a box in the corner that hadn't been there the night before.

"Hi," she said happily, as if she hadn't tearfully dumped him in a restaurant two weeks ago.

"Hi," he said, playing along. He pointed to the box. "What's that?"

"Don't know. Kenny just said to make sure it didn't go anywhere, that he'd explain it to you later." Cutting him off before he could escape behind his desk, she moved close to take his hand and press it against her heart. "Did you miss me?" she asked softly.

He opened his mouth but she put a finger against it.

"Wait." She shot him a little smile. "I should go first." She drew a slow breath. "There's no smooth way to say this so I'm just going to spit it out. I shouldn't have let you go, Joe." She arched a little, making sure to press all her good parts, of which there were many, against him. "I missed you."

He waited for the usual zap of arousal to sing through his body, but nothing happened. He looked at her and felt warmth and affection for the time they'd spent together, but no heat. "Cindy—"

"Mm-hmm?" She slipped her arms around him, glided them up his back, and then down to cup his ass. "Let's go to my place."

Reaching back, he took her hands in his, brought them between their bodies.

"Uh oh." Smile fading, she pushed back so they weren't touching. "What's going on?"

"We stopped seeing each other, remember?"

"Oh, that. Just a little tiff really."

"Cindy. We both know my work isn't conducive to a relationship—"

"Don't be ridiculous, we can work through that."

"You didn't think so when you left me over that very thing."

She studied him closely. "Is there someone else already?"

That it was even possible shook him deep, but there was. Beautiful, lazy-smiling, easygoing, come-what-may, churn-him-up Summer. "This is about you and me," he said.

"You enjoyed what we had. I know you did."

"I did," he agreed. "But—"

"I really hate buts, Joe."

"I'm sorry, because this is a big one. You asked if I

missed you. It's easier to tell you what I didn't miss. I didn't miss worrying about disappointing you, or stressing over how mad my work made you—"

"You . . . didn't miss me," she said, shocked, making him wince. "Wow." She seemed bowled over by this, and backed away to think. "I pictured you so miserable. I even waited an extra few days to dig that misery deep." She sank back to his desk. "I can't believe it. You didn't miss me. *Me.*"

"I'm sorry."

"Me too." She stood up again. "But that's my problem, right? I mean I took the risk of leaving you. I actually thought I'd get a diamond ring out of it."

He felt himself pale, and she let out a mirthless laugh. "Don't worry, Joe. I think I get it now." She looked him over from head to toe, put her hand to her heart and gave one little fluttering sigh. "If only you weren't so damn gorgeous." She sighed. "But so am I. I'll recover."

"Yeah, you will." He hugged her when she leaned in, then watched her go, thinking he must be insane, because being with her had been a piece of cake compared to being with Summer.

Too bad he'd never taken the easy route in his life.

He blinked, then backed to his chair and fell into it, because he'd just realized where this thought process had taken him. He'd told Summer they were going to be just friends, that that's all he wanted, and he'd lied through his teeth. He wanted more. He wanted it all. If that didn't make him the biggest fool alive, he had no idea what did.

Kenny poked his head in. "Cindy cut you loose again?"

Still stunned by the revelation, Joe stared at him. "Huh?"

"Did Cindy—"

"*Woof.*"

At the unmistakable sound of a puppy's bark, Joe nearly had a coronary. He rushed past Kenny and looked inside the box. Inside was a downy soft blanket and a dark muddy-colored spot.

A muddy-colored spot that wriggled, whimpered, and then barked again. "A *puppy*? What's a puppy doing here?" It looked like a chocolate lab, complete with melting eyes and a pink tongue lolling out of its mouth as it sleepily contemplated Joe.

"She's our new arson partner," Kenny said. "Do you like her?"

"If she's yours, I like her a lot."

"Yeah, about that." Kenny pasted an apologetic look on his face. "She was going to be mine, but then my landlord said no dogs."

"You live in your own house."

"I'm awfully strict."

The puppy began to try to crawl out of the box. She fell on her back twice, crying in frustration, shooting Joe those dark, dark puppy eyes. Caving like a cheap suitcase, he scooped her up, and immediately got a face licking from chin to forehead.

"Look, they were giving away puppies at the pound yesterday," Kenny said. "I drove by as they were cleaning up. She was the last one left. I mean look at her, I couldn't just leave her, right?"

"You should never have stopped."

"I know. But she'll make a great arson dog, don't you think? Check out that nose."

As if on cue, the puppy wriggled her nose, and then set her head down on Joe's chest, panting happily.

"She's got your name all over her," Kenny said hopefully.

Although she couldn't have been more than a few
pounds, she felt like the weight of the world. She was a responsibility, a huge one, and he was a man who couldn't see
himself making it work. "I don't need a dog," Joe said, and
stroked her soft fur.

"Look her in the eyes and tell her that."

Joe stared down at the puppy, then back at his partner.
"Don't do this. Why are you doing this?"

"She ate everything that wasn't tied down last night,
man. I thought I was ready for a dog but she's crazy."

"Take her back."

They both looked at the puppy, who cocked her head at
them and whined softly.

"I can't do it, man," Kenny said miserably. "I thought I
could but . . . you take her."

"No."

"Come on. Would it be so bad to have a real attachment?
An emotional connection?"

"You know what? Don't even start." He'd had a hell of
an emotional attachment just two nights ago, and yet it
wouldn't be *him* that put a halt to things, but Red's own issues with a so-called commitment. "I live on a sailboat.
How do you walk a puppy on a sailboat?"

"Very carefully."

"This isn't funny. Take her back."

"Ooops," Kenny said, picking up his pager, reading the
display. "Gotta go."

"Don't you even think about—*Kenny*!"

But it was too late, he was gone.

Joe swore colorfully but that didn't change a thing. He
was still alone with the puppy. "Great. Well, I have to go,
too," Joe said. To no one. To the puppy. He set the thing
down in the box and headed to the door, stopping at the

sound of a long, pathetic whine. "You can't just come with me."

She tilted her head. Her ear hit her in the face and she sneezed.

"Okay, you're cute. I'll give you that. But you still can't come."

She let out another heartbreaking whine.

"Ah hell." He moved back to her and picked her up. "You plan on being good, right?"

She licked him again, and he sighed into her happy little face because as he knew all too well, even the best laid plans got screwed up.

The next morning Summer took a few customers on a kayak trip, and was shocked when they booked her again for some of their friends. She set up a calendar to keep track of her trips, then worked on the insurance paperwork for her mother, a chore that seemed never ending. At the end of the day, she went for a run to ease her stress.

She took the streets instead of the beach, telling herself she wanted a change of pace, but when she found herself standing in front of the three-day-old burned-out shell of Creative Interiors II, she knew she'd meant to come here. She wanted to see it for herself in the light of day.

There was yellow tape wrapped around the building, warning people to stay out. *Caution.*

It seemed to Summer that her entire life had a yellow tape around it.

Caution—don't run so far that you forget where you came from.

Caution—don't turn your back on the people that matter. It's not easy to find them again.

Caution—don't try to get back to the last place where things made sense. You'll only find yourself more lost.

She ducked beneath the tape and saw the fire vehicle parked in the lot. *Joe's*. She moved up the three front steps and peered inside. The front had been boarded up but someone had removed the barrier and let themselves in. She did the same.

The destruction was both shocking and numbing. The walls were black, the windows broken, the furniture unrecognizable as anything other than drenched, charred rubble. It smelled horribly acrid, and at her first whiff, she was assaulted with the memories of being surrounded by fire. Like a one-two fist to the belly they hit her, and she doubled over.

Joe popped his head out of one of the alcoves and saw her clutching her stomach. "Christ," he said, and rushed toward her.

"I was just in the neighborhood . . ." She tried a smile but it was difficult with the breath backing up in her throat, and finally she gave up. "Oh, damn," she whispered, and sank to her knees in the wet muck. "These damn spots in front of my eyes are getting really annoying."

"You shouldn't be here." He wore coveralls, gloves, and boots, and was streaked with dirt from head to toe. He tore off his gloves, threw them aside and crouched besides her. Tugging on her ponytail, he tilted her head up. "You're pale."

She looked into his face, sooty and streaked with sweat, and found there was nothing else in the world she'd rather be looking at. "I am not going to throw up." She had no idea if she was trying to convince him, or herself.

"Are the spots still dancing?" He shifted his face even closer as if he could see them himself.

"No."

He relaxed slightly but remained close enough that she could have counted the gold flecks swimming in his whiskey-colored eyes, or each individual thick eyelash. She could see the inch-long scar above his eyebrow, which she knew was courtesy of taking a flying leap out of his father's hands and into their TV set. He had other scars, too, and each of them had broken her heart.

Just, as she suspected, she'd once broken his.

She wanted to make that up to him, wanted him to smile at her, feel the warmth and affection he'd once had for her. God, she needed that from him. "It's . . . not as bad in here as I thought."

"Well, the bathroom's gone. That's where the fire started. But this room . . ." He looked around. "It's actually salvageable. The back is trashed though, needs new flooring, paint, and there's a lot of water damage—" He took a look at her face and broke off. "And you don't need to hear this right now, I'm sorry. Why are you here, Red?"

"I told you, I was just in the neighborhood—"

"Truth."

Because I'm lost. Floundering. My foundation's slipped.

He didn't rush to fill in her silence, but waited her out. Silence had never bothered him the way it had her. "I wanted to tell you another secret," she said.

"Do I have to tell you one first?" he asked cautiously.

Such a guy. "No, this is a freebie. I told you I came back to Ocean Beach for my mom. Remember?"

"Yes."

"And I really thought that was it, but now I don't think that's the whole truth." She looked around. The soot and water were pervasive and depressing. "I came for me, too. I needed to connect. Emotionally."

He stared at her. "Have you been talking to Kenny?"

"What?"

"Never mind. Go on."

"That's all I've got." She shrugged. "Only there's a problem. When it comes to actually executing the emotional connections I think I want, I keep screwing up. I'm pretty sure I'm doing it on purpose."

"Maybe you're not ready."

"Maybe." She shot him a smile. "I guess I'd kind of hoped you'd say that I haven't screwed anything up at all, especially between us."

"You haven't. But you have to see that yourself."

"So we're really okay?" She looked at him, so big and tough and brutally honest, and had to ask. "We're really going to be friends again?"

He nodded, and that more than anything made her feel better. He was so strong, so sure of himself. She wanted to ask him how he'd gotten to this point. She wanted to know the path he'd taken, and what he'd done to become so comfortable with who he was, but before she could ask any of that, a small bundle of fur bounded toward them.

"Woof."

The bark belonged to the sweetest chocolate lab puppy Summer had ever seen. It launched itself at Joe, who caught it in midair.

"I told you to stay," Joe said sternly, but sighed when the puppy licked his chin. "We're going to have to work on that," he muttered.

"She's yours?" Summer opened her arms and the puppy jumped into them.

"A misbehaving little tyrant is what she is. She's already eaten two files in the truck, and chewed through a bag of evidence. Not to mention she has no manners and can't sit or stay to save her life."

"You sound like a dad."

"Bite your tongue."

"Oh, Joe. Not all dads are bad."

He looked away. "I know that."

He broke her heart. He always had. But he'd no more welcome her sympathy now than he ever had. She stroked the puppy. "She can't be more than twelve weeks old. Telling her to sit or stay means nothing to her. And she's probably teething— Ouch!" She pulled her hand free— now sporting teeth marks—and laughed at the puppy's startled expression.

"I have matching marks all over me," Joe said, but reached out to pet the dog's head.

Summer nuzzled the soft fur. "So what's an adorable thing like you doing with such a grump?"

"She's not a grump," Joe said.

Summer laughed. "And do you really think you're so adorable?"

He looked down at his coveralls. "Not at the moment."

But sitting next to her on the dirty floor, surrounded by chaos and soot and grime, his hair scruffy and untamed, his mouth curved in a slight grin, he was. Absolutely adorable. Reaching out, she ran her finger over his dimple. She wanted to run her finger over more of him. All of him.

As if he could read her thoughts, he got to his feet. Kept his distance. "You shouldn't be in here."

"Yeah." She stood, feeling awkward. Unwanted. "I know I'm keeping you from your work."

"And my sleep, too, but since when has that bothered you?"

Her heart hitched. "I'm keeping you from sleep?"

"I thought that was your new mission in life."

"Oh, it is." She backed up a step and forced a smile. "Along with driving you wild."

"Baby, that's a given." He put his hands on his hips. "You done making light of this?"

"Probably not."

"Because it's sure as hell easier than talking to me, right?"

"Is that what you think? That I don't want to talk to you?"

"You tell me what I'm supposed to think. You come into town after years of silence, wanting to pick things up right where they were left. With benefits. Well, things change, Red. People change, damn it. I'm not that same idolizing, stupid, pathetic kid who would have rolled over like this puppy if you so much as smiled at me."

She stared at him, as disconcerted by his self-derisive tone as by the words. "I never knew that's how you saw yourself. I never saw you that way."

"You never saw me at all."

She searched his fathomless gaze, her heart melting when the puppy in his arms stretched to lick his jaw and he leaned into it, nuzzling the puppy's face beneath his neck.

Summer wanted to be right there. *She* wanted to nuzzle that spot. *Jealous of a puppy.*

"You said being friends works for you," he said. "But you still won't open up to me about anything that matters—" He froze a moment, then scrubbed a hand over his face. "Jesus. I can't believe I just said that." Turning from her, he stared off into space. His broad shoulders were filthy and looked like he carried the weight of his world on them. She put her hands there, gently squeezed, woman enough to love the feel of the hard strength of him.

"Would you like to know why I usually get dumped by women?" he asked.

"Um, they're farsighted?"

A low, harsh laugh escaped him. "Because I don't open up. I don't share myself."

The implications of that, mixed with what he wanted from *her,* sank in. "Oh."

"Yeah, how's that for irony? I'm standing here hounding you for the very thing I've never given. I'm sorry for that." He shook his head and still didn't look at her. "Look, I've got to get back to work."

"Joe—"

"And like I said, non-fire personnel aren't allowed in here. I'm sorry, but you'll have to go."

Right.

She had to go.

Story of her life. Her own fault, she'd written it herself.

Chapter 15

Joe named the puppy Ashes for her rather disgusting love of rubbing her nose in soot. A friend of Kenny's was indeed an arson-dog trainer who agreed to begin working with Joe and the puppy. Given that Ashes fell asleep in the middle of their first session, Joe didn't expect any miracles.

The next day, San Diego was hit by a hot, violent summer storm. Joe and Kenny set out in it to talk to the people involved with the Creative Interiors case again, going to Ally's Treasures first. As they ran from the truck, getting drenched in the process, the unhappy Ashes began to howl from her perch behind the wheel.

"She could wake the dead," Kenny yelled over a boom of thunder.

"I need a dog sitter!" Joe yelled back, eyeing the pathetic puppy face plastered to the window, woefully watching them run away. "Or someone to just shoot me."

"I'll shoot you later," Kenny promised, and pulled him inside Ally's Treasures.

Ally was a tall, lean, haughty beanpole, with sharp eyes and a sharper tongue, who clearly did not like dripping wet fire marshals. "I'm busy," she said when they identified themselves.

"This will only take a minute," Kenny promised, and smiled his charm-the-witness smile.

Immune, Ally frowned. "Make it quick."

"How do you feel about Creative Interiors?" Joe asked.

She lifted a shoulder. "They have the better building and street visibility, but since I do a better business, I don't lose sleep over it."

"How do you know?" Kenny asked, looking at a shelf of seashells filled with sand, all marked with shockingly astronomical prices.

"How do I know what?" Her tone was holier-than-thou, her nose so high in the air she was in jeopardy of a nosebleed.

"That you do a better business," Kenny said patiently.

"Because I snoop, if you want the truth. I go into their stores and check out their stock and what their customers are buying. There's no law against that. Camille does it to me right back."

"Camille spies on you?" Kenny asked.

"Of course she does. She sends one of the twins, the one who smokes, to buy a *Cosmo* off my magazine rack, then she presumably goes back and tells them everything. If I were Camille I'd be more concerned about how much more work she does than her spacey sister, or that seriously creepy bookkeeper she just hired, or even that wild and crazy roam-the-planet daughter of hers, but whatever. To each her own."

Joe bit his tongue with effort. "One of the twins smokes?"

"Yes. Don't know which one."

"Have you ever been to their warehouse?" Joe asked.

"The one that burned?" Her eyes narrowed. "Why?"

"Have you?"

Her cool veneer slipped a moment. "I don't like where this is going."

"Yes or no."

"No."

"What about the new store site?" Kenny asked. "Creative Interiors II. Were you there at all?"

She paled and shook her head.

"Are you sure?" Joe asked.

"Once," she admitted. "At the opening party. They had quick-serve hors d'oeuvres set out. *Please.*"

"What about the next day?" Joe asked. "Were you there at all on opening day?"

Some of the snide light and superiority drained out of her eyes. "I drove by," she said quietly, finally taking them seriously. "Right at ten o'clock. Just to see how many people they had, that's all. I never went in."

"Where were you between the hours of six and ten that night?"

She straightened her shoulders and looked him right in the eye, all attitude gone. "I was here. I closed at six and spent the next few hours working on my books. I was alone. I have no one who can verify that, but I can tell you right now, you'll find no evidence of my doing Creative Interiors any harm. I don't need to, they do enough harm to themselves."

Next up on the interview list was Braden. Joe and Kenny crossed the street from Ally's Treasures to Creative Interiors, getting drenched all over again. Halfway across, Ashes saw them from the truck and resumed her howling.

Kenny laughed, and because of it, Joe made him go back and get the damn puppy.

Kenny ran and opened the truck, scooping the puppy against his shirt. "She's shedding."

"Bummer for you." Joe no longer bothered to swipe the rain out of his eyes. It was six o'clock, closing time, and as they came up to the door of Creative Interiors, Braden walked out.

"You're looking for me," he said, and opened his umbrella, tucking himself and his laptop neatly out of the way of the slashing rain.

Joe and Kenny, neither of whom had an umbrella, stood there with water running down their no longer repellent clothing. Ashes licked the rain off Kenny's jaw.

"Make it quick." Braden eyed them both with a cool gaze, not offering to share his umbrella or to go back inside. "Or do I need an attorney?"

Kenny squinted through the drops on his glasses. His blond hair was sleek to his head, his shirt clinging to him, and there was a squirming puppy in his arms shedding all over him. He was not a happy camper. "Can we take this inside?"

"Do I have a say in that decision?" Braden asked.

"What? Of course you have a say." Kenny's irritation was beginning to show, the way it always did when things weren't neat and tidy. Or dry.

"Then no," Braden said. "I don't want to go inside. I'm perfectly comfortable out here."

Kenny opened his mouth but Joe put a hand on his tense, wet arm. "We'd like to ask you a few questions," he said calmly. "You don't need a lawyer, unless you want one."

Braden just looked at his watch.

"You don't seem all that surprised to see us," Joe noted.

"Look, I'm not stupid. I'm the new guy and I don't talk

much. Plus, I was there the night of the fire. I was alone in the room where the fire originated."

"Were you?"

"You know I was."

Joe sighed. "Can you elaborate? Tell us how you came to be alone there?"

"The whole staff was around, working. Then they left, and it was just Summer and me. I think I scared her."

"Why?"

"Didn't mean to. I thought she knew I was still there."

"What were you doing?"

"In the bathroom?" He arched a dry brow.

Joe just waited, not at all bothered by the way his clothes had begun to stick to his entire body. He liked the rain, always had. But Kenny was a rare lit fuse. He was wet, wrinkled, holding a squirming puppy, and ready to blow.

Braden stayed rigid for a long moment, then caved when neither fire marshal moved. "I used the toilet," he said. "And then the sink."

"Anything else?" Kenny asked.

"Like? . . ."

"Did you have gasoline in there for any reason?"

"Christ. No."

Joe looked down at Braden's black boots, still dry on the tops—unlike his own soaked athletic shoes. "What size shoe do you wear?"

"Depends on the shoe."

"Approximately," Kenny said tautly.

"I don't know. An eleven."

"Do you smoke?"

"Used to."

"What does that mean exactly?" Joe asked.

"It means I quit."

"How long ago?"

"I've quit several times. The last was a few weeks ago." Braden swiped his hand over his mouth. "Is that all?"

"For now, thanks," Joe said, and they watched him go.

"He's involved with Chloe." Kenny set the puppy on the ground. "Heel," he commanded with quiet authority.

"She has no idea what that means." Joe rolled his eyes when Ashes plopped to her back on the wet concrete, waiting for someone to squat down and pat her belly. "They're dating then?"

"In a manner of speaking."

Joe looked at the building and sighed. "They're all connected."

"And so are we." Kenny smiled grimly when Joe closed his eyes at that. "Let's finish this. Camille's still inside."

"She won't thank you for this."

"The job comes first," Kenny said in a carefully even voice.

They stepped inside and stood by the door, not wanting to get anything wet. Kenny passed the puppy to Joe. "Your turn."

Camille came out of the back and gasped. "A puppy!"

"A wet puppy," Kenny warned as she scooped Ashes close.

"Oh, she's adorable." She lifted her smiling eyes. "You're wet, too. You're all going to get sick." She ushered them to the back and went directly to the teapot in the sink. "Let me make some hot tea."

"Don't trouble yourself," Kenny said gently. "Why don't you come sit down, Camille."

"Oh. Okay." She put Ashes down.

The puppy skidded her way toward Joe. He looked her right in the soft chocolate eyes and said, "Stay."

Ashes set her butt to the floor, wriggled and panted, and shockers of all shockers, stayed.

Camille came close, sat in the chair Kenny pulled out for her and folded her hands. "You've found something." She divided a gaze between them. "Tell me."

"The accelerant in the bathroom of the store proved to be the same mix of gasoline found at the warehouse fire," Kenny said.

Her eyes went wide. "But— Oh my God."

"And you're still certain gasoline isn't something any of you would use?" Joe asked.

"I'm sure."

"Do you or any of your employees smoke?" Joe asked.

She paused. "Is that relevant?"

They'd found two cigarette butts now. They were being tested for DNA, which wouldn't help them unless they matched in their database with a convicted criminal. But both butts were the same brand, smoked down to the same length, and couldn't be discounted.

Nothing when it came to this fire would be discounted, not now.

"It could be relevant, yes," Kenny said.

"Well, no one smokes in the store, of course."

"But what about outside? Anyone?"

For the first time, she looked away. Down at her clean, neat fingernails.

"Camille?" Kenny said.

"I can't think of anyone off the top of my head."

"Do any of your nieces smoke? Or your sister?"

"Oh, you know kids. They're bound to try stupid things."

Over her head, Joe exchanged a look with Kenny. She was holding back. Camille, holding back. He couldn't believe it. "What made you call Summer on her cell phone the night of the fire?"

"I . . . she's my daughter. We call."

"But you don't," Kenny said very quietly. "You don't call her."

"I don't want to bother her. But that night . . . she was leaving the next day. I wanted— I thought maybe—" She covered her mouth with a shaking hand.

"You thought what, Mom?"

Everyone turned in unison to see Summer standing in the doorway. Ashes, at the end of her restraint, leapt to her feet and bounded over to her.

Summer bent and scooped her up. She wore one of her long, loose, sleeveless sundresses with a tank top beneath, both in the color of a California poppy, which showed off bronzed, toned limbs and all that shiny fiery hair. Joe imagined he could smell her, some complicated mix of spring flowers and sexy woman. On her face there was a somber, unreadable expression, though her eyes lighted right on Joe's. "Sorry," she said, petting the puppy. "I'm eavesdropping."

"I called to see if you were busy," Camille said, tears in her voice. "On your last night in town."

"I'd've liked to see you." Summer came into the room. "I'd been feeling alone."

The statement sliced right through Joe. He hadn't gone to her that night out of self-protection, but he should have thought about her being alone, feeling as if she has no one to turn to, no reason to stick around. Some friend he'd made.

"So you've connected the two fires." She sat heavily. "Which means, of course, you'll be looking at that first fire again. And the one where my dad died."

Camille gasped, and when everyone looked at her, she swallowed hard. "I hadn't thought— Oh my God."

Summer leveled Joe with those deep jade eyes. "Am I right?"

"Yes," Joe said, sorrow filling him at the pain this was going to cause all of them. "You're right."

Camille abruptly pushed up from the chair and walked out of the room without looking back.

Summer sighed and got to her feet as well but Kenny stepped in front of her. "Let me," he murmured.

"Do you think she'll talk to you?"

"I do, yes."

"She's even more stressed than I imagined," Summer said when Kenny was gone, staring at the door. She set Ashes down and hugged herself in a gesture Joe wasn't even sure she realized she made.

Socks appeared in the doorway and glared at the specimen of puppy.

Ashes let out one hopeful, excited bark.

"Ashes, sit. Stay," Joe said firmly. *"Stay."*

Ashes didn't sit but she did stay, her entire body quivering with the effort to hold herself back. One small whine escaped her.

"Stay," Joe said again softly.

Socks, not being under any orders but her own, walked into the room and right past Ashes.

Ashes barked again, and leaned in and licked Socks's face. That proved too much for the cat, who hissed, which invited Ashes to bound after her.

Socks leapt over the backs of two chairs, jumped onto the table and off again in a single graceful bound. Ashes became a frantically barking mass of excitement, chasing the cat around the table in circles. They both vanished beneath the table, from which emerged more wild barking and ferocious growling.

"Goddamnit." Joe dove beneath the table, snagged the puppy, and came face to face with Summer, who'd dived under the table from the other side to grab Socks.

"Your puppy is short on manners," Summer said with a smile.

"You're telling me?" The puppy licked Joe's chin. "What am I going to do with you?"

"Keep her, of course." Summer was close enough that if they hadn't had the puppy and the pissed off cat between them, he might have been able to lean in and do something stupid.

Ashes did it for him. She craned her neck and licked Socks again. Socks retaliated by lifting a paw and bitch-slapping the puppy across the face. Ashes yelped and Joe jumped, cracking his head hard on the underside of the table.

He swore at the cat, at the puppy, at Summer who was laughing at him as he backed out from beneath the table. He sat right on the floor while the stars cleared from his vision. "I'm beginning to see why that dog was at the pound."

"You wouldn't give her back."

He rubbed his aching head. "In a heartbeat, I would."

Summer kneeled in front of him and put her hands on his shoulders, peering into his pupils. "How many of me do you see?"

"One, which is more than enough." He grabbed her hand when she would have pulled away. He understood the stress he saw behind her smile, but didn't like it, nor the fact that he worried so damn much about her.

Socks jumped up to the couch, twitched her tail and scowled at them.

Summer ignored the cat, made a soothing noise in her throat at Joe, and sank her fingers into his hair, unerringly finding the nice bump he'd just given himself. "You always had bruises all over you. I hated that."

He closed his eyes. "Red—"

"I cared about you. So much."

"And now?" he asked before he could stop himself.

"I care about you now too." She kissed his jaw, first one side and then the other, but then rose to her feet and gave him a hand.

He let her pull him up and eyed the delicate purple shadows beneath her eyes. "Are you off work?"

She nodded.

"I have more to do at the office but I could use a fun little run first."

She arched an amused brow. "You were going to go for a run. Now. For fun, no less."

It felt so good to see her knowing grin, he felt one split his face as well. "You know it. You could come with me."

"You, Joe Walker, are a very sweet man."

"Sweet?"

"Oh, is that not a manly enough adjective? How about strong. Smart. Gorgeous. Sexy—"

"Keep going." He let her tug him to the front. Camille was gone, and so was Kenny. Summer locked the store up and they dashed out into the rain, which seemed to be coming down in sheets.

"Darn, I forgot about the storm," Joe said, tongue firmly in his cheek. "Probably we shouldn't run in this."

"I happen to remember you love the rain."

Yeah, he did. In the old days they'd wait out a storm in the back of the library, or the warehouse, or her house. It didn't matter where. They'd watch MTV or play games or just talk. But he kept the memories to himself as they ran to the parking lot.

"Your car," she said, hand out palm up for his keys. "My turn to drive."

He grinned. "We drove the truck. Looks like Kenny took it and Ashes. You'll have to drive us in the Bug. I need a ride home to get clean clothes."

She navigated the storm and traffic with easy precision. By the time they parked at the marina and ran down the dock toward his boat, they were once again soaked. "I don't know . . ."

"Baby," she said. "Get your running clothes on."

The sailboat he lived on was forty-six feet long, all sleek polished wood and white trim. Below deck, they stood dripping in the galley that had wood floors, shiny wood cabinets, a wood booth for dining, and a stainless steel sink and refrigerator. The counter was clean except for two cameras he'd left out, which made Summer smile.

"Make yourself at home," he said, and tossed her a towel. "I'll be right back." He moved through a small archway into the captain's quarters, slid the door shut behind him and stripped out of his soaked work clothes.

"Wow, I'm impressed," Summer said.

Butt ass naked, he whipped around, but the door was still shut. The walls were just incredibly thin, and he had to laugh at himself. "Impressed at what?" he asked, rifling through his drawers for something clean to wear.

"You actually have healthy food in here. Salad makings, yogurt, fruit and veggies—"

"Why are you going through my kitchen?"

"Because you said to make myself at home. Ah." He heard his cupboards opening. "You do have a vice. Frosted Flakes."

He pulled on the first pair of sweats he came across and began the hunt for clean socks. "A guy's gotta have something good for breakfast."

He heard her opening and shutting some more cupboards and shook his head. Nosey wench. He'd have sworn he heard the clink of a spoon against a bowl, but that was ridiculous. She'd never stoop to eating Frosted Flakes. It wasn't green and didn't have the required amount of good nutrients per ounce. Locating two socks that he wasn't quite sure were an exact match, he turned around, looking for a shirt. Snatching one off the foot of his bed, he cocked his head at an odd crunching noise.

Holding the shirt in his hand, he slid open the door between his bedroom and the galley, then gawked at her sitting at his table with a huge bowl of Frosted Flakes, shoveling them into her mouth. She'd stripped out of her sundress, leaving her in the coral tank top and black biker shorts that hugged her hips, leaving her belly bare. The ring there flashed. Her tank was wet from her hair, and her nipples were hard.

"These are amazing," she said around a mouthful, dribbling a little milk out of the corner of her mouth, lapping it up with a quick dart of her tongue.

"Slow down, sailor, we aren't going to be able to run if you eat that entire bowl." He felt his body quiver when her tongue darted out again, at the other corner of her mouth this time.

Her hair was still dripping down her shoulders. If she'd had any makeup on, it was all gone now. Her expressive jade eyes never left his. "We aren't going to run, Joe."

"We're not?"

Now her gaze dropped, caressing his bare shoulders and chest, before dipping even lower. "Nope."

"You said you wanted—"

"You. I said I wanted you." Standing up, she came toward him. She stroked a finger over his collar bone, his shoulder, then his pec, right over his nipple.

An involuntary hiss escaped him as she slid her wet body up against his. "Red. *God*—"

"Remember the other night?" She pressed her mouth to his neck. "When you touched me? When you—"

"I remember," he said tightly, his knees wobbling at the feel of her mouth on his flesh.

"It was the first time since I'd been home that I felt like I could breathe." She glanced at him from beneath her long lashes. "That was because of you. I want to breathe again, Joe."

"You just want the release."

"Oh, yeah, I do."

He had no idea how he found the strength to put his hands on her shoulders and back away, putting some air between him and her glorious curves. "We're going running. Damn it."

Her eyes were dark, and filled with what she wanted, and it wasn't a little jog. "Stop looking at me like that," he demanded, fisting his hands at his sides to keep from reaching for her. "I told you. I can't do this and keep it light with you, I just can't. Don't ask me to."

She stared at him for a long time, disappointment, regret, and something else crossing her face. She slid the towel off her neck and reached for her dress, which she had lying on the back of a chair. "Don't worry, Joe. I won't. I won't ask you to do anything." And she headed toward the stairs.

Damn it. "Red—"

She kept walking.

And he let her go. He had to.

Chapter 16

Summer drove in the wild June storm, her emotions as battered as the roads. Only for her it had nothing to do with the wind and rain and everything to do with the storm raging inside her.

Yes, she'd wanted the quick, fast, hard release that she knew damn well Joe could have given her. Yes, she'd gone there for it. Was it such a crime that she found him so deeply, unfailingly attractive? That with him, it felt more right than it had with anyone else in a very long time? That with him maybe it was much more but she didn't yet know how to deal with that?

She gripped the wheel tight.

This sort of a thing needed to be obsessed over, thought about, given its space. She hadn't given it enough space. It was still too deep and terrifying, and far too real.

Really, Joe just needed to follow her lead and make do with what they had for now, because it was far better than most ever got to experience anyway.

A burst of lightning startled her. Another came on its heels, lighting up the sky like the fire that had been burning her dreams and waking hours, and sent her thoughts skittering back in time.

Fighting with Joe.

Running up the stairs.

Screaming for her father.

Hearing his hoarse cries for help.

Standing in the doorway, stunned by the smoke and flames . . .

And seeing a shadow. The shadow of another person as they ran past the window just outside the main floor of the warehouse.

Oh, God. She whipped to the side of the highway and set her head to the steering wheel, shaking. Had that been a real memory? Heart pounding, she sat there and struggled to pull more from her brain, but nothing else came. After a long while she lifted her head.

The rain had stopped. It wasn't dark yet, not for at least an hour, and unnerved, she drove up through the winding roads into the hills for the trails she knew would soothe her.

She kept her running shoes in the back of the Bug so she was able to park at the trailhead and go for it. She ran for several miles through a deep foggy mist before sinking to a rock on an overhang where on a clear day she'd have been able to look down on much of San Diego County, and the green hills lining the brilliant shiny azure blue of the ocean. God, she loved the smell after a rain. The wet gravel, the thriving wildlife, the sounds of small animals scurrying around chirping at one another. Gradually her pulse slowed and her head stopped throbbing with the memories.

When she left here, the memories would ease back to leave her alone, she knew that.

But her mom needed her. And maybe she needed her family as well. Getting to her feet she began the jog back. The soggy ground squished beneath her shoes. The trees dripped down on her damp, heated skin, soothing, cooling her down. By the time she got back to her car, she thought maybe she could function as a human without having a breakdown. Sliding into the driver's seat, she picked up her cell phone, with some ridiculous little hope running that maybe she'd have a message from Joe.

She did have a message, but not from Joe. The ID display read *out of area*. The text message was simple.

Go Away. Please, go away.

"Not funny, Diana," she muttered. "Or Madeline. Or . . ."

Or who? Who else would do this? She nearly deleted the message, but at the last minute didn't, instead tossing her cell to the backseat.

No she wouldn't go away, thank you very much.

Instead she drove without a particular destination in mind, trying not to think. That was her new objective for the rest of the night, no thinking allowed.

She ended up back in O.B., where it was raining again. Or still. Ahead on the right was Tooley's Bar with its pink neon palm tree sign blinking through the misty rain. Chloe's beat-up old Toyota was there in the lot, and on impulse Summer parked next to it, slipped her damp sundress back over her tank and biker shorts, fluffed her hair with her fingers and called it good. She ran through the drizzle to the building and opened the door. The interior was mostly beat-up old teakwood, with baskets hanging from the ceiling and sand and peanuts scattered on the floor like a Jamaican beach. It was large and roomy, and not crowded, which sent relief through her, and she took a few steps inside.

Stella and Gregg were standing on the edge of the dance floor, arms around each other. "Surprised to see you," Stella said, her smile not quite as warm as usual. Summer knew they'd been questioned about the fire, specifically about how Summer had reported Gregg being downstairs before leaving the shop, and how Gregg had offered to close up for her. Summer was sorry for it but she couldn't have done anything differently.

"You don't usually show up here," Gregg said.

"Just looking for some company." Summer smiled, hoping it'd get friendly again, but neither returned the smile or asked her to join them. In fact, Gregg nudged Stella away, and off the dance floor. "Enjoy yourself tonight," he said over his shoulder.

"Oh, yes," Stella agreed as Gregg slipped his arm around her. "Please, enjoy yourself."

Please. *Go away. Please, go away.* Summer blinked. "Um, what did you just say?"

Stella looked at her strangely. "I said enjoy yourself."

"No, you said please. Please, enjoy yourself."

"Okay." Stella glanced at her husband and lifted a brow. "You're right. I said please enjoy yourself." As her anonymous caller had.

"Right. I will, thanks." But they were already gone. Summer moved toward the bar, thinking this had to stop. *She* had to stop.

Chloe was sitting on a bar stool wearing a black denim mini and a dazzling pink halter that should have clashed with her green-tipped hair but somehow didn't. She had a tattoo on her bare shoulder of a hummingbird that looked brand new, and was accepting a very tall pink frothy drink from the bartender.

"You've been busy," Summer said, and gesturing to the new tattoo, sat next to her.

"Yeah." Chloe ran a finger over the hummingbird and smiled. "I know the image better suits you, but I like the idea of being so free."

"It's not all it's cracked up to be," Summer muttered.

Chloe arched a perfectly plucked brow and wordlessly slid the brand-new drink over. "You look like you could use this. Strawberry daiquiri," she said to Summer's unasked question. "Most excellent. Cheers, I'll get more." She gestured to the bartender, who served them an entire pitcher.

Summer would have rather had a peach smoothie, but she sipped at the drink and had to agree with Chloe. Most excellent. Leaning back, she watched the few singles standing around scoping each other out. If things had been different, she might have been in the scoping mood herself.

But damn if a certain fire marshal hadn't ruined her for other men.

Not permanently, she promised herself. Just temporarily, very temporarily, and when that made her start thinking too much again, she sipped her drink some more, trying to empty her mind. "You didn't by any chance text message me earlier?"

"On your cell?" Chloe asked.

"Yeah."

"I don't even have your number."

Summer stared at her as that sank in. It was true, Chloe didn't have her number. How sad was that? "Chloe, why aren't we closer?"

"You don't like people too close."

That made her suck harder at her straw. "I'm sorry. For what it's worth, I'm trying to fix that."

"I know."

"You do?"

"You're still here, aren't you?"

Summer smiled. "Yeah." She sipped some more and realized Chloe wasn't being her usual sarcastic self. "So what's up?"

"Nothing."

"Where's Braden?"

Chloe looked away. "Who?"

"Oh, no. You dumped him. I thought you were crazy about him."

"Don't be ridiculous. I just wanted his body."

Summer saw through the tilted chin and pride to the misery beneath. "What happened?"

"He dumped *me*," she confessed. "Not that you'd understand. I'm betting you've never been dumped."

Summer thought of tonight, and Joe, and took another long sip of her drink. "Don't bet anything important on that. Did he break your heart?"

"Of course not. I've got a heart of steel, no one could—" She broke off, her voice soft and husky as she studied her drink carefully. "He broke it in two, actually."

"Oh, Chloe. What happened?"

"That's just it, I don't know. Things were great. Then today he tells me this isn't working out for him, he can't see me anymore. That maybe he's going to be moving on."

"You mean, leaving town?"

"I guess. Whatever." Her thin shoulders sagged slightly. "Good riddance."

Without the usual cynical light in her eyes, Chloe looked so young. So hurt. Summer put her hand over hers. "You really cared for him."

"Yeah, the rat bastard. And I thought he cared for me back. He said he did. He did," she said into Summer's shocked face. "I know he doesn't say much at work, but we talked. We laughed. We . . . Well." She clinked her glass to Summer's and they both went to take a sip, but Summer was startled to hear the slurping sound of her straw on empty glass. "Guess I was thirsty."

"No problem." Chloe poured them both another from the pitcher, then tipped her glass to Summer's and knocked back a good half of it in one sip.

Summer did the same. Things were beginning to look different under a nice alcoholic buzz. For one thing, she could no longer see the front door clearly, which meant as the place filled up, she didn't feel the usual sense of growing panic. That was nice. Very nice.

"So." Chloe grinned. "You getting lucky tonight? I'm going to have to live vicariously through you for now."

"I've told you. Joe and I are just old friends."

"That's just a damn shame."

"Yeah." Summer held up her glass and Chloe topped them both off again from the pitcher.

"You going to miss him when you go?" Chloe asked.

"Joe?"

"No, the man on the moon. Yes, Joe."

"Yeah," Summer admitted. "I'll miss him."

"Maybe he could go with you and become a river guide, too. You could stay out there in the wilderness until you have kids, and then—"

"Chloe." Summer laughed. A real one. "Come on. I don't think about that kind of stuff."

"Why not?"

"Well, because . . . I don't know," she said honestly.

Chloe grinned. "You know, you act so tough, but I think you're really just a big chicken." She flapped her arms and made a clucking noise. "Want to know a secret? I'm chicken, too. My dad walked out on my mom, and granted, she got lucky the second time around, but I don't think I inherited any of the luck at all."

"If Braden walked, he's not worthy anyway."

"Don't say his name," Chloe said with a pout.

"He doesn't deserve you."

"No, he doesn't." Her eyes filled. "Damn it. I fell hard for that jerk. It was the real thing, too. True love." She sighed. "At least for me."

"You were okay with falling in love?"

"Are you kidding? *Yes.* Look, I know we both come off so tough and independent, but the truth is, while you're the real deal, I'm not. I *want* to share my life."

Summer had seen how love worked. She'd watched it bloom like a new rose between her mother and father every day of her life. It'd been the can't-eat can't-sleep kind, heart-wrenchingly real to the point where for Camille and Tim, little else had been able to penetrate. Little else had mattered.

Summer had lived with that, knowing she was an afterthought, a result of their bond but not really part of the circle. She even understood it, though she'd never really felt such a bond herself. And she'd decided life was too big, the possibilities too endless to tie herself down to one person to the exclusion of everything else.

She'd been told more than once that she had a rather masculine approach to relationships. She was fine with that. Had always been fine with that. Until now. Being here reminded her how nice it could be to have those ties she always avoided like the plague. Being here reminded her that love could be a nice, warm, sort of fuzzylike emotion that maybe could grow on her quite nicely.

At the thought, a little tiny flicker came from deep inside. Maybe she *could* want to belong to a specific place rather than roam, be part of a group that didn't change with each trek she took, to be a part of a relationship that mattered, that stuck. "You're definitely the strong one here," she said to Chloe. "Being able to admit what you want, being able to go for it."

"Wow, look at us," Chloe said. "Bonding. Who'd have thought?" She tipped up the glass, downed it, then slapped it down to the bar. "We should go get inked together next time."

"As in tattooed?"

"Yeah."

"Um . . . thanks, but no."

Chloe shrugged and topped off their glasses with the last of the pitcher. "We could go get a Brazilian wax. I'm due."

"Ouch."

"You get used to it."

"Really?"

"Well, no. But then I reward myself by getting a massage and Sven is so gorgeous . . ."

Summer choked on her drink and Chloe's grin nearly split her face.

"And you think *I'm* crazy," Summer said.

"I'm plastered," Chloe said cheerfully.

"I can tell." Feeling superior, Summer pushed her empty drink away, then swayed. She put a hand to her head. "Whoa."

"The drinks were doubles. And we had two. Or four. So that's like . . ." Chloe began counting on her fingers, weaving a bit in her chair. "A lot."

The bar had begun to fill up. People shifted in closer, and Summer wasn't so far gone she couldn't focus on the faces. An unmistakable desire to giggle overcame her. "Uh oh."

"Huh?" Bleary-eyed, Chloe took a look and gasped. Braden was heading purposely their way, his mouth grim, his face granite.

Nothing unusual there.

But his eyes. Those dark, usually unreadable eyes blazed with hunger, with need and temper and heat as they lit on Chloe and no one else.

"Chloe," Summer said carefully, enunciating each syllable. "That's not the look of a man who doesn't give a shit."

"I know. Oh God, I'm sweating. Look at him, he's so pretty. And I can't hardly see straight, I'm *drunk*." Chloe sounded panicked. "What do I do?"

Summer had never seen her cousin look so open, so vulnerable in her life, and her heart swelled in sympathy. "Well, I think you should stay seated, for one thing." She glanced at Braden, and her heart started to beat faster for Chloe. God, to be looked at like that. Joe had, when he'd been buried deep in her body, so deep she'd lost herself in him.

She'd loved it. Why hadn't she told him she loved being with him like that?

"What do I do?" Chloe whispered desperately.

"Smile?"

"I don't know if I can. I want to cry."

"No. Crying would be a mistake. Don't let him see how much this means to you. Suck it up," Summer demanded.

"Okay." Chloe forced a smile that hardly quivered at all. "How's that?"

"Good."

"I'll just keep remembering he wants to throw me away simply because it's time to move on."

Summer didn't respond because she'd thrown plenty of good people away simply because it was time to move on. The wrongness of that was something she'd have to live with.

Braden wound his way through the other customers and

came close without so much as a glance at Summer. And the cool, bad, tough Chloe threw her arms around him and buried her face in his neck.

Braden stared down at her, his cool visage nowhere in sight as he hauled her up from her bar stool, wrapped his arms around her and held on tight.

"I thought you were leaving," Chloe murmured.

"I couldn't go without seeing you again." The look on his face broke Summer's heart. He did love Chloe. He loved her with everything he had.

So why was he leaving at all? Feeling like a voyeur, Summer slipped off her bar stool. She wobbled and had to blink to clear her vision. Wow. Strong drinks.

The bartender was watching her. She hitched her chin toward Chloe, who was now kissing Braden as if their tongues were fused. "Make sure he drives her home, okay?"

"Will do," he promised. "How about you?"

"I'm going to call for a ride."

"Good idea."

She made her way outside. Night had fallen, and it was still drizzling. She leaned carefully against the building and pulled out her cell phone. It was midnight. Later than she'd thought.

Who to call? She hit the ON button and dialed Tina.

But the very male, sleepy "hello" that resonated through the phone into her ear and through her body was not Tina's. It wasn't Bill's either.

It was Joe's. Huh? Stupefied, Summer clicked the phone off. She glanced at the number she'd dialed and groaned.

Her fingers had dialed Joe without her brain's approval. Bad fingers. She tried again with the slow precision of a person who'd had three double strawberry daiquiris. This time she went for the twins's cell. Sure they enjoyed hating her guts but this was a family emergency, and even dysfunctional families stuck together. The rain sifted down over her like cooling fingers on her hot face as she waited.

"Are you going to hang up on me again?" asked a slightly bemused Joe.

Ohmigod. *What was the matter with her fingers?* "Sorry," she said quickly. "Dialed wrong." She hit OFF and touched her forehead with the phone. "Concentrate, damn it!"

Before she could call her mother next, the cell vibrated in her hand. Knowing what she'd see, she peeked at the caller ID, then winced. "Hey," she said casually.

Joe no longer sounded sleepy. "What are you doing?"

"Sorry I woke you."

"You don't sound like yourself."

That he knew her so well no longer surprised her. That it made her want to cry did. She wasn't going to get mushy over just the sound of him, she wasn't. But why hadn't she called a cab? The answer was rather revealing she decided shakily. "Look, I dialed wrong."

"Twice."

"Huh?"

"You dialed wrong twice. Who were you trying to call this late?"

"I don't know." She tipped her face up, closing her eyes as the rain soothed her. "I'm a bit off my center here."

"Yeah. Join the club."

The utter weariness in his voice cut right through her happy little fog. "Joe?"

"Good night, Red."

He was going to hang up. Panic gripped her. Not her typical kind of panic attack, where she couldn't breathe, but a new kind, a vice on her heart, squeezing out terrifying emotions that she nearly choked on. She imagined him sitting in his bed, all rumpled and sexy with it, maybe without any clothes on, and her body tingled. "I got a phone call tonight. It threw me off. And then I drank Chloe's stupid pitcher and it turned out to be doubles, and now I can't—"

"You've been drinking? Where are you?"

"Outside of Tooley's."

"By yourself? In the rain?"

"Yes, but—"

"Get back inside. I'll be right there."

"Joe, wait. I—"

But he'd already clicked off.

"Fine." She sighed. "I'll wait."

For him, she had the feeling, she'd always wait.

Chapter 17

Joe hung up the phone, got out of bed, and staggered into clothes. Ashes lifted her head from her spot at the foot of his mattress and eyed him sleepily.

"Come on," he said, and she jumped down and ran happily to his feet, ears flapping, tail wagging.

She was always thrilled to be with him, no matter what was going on. Odd how nice that was. He scooped her up because it was faster than waiting for her to try to keep up, and they headed off the boat, down the marina, and to his car.

The rain came down steadily, looking like silver sheets beneath the streetlight's glow. Joe took I-5, heading toward O.B., and pulled into Tooley's. Before he could get out of the car, Summer appeared at the passenger side. She put both hands on the window, fingers spread wide, then grinned at him. "Hi."

"Hi yourself." He came around for her, and bent to open the door but she had all her weight planted as she leaned on the window. She was staring at her fingers. "You got here fast."

"I had visions of you deciding to jog home," he said dryly.

"Nah. I already ran tonight."

"You did?"

"After you wouldn't jump my bones."

He hardened himself to her dubious charms. "I thought you were going to wait inside for me."

"I knew you'd come fast." At that she lifted her head and grinned at him again. "No pun intended."

At that, he had to laugh. "I have no defense."

"Well, actually, you do. By the time we ended up on my floor that night, we were both charged, lit, and ready to go off like a firecracker." She grinned. "Hey, you outlasted me."

"By about two seconds." Her casual recount of what had been one of the most memorable two minutes of his life, both aroused and embarrassed him.

"Joe," she said simply, and set her forehead to the window. Then she straightened and leveled him with her eyes. In them there was a lingering amusement, but also a sadness that nearly brought him to his knees. Reaching out, he stroked a wayward strand of hair from her eyes, and then because he was a glutton for punishment, let his fingers trail over her cheek just for the sake of feeling her soft skin.

Closing her eyes, she pressed her lips to the palm of his hand, and then without another word, let herself into his car, where Ashes mauled her with lashes of her tongue.

Joe came around, slid behind the wheel, and hauled the puppy off her. Summer smiled at him as she reached for her seat belt. Her hair lay in soft fiery wet waves about her face, which was slightly flushed. Her eyes were glossy, too glossy, and she couldn't match up the seat belt fastener to click it in. "It's broken," she said.

He took it from her and popped it into place.

"So strong, Superman Joe."

"Cut it out." He revved the engine and drove out of the parking lot.

With a smile, she leaned back and closed her eyes. "I love this car. All powerful muscle, like its owner."

He glanced at her but she didn't open her eyes. Hair whipping around her face, she wore a small, secret little smile on her lips that said she'd have a good time no matter what was going on because life was too short. She'd learned that lesson long ago, and so had he.

Ashes hadn't learned anything but the joy of sticking her head out the window and drooling on the glass.

"Nothing beats this," Summer said after a few minutes. "A nice drive, a nice, rainy night, a nice . . ." At that she opened her eyes and looked at him. "Friend?"

He nodded, and she relaxed again, closing her eyes.

A nice friend. It's what he'd promised her, though it was going to kill him. *She* was going to kill him. He pulled onto her street and turned off the engine. "Wait here," he said, and was rounding the trunk of his car when she opened her door and tripped getting out. She sat on the wet curb and grinned up at him as Ashes bounded from her seat to Summer's legs.

"You never listen." Joe bent and scooped Summer up in his arms. "Ashes, come."

Summer sighed a dreamy little sigh, slipped her arms around his neck and settled her face against his throat. "Love it when you do the he-man thing." She pressed her lips to his skin.

"Stop that," he said.

"Okay." She bit him instead.

The feel of her teeth sinking into him shot arrows of heat straight to his groin. "Red—"

"I love the way you say my name." Pulling back, she

smiled at him. "All thick and husky. Like you're turned on."

He was, but it was more than that. It was the warmth and affection in her eyes, the way her right eyetooth was slightly chipped from that headfirst fall she'd once taken off the monkey bars in third grade, the light smattering of freckles across her nose. It was the way she held on to him, like he was the most important thing in her world, at least at the moment.

She laughed a little, and he looked into her face and thought, *you are the silliest, more adorable, sexy drunk I've ever seen.*

"You have the prettiest eyes," she sighed. "All four of them."

Asking her for her keys would be useless, so for the second time he let himself in the back door of her cottage. "You should lock this thing up better."

"I know. But then how would you tuck me in? You are going to tuck me in, aren't you?"

He didn't bother to answer that question because in all truth, he had no idea what the hell to do with her.

"I want a bubble bath."

"You'll drown yourself. Maybe a shower." He took her into her bathroom and set her down. When her feet touched the floor, she weaved and sat down right there on the tile. "I think I need help."

Oh no. No, no, no. *No.*

She removed each sandal with the exaggerated care of the elderly or the extremely inebriated. Then she began to wriggle out of her loose sleeveless dress, which took her a long moment, several curses, and finally a giggle as she got stuck with her arms tangled in the material, stretched over

her head, her belly softly jiggling as she laughed breathlessly. *"Uncle."*

He stared down at her, having to laugh too. God, he
wanted to gobble her up.

She flopped to her back. She still wore her coral tank
and matching biker shorts, and according to the muffled
snorts he could hear beneath the dress covering her head
she was still cracking herself up. With a sigh, he bent and
grabbed the soft dress and pulled, freeing her.

"Only a few more garments to go," she said, grinning
stupidly at him from flat on her back.

He stood over her, his hands now jammed in his pockets
to keep them to himself. "You're on your own, baby."

With a big huff she rolled over and got to her knees. "If
you could start the water."

He flicked on the tap and turned back to her, immediately closing his eyes because she'd wriggled out of her
tank and was shoving down her shorts.

She wore nothing beneath either and her glorious long
tough body imprinted itself on his brain as she stood.

"You can look," she assured him, stepping toward the
shower, doing a little shimmy that made his eyes cross and
all the blood drain out of his head for parts south. "And you
can touch." She waited a second, standing there free as a
bird and more beautiful than any single mischievous
drunken minx should ever be allowed to look. *"Please*
touch."

"No."

She looked so disappointed he might have laughed but
he had no working brain cells left. "Get in the shower,
Red."

"All right." She opened the glass door, then weaved for
a second, forcing him to leap forward and grab her. Hands

full of naked woman, he gritted his teeth, steadied her, then shoved her into the water.

Her scream pierced the air and made him smile grimly.

"It's cold!" she shrieked.

"The better to sober you up," he said, suddenly enjoying himself immensely, and left the bathroom. Ashes was asleep on the couch, curled up with a pillow like she belonged there.

The wind had picked up again, and branches of the trees alongside the cottage brushed the windows. The lights flickered a few times as he paced the living room. He needed to get home, needed to be at work early in the morning, but he didn't want to leave until the water turned off, until he knew Summer was in bed and safe.

She was a grown woman, he reminded himself. There was absolutely no reason to tuck her in, to make sure—

"Oh, good," she said softly from the doorway. She was wrapped in a light peach terry cloth robe, her long hair combed and dripping, her feet bare, her eyes unusually dark and solemn. "You're still here."

"I was just leaving—"

"I think the power's going to go."

Indeed, it flickered and she looked around uneasily.

"You're used to being without power," he reminded her. "You're outside for weeks at a time."

"Yeah." She bit her lower lip. "But it's not exactly the dark I'm afraid of."

Against his better judgment, he moved close. She had a light sunburn on her nose, and a small smile on her naked lips. Even as he looked, her tongue darted out and nervously dampened them. Her eyes were clearer now, her earlier joviality replaced with far more complicated things. "What are you afraid of?" he asked quietly.

"Being alone."

A drop of water ran from her jaw, down her throat, and into the robe. He thought about the body beneath the terry cloth and felt his knees wobble. "Look, I'm trying to be the good guy here. You're under the influence—"

"You ruined that buzz with the icy shower." She slipped her hand in the robe pocket and came up with a condom that made him want to groan.

"I'm leaving," he said, feeling like a damn saint because hell if he wasn't every bit as head over heels for her as he'd always been. But he couldn't let her do more damage, not when she had one foot out the door.

He couldn't live through that again.

A gust whipped around the outside of the cottage, and again the branches brushed the windows. Summer jerked and stared wide-eyed at the dark windows. "I wish there were shutters here."

"It's just the trees—" He frowned at how pale she'd gotten. "This isn't you, you're not jumpy over a storm. You love storms."

"Yeah." But she eyed the bare windows uneasily.

"Red." He put his hands on her shoulders and waited until she looked at him. "Talk to me."

"I'd rather . . ." She glided her hands up his chest, wound them around his neck and tugged, then planted her mouth to his, making him groan. He tensed, planning on pulling away because hell if he was going to let her distract him with sex again. Hell if—

She slid her fingers into his hair, and God, he loved that. Loved the feel of her hands on him, the way she tilted her head to gain better access to his mouth, loved the way her tongue danced slow and sinuous over his.

A crash from the kitchen had them both jumping in surprise. Joe whipped around in time to see the back door blowing in the wind after slamming open against the wall. "I must not have kicked it shut hard enough," he said, and moved toward it.

Summer flattened herself back against the archway between the hallway and the living room, her heart ramming against her ribs. Just the door. Her fear was definitely irrational, even to her own murky brain, but for the moment she couldn't think, couldn't put it all together.

Joe came back, gazing at her face as if he might gobble her up if given the chance, and her nipples went hard and her thighs trembled. She launched herself at him, with one goal in mind.

Sexual oblivion, the way only he could offer it.

His hand stroked down her back and then up again as she burrowed against his big, warm, wonderful body. She slid her arms around his waist, sighing at the solidness of him, how it felt to be pressed tight, held tight. She arched a little closer and felt his mouth on her neck, just beneath her ear.

He unclipped his pager and gun, set them on the end table, and backed her against the archway, trapping her, kissing her neck again, making her moan. At the sound, he dragged his mouth down a little, burrowing beneath the terry cloth.

It wasn't enough, it still wasn't enough. A voice deep inside told her that this, with him, might never be enough but she shoved that aside, and reached down to untie the belt on her robe.

"You're going to kill me," he said huskily, eyes locked on hers.

"Then you'll die a happy man tonight."

He choked out a laugh at that. His gaze ran down her

body. Her thighs trembled, and between them, she went damp as she shrugged and let the robe fall. "Touch me, Joe."

His jaw was tight and bunching with tension as he lifted his hands and cupped the weight of her breasts, letting his thumbs rasp over the tips like the material of her robe had, only better. They hardened further.

With a rough sound, he once again backed her to the archway. The plaster was cool against her back and buttocks, while Joe was hot against her breasts and belly and thighs. There was something erotic about being naked while he was fully dressed. It made her feel weak and quivery, and yet so powerful at the same time, but then he sank to his knees, nudged her thighs apart and kissed her between them, and thinking became optional.

He glided his big, knowing hands up her legs, used his thumbs to spread her open to suit him, and then bent in and put his mouth on her.

Her head thunked back against the wood.

"How am I doing?" he murmured.

What? How was he doing? Couldn't he tell?

"Red?"

And then she remembered. He wanted her to stay with him, no escaping, no vanishing in the moment, and suddenly she felt very, *very* naked. "Uh . . ."

"Good?"

"Yes," she managed. "Good—"

He laughed softly and did something with his tongue . . . and added a finger . . . oh god . . . and then he hummed a little "mmm-mmm, nice" or something equally dizzying, and then she was a panting, writhing wreck, trembling on the very edge. The bastard held her there, pulling back just enough to make her sob in frustration. She tightened the grip she had on his hair and looked down at him, vulnerable not because of her position but because she was letting him look deep into her eyes.

You don't see me, he'd said. But she did. God, she did. Didn't he know that was the problem? That every time they did this, he dug himself further into her heart? "Joe," she whispered, her throat tight, her eyes burning. "Don't you even think about stopping."

He let out a slow smile, his eyes hot and hungry, and bent back to his task, and this time let her take the plunge. When her knees collapsed, she fell right into his arms on the floor. Engine still revved, she tumbled him over to his back and tore at his clothing just for the joy of having his hot, sleek, hard flesh beneath her fingers, and then her mouth. She kissed his shoulder, a pec, making her way past his rib cage, his quivering belly, swirling a little lower until he hissed out a breath. And when she got to the prize and took him into her mouth, he let out a guttural, rasping moan. His hands came up and fisted in her hair. "Red—"

She shut him up with a single swirl of her tongue and was well on her way to driving him as insane as he'd driven her when suddenly she found herself flat on her back, his big hard body towering over hers, his eyes glittering as he reached out and picked something up off the floor.

The condom.

He tore the packet open with his teeth, his eyes never leaving hers as he covered himself, as he nudged her thighs open and made himself at home between them and cupped her face in his hands.

"I love you," he said, and began to move. He took them both right out of themselves and back again, wild and free, simple and beautiful.

And terrifying. So damned terrifying.

Chapter 18

Summer lay beneath Joe, listening to him breathe. Her heart was still beating so wildly in her chest she thought maybe her ribs would crack.

He'd said he loved her.

She'd spent the last twelve years avoiding emotional attachments. She hadn't put a name to it, or really even made a conscious decision to do so, but that's exactly what she'd done. Until now. Now she faced the very dilemma she'd never wanted.

She'd let a man into her life, and not just any man, but one that knew her better than anyone else, giving him the tools he needed to break her heart.

How did they move on from here? Could they really pretend he hadn't said what he had in the thick of the moment? And surely, that was all it had been.

Though *she'd* been in the moment many times and had never felt the urge to let those three little words fly.

Joe rolled with her so that she lay sprawled over the top of him. He slid a hand down her back to cup her butt. "Now you can cut off the circulation to *my* legs and other vital parts. Seems only fair."

There was a teasing light to his voice, thank God. "Complaining?"

"Hell, no." He added his other hand to her ass.

From outside the wind still whistled and howled, brushing tree branches against the windows and providing quite a bit of noise but not enough that she couldn't feel his heart still pumping strong and steady beneath her cheek with enough force to provide electricity to the entire town. She lifted her head and stared down into his face. "Do you need a glass of water?"

"Sure, if you could give it to me intravenously."

Okay, good. Lighthearted fun, which happened to be right up her alley. She went smug. "Can't move, huh?"

"That would be because you're holding me down."

"Which is handy if I want round two."

He laughed and she licked his nipple, and his laugh turned into a moan as she felt his body stir.

"I need a recovery period," he said.

"You've had it." Because her world felt right again, or at least not upside down anymore, she sat up on him.

"Ooof," he said, but his hands went gamely to her hips.

She looked into his face. Unlike her, he was not still grinning broadly. In his eyes sat his entire heart, and it made hers clench. He'd tried to warn her, he'd even tried to joke it away, but she was doing the one thing she'd meant to never do again, and that was hurt him. Her smile slowly faded. And her own heart began to swell until it felt like she might pop a rib. "I'm sorry," she whispered, and got up.

Behind her, she heard him sigh, and when she turned around, he was pulling up his Levi's. He reached for his shirt, then his gun. When he was dressed, he looked at her.

She wrapped herself in a chenille throw from the back of the couch and turned away to stare out the window into the black, stormy night. Her earlier euphoria had drained right out of her. Holding on to any pretense seemed exhausting.

"You okay?" He spoke quietly from behind her.

He'd come out into the night to rescue her when he hadn't necessarily wanted to see her. He'd given her a mind-blowing orgasm—two actually—when he hadn't meant to have sex with her. He'd given and given, and she'd taken and taken. It was a terrible pattern, a revealing one that filled her with self-loathing, and yet she didn't possess the courage to stop the madness. "Did you mean it?"

"Yeah," he said, knowing exactly what she was asking. "I meant it."

"Joe." She felt hot, cold. Anguished.

He let out a sigh and moved to the door.

"Joe, wait."

"For what?" His eyes glittered with dark emotion as he rounded on her, stalked back across the room to go toe to toe. "Round two? You need me to screw you blind again?"

Embarrassed, she tried to turn away but his hands came up to hold her still. "You don't like it worded like that? Well, here's a bulletin. I don't like feeling it."

"It's not like that."

"No, it's not. It's not like that at all, not for me. Red, when I'm in you and you look at me . . ." He let out a rough sound and backed away. "I *feel* like Superman," he admitted. "How's *that* for being embarrassed? You make me feel like a damn hero."

She hugged herself, silent as she contemplated his words. He *was* a hero, in her eyes. He was the only one always there for her, no matter what, and yet she didn't know how to say it.

"You said for me to wait. What for, Red? For you to stop shoving me away when I get too close? You to open up and talk to me? Christ, I'm only human here. I see you hurting and it kills me, but you won't let me in." He turned away. "I have to go."

"Did you . . . did you love me like this back then, too?"

He was quiet so long she wasn't sure he'd answer, then he slowly turned and looked at her, eyes solemn, hair wild, no dimple in sight. "That was years ago. What I felt then no longer matters."

"Yes, it does."

He looked away, into the night. "You were all I had. You were everything to me."

She thought maybe now she understood for the first time how much she'd really hurt him, and felt sliced in two. "What could we have done? Get married and live happily ever after, and forget the warehouse fire ever happened?"

He shoved his hands into his pockets, the same hands which had taken her to bliss and back only moments ago, and now they were as apart as strangers. "I don't know." He shrugged. "I didn't believe in happily ever after. All I know is I believed in you, and how you made me feel. Which was alive." He slowly shook his head. "When I'm with you, it just bursts out of me. But I'm a selfish SOB. I need it back and I need to know, Red. Is this going anywhere other than your living room floor?"

Her breathing had already gone to hell. At his question, her chest tightened. Admitting her burgeoning emotions to herself was hard enough. "What if I know I have feelings, I just haven't been able to sort them yet?"

"Then sort them. But I know you, Red. You'll tell yourself it's not real, it's just temporary. You'll tell yourself whatever you have to so that when you leave, you can do so without looking back."

She gaped at him. "You think I'm pushing you away so that I can leave again?"

"I don't know what I think." He waited, giving her a chance to help him.

But she couldn't seem to think under a spotlight.

"You know, Summer," he finally said. "No one can disappoint me quite the way you can." And with that knife to the heart, he walked out the door.

She clung to the doorway and watched him get to his Camaro before she remembered something that pierced through her pain. "Joe." She ran after him in her robe, blocking him from getting into the car, getting wet all over again.

"Go inside," he said, sounding exhausted.

"Wait. I forgot to tell you something." She grimaced because she couldn't believe it. "Several somethings actually."

As wet as she was, he looked at her. "What?"

"I forgot to tell you about the phone call I got earlier. I think I said something about it at the bar—"

"Tell me."

"I was asked to go away. They even said please. Can you imagine?" She forced a laugh. "A polite stalker."

He suddenly had his fire marshal face on. "This happened when exactly?"

"Earlier."

"Did you recognize the voice?" he clipped out, no longer her giving lover, but a man on the job.

"It was a text message. Out of area phone number."

"Let me see it. Don't tell me you erased it," he said when she just stared at him.

"I didn't." She had to smile. "It's just that you look so tough and in charge when you talk in your cop voice."

He narrowed his eyes. "The phone, Red."

"Right. I left my purse in your car." She brushed past him and bent inside the car, feeling around on the floor where she'd tossed it earlier.

She felt him watching her, and wondered if her robe was covering her bare butt or not. "Got it," she said, and pushed herself to her knees in his driver's seat, rifling through her bag, her hair in her face. "Here."

"Scoot over." He added his hands to the command, giving her a little push so that he could climb in after her. He shut the door, creating a tight intimacy she didn't know how to face after all they'd said to each other. The air felt charged, and not just sexually, but emotionally.

While he looked at her text message, she looked at him. He'd been tense before their little tryst on the floor, but then afterward had become more relaxed than she'd ever seen him.

Now he was tense again. She knew he was shocked that this had happened, and frightened for her safety. Bungled in with that was anger and frustration that he couldn't fix it for her right here right now, all complicated by what they were, or weren't, to each other.

Finally, he lifted his head and looked at her. "Is this your first call from this number?"

"Yes."

"Your first threat?"

"Well, it's not exactly a threat— Yes," she said at the irritation in his face. "It's my first prank."

He nodded, pulled out his own cell. "Kenny," he said into it. "We need to meet— Yeah, I know what time it is. Bring caffeine." He clicked off and looked at Summer across the console, his eyes dark and unreadable.

Distant.

She'd done that. "Joe—"

"I want you to come home with me." He glanced at the house behind them. "I don't want you to be alone."

She took in the small cottage, lit in the night like a beacon, with darkness all around. The other cottages either weren't filled at the moment, or their occupants long asleep.

"I'm going to go into work after I drop you off," he said. "But I'd like it if you stayed on the boat until daylight, and then kept me informed of your day as you go."

"I'm sure I'm not in any real danger—" At the unbroachable look in his eyes, she broke off. He wasn't going to bend on this. "Okay. I get it. I don't like it, but I get it."

He let out a long breath. "Nothing about any of this is fair, I know."

She closed her eyes and nodded, surprised into opening them again when he touched her jaw. She turned her cheek into his palm and closed her eyes, unbearably reassured by just the feel of his callused fingers on her.

"I was an ass in there," he said. "I'm sorry."

"You weren't." She kissed his palm. "You weren't. It's me. I'm the ass."

A low, rough sound escaped his throat, one that might have been pleasure, pain, or a combination. His eyes were shadowed as they met hers, lit only by a quick flash of lightning that burst around them. Then he pulled away. "Let's go get you a change of clothes."

Afterward he drove south on I-5, toward Mission Bay. Given the amount of alcohol she'd consumed, and the energy they'd burned on her living room floor, she was beat. And punchy with it. "We didn't really solve anything," she said softly as he drove. "And yet you're sort of stuck with me."

"Or you're stuck with me. Depends on how you look at it, I suppose."

"Maybe we should start over," she said. "We could even pretend we don't know each other."

"What, to buy you time to sort through your feelings?" he asked dryly.

Damn it, maybe. "It's not a bad idea."

He slanted her another glance.

"This has nothing to do with you, you know. I'm just not a successful dater. In fact, usually, once I—" She broke off at his expression and decided she'd probably let her mouth run a moment too long.

"Once you sleep with him, he's gone, is that is?" he asked.

"Maybe we shouldn't talk."

"No, maybe we should. I don't want to be your dick-of-the-week, Summer."

A laugh burst out of her at that. "Well, then. How about we take this one day at a time?"

"I think with you, we'll go minute to minute. And now that you've turned me around so many times I don't know whether I'm coming or going, are you going to tell me the other thing you needed to tell me?"

"Oh my God, I'd nearly forgotten."

"What now?"

"Did you know Braden's leaving?"

"What do you mean, leaving?"

"He's with Chloe tonight. It's their good-bye. He said he isn't the stick around type." A stab of guilt went through her because she'd become the same type. "I thought you'd want to know."

"Yeah. I want to know."

He said this so grimly she frowned. "What aren't you telling me here?"

"Nothing I'm supposed to."

Her heart sped up, and her stomach dropped. "I know Braden's quiet and sort of mysterious, but he wouldn't hurt anyone. If you could have seen the way he looked at Chloe tonight . . ."

He swore at that, muttering to himself, then glanced at her again. "He has a police record."

"He's been arrested?"

"Yes. And his name isn't Braden Cahill. His real name is Brian Coldwell. Did you know that?"

"No." Her thoughts raced uncomfortably. "You've been busy," she said slowly.

"It's my job."

"You're good at it."

"Not good enough." He slapped an open palm on the steering wheel in frustration, shook his head, and sped up.

Chapter 19

It was somewhere near one in the morning by the time Summer watched Joe walk away. He'd taken her to his boat, waiting until she'd gotten into his bed and closed her eyes before he'd left. Though he'd told her he had to work, she still felt as if she'd pushed him out of his own home.

His bedroom was small and shaped like the top of a torpedo, with the bed against the curved wall, which was lined with high, narrow windows. He had a heavy blue comforter and soft matching sheets that smelled like him, which was to say incredible. She kept pressing her face into his pillow.

Pathetic.

Reaching for the phone, she called Chloe. She knew the call wouldn't be welcome but she had to check on her after what she'd learned tonight about Braden.

Chloe answered her cell phone with a very breathless, annoyed "Yeah?"

"I just wanted to see how you're doing," Summer said.

"I've had three orgasms and I'm going for four, thanks for asking. Now don't call back."

"Chloe."

Chloe sighed. *"What?"*

"I need to talk to you about Braden."

"No."

"Chloe—"

"Okay, stop. Stop right there. You always followed your gut and it got you the world. Now I'm going to do the same, only my world is right here lying next to me."

"He has one foot out of that world, remember?"

"Hold on a sec."

Summer heard her cover the phone and murmur something softly, and then Braden's equally soft reply. After a moment, Chloe came back. "I sent him to the kitchen for whipped cream. So what is it? What aren't you telling me?"

"Braden has a police record, and he's using a different name from his last job."

Chloe was quiet a moment. "Are you sure?"

"Yes. I'm sorry. God, I'm so sorry. Want me to come over?"

"I don't need a babysitter. Look, whatever this stuff's about, I believe in Braden. He's a good guy, Summer."

"I want to believe that too. I really do. Just . . . be careful."

"Yeah. I will." Chloe clicked off, sounding much more subdued than she had, and Summer hated that she'd been the one to cause it. She picked up her phone again to let her mom know where she was. She didn't know if Camille would worry, but maybe it wasn't about that so much as Summer just needing to connect.

But Camille didn't answer her phone. Concerned, she called Tina's house.

"Yes, she's here," Bill told her. "The two of them are in the hot tub singing show tunes over a bottle of old scotch."

Summer laughed in surprise. "They don't drink scotch."

"They don't usually hot tub it either, but your mom

found some old stuff in the boxes that came out of the warehouse."

"What stuff?"

"Your dad's. Just an old partially written manuscript and some notes. And the bottle of scotch. She decided it'd aged enough."

"Maybe I should come over and try to cheer her up."

"Actually, she's not sad," Bill said. "They're out there laughing and talking. And singing, let's not forget the singing. I think it's therapeutic. Me, I need a run to the racetrack for my therapy."

"Too bad Del Mar isn't open all night, huh?"

"Babe, you ain't kidding." He huffed out a breath but she could tell he was smiling. "Want me to give her a message?"

"I'll call her tomorrow. Just watch after them, okay?"

"I always have."

In the early dawn light, Joe leaned back against the trunk of the Camaro. He was watching Chloe's condo and sipping a Red Bull. It'd been that or a dozen doughnuts, but he refused to go back to stress eating simply because his life had been turned upside down.

And it had been turned upside down. It wasn't work either, though he was in the middle of several difficult cases, with Creative Interiors at the top. He'd had many such problems this year. He'd learned to separate out his emotions from the practical aspect of his job.

Or so he'd thought.

But enter one Summer Abrams. Or reenter.

From behind him came a whine. He'd left Ashes asleep on the passenger seat of the car, having some sort of a dream that involved twitching her feet and ears. Probably dreaming about eating his files, her favorite pastime. Reaching through the window, he stroked a hand down her little body, over her plump belly, and she quieted. Just because of his touch.

Hard to believe he'd gotten to the ripe old age of thirty and could still have such a small thing grab him by the throat, but it did. He'd never had any pet as a kid, hell it'd been hard enough to survive without that worry. As an adult, he'd always been too busy. The people in his life were important to him: Kenny, his other coworkers, the women he'd dated . . . but none had ever required his care the way Ashes did. He'd always figured he'd think of such a responsibility as a chore.

But he didn't.

With the jolt of caffeine humming through his system, he straightened as the front door of Chloe's apartment opened, and out came the man he'd been waiting for.

Joe knew the exact moment Braden saw him. Not that the younger man's feet faltered, or that his body language changed in any noticeable way.

But his face went carefully blank.

Dead giveaway.

"Morning," Joe said, and reached into his car to bring out another can of Red Bull.

Braden eyed the can, then Joe. "You waited out here for who knows how long to offer me a kick of caffeine that tastes like cow piss?"

"I don't think it tastes like cow's piss. At least not if it's good and cold." With a shrug, Joe opened the can himself. What the hell. "And for your information, I waited out here—for two hours, thanks for asking—to find out what the hell you think you're doing, skipping town right now."

Braden lifted a shoulder. "What's wrong with right now?"

Joe took a long sip of the drink. Between realizing he'd done the unthinkable and moved Summer in with him, then getting no sleep while he sat in his office staring at the files of the fires, and now all this caffeine, he'd be lucky if poof, his head just didn't explode right off his shoulders. "Leaving now makes you look guilty. You know that."

Braden eyed him for a beat. "Makes me look guilty, or makes me guilty period?"

"Semantics."

Braden cocked his head. "Are you here to arrest me for something?"

"Well, it wouldn't be the first time, would it?"

Braden closed his eyes. Swallowed once. "Don't fuck with me."

"Actually, that was going to be my line to you. I interviewed you after the warehouse fire. After the store fire. Both times I could tell you were nervous and I asked you point blank if there was something I needed to know. You said no."

"I stick by that."

"All right." Joe opened his clipboard. "You have a record. I pulled it."

"How did you—"

"You used the same Social Security number for your alias, so they're linked at the DMV. Not smart."

Braden's mouth tightened.

"Does Chloe know your real name is Brian?"

No answer.

"How about that you're an alcoholic?"

"Recovering. I haven't had a drink in eighteen months."

"You have proof of that? Or the fact that you supposedly haven't smoked?"

Braden looked at Chloe's condo.

Joe sighed. "Does she know any of it?"

"She doesn't know anything about me other than what she's seen. I wanted that."

Joe knew all about wanting to be impenetrable. Unbreakable. What he didn't know was if Braden's reason was legal or not. "We want to search your place."

"Wouldn't it be easier if I just showed you all my size eleven-and-a-half shoes so you could check for traces of gasoline?"

Joe looked at him for a long moment. They'd let everyone know about the size eleven-and-a-half prints found at the fires. What they hadn't said was that the prints were a work boot, not a shoe.

So was Braden innocent, or just very, very good?

Joe flipped through the pages on his clipboard. "Interesting how Braden Cahill is this model citizen. No tickets. Not so much as a blip on his record anywhere. Brian Coldwell however . . . not so lucky."

Braden snatched the opened Red Bull out of Joe's hand and sat on the curb as he downed the contents. "I didn't do anything wrong."

"Embezzling from an antique shop—"

"It was my uncle's shop. He owed me back wages that he refused to pay. So I helped myself."

"He prosecuted."

"He's an asshole."

"Okay." Joe could buy that easily enough, he'd been raised by an asshole. "You were also held and questioned about another matter. Money laundering."

"Again, my uncle. When I discovered the truth about his

business, and how he was laundering drug money through his shop, I quit. But then he was caught and they thought I'd helped him."

"You hadn't?"

"No, and I was never charged for anything."

"True." Joe tossed his file into the truck. "You have access to Creative Interiors's books."

Braden swiped a hand over his mouth. It was shaking, and Joe had no idea if that was nerves or the caffeine jolt he'd just given his system. "I've done nothing wrong," he repeated.

"Then why are you leaving town?"

Braden closed his eyes and let out a harsh laugh. "To avoid this."

"Haven't you watched *Cops*? Running is always a bad thing."

"I didn't think of it as running. More an avoidance technique."

"Well, you might want to rethink it," Joe said. "Seriously rethink it."

Braden got to his feet and pulled out his keys. "Are we done here?"

"For now." Joe watched Braden stalk away before he got into his car just as his cell phone rang. "Walker."

"So official."

His entire body softened at the sound of Summer, even as a certain part of him went hard. Jesus, he was worse than Pavlov's dog.

"Did you find Braden?" she asked.

"Yes. I think he's going to rethink leaving for now."

"Any news on the text message I received?"

"We're tracing the number it was made from."

"Did anyone else get a text message?"

"Not that we know of. Red, I'm telling you more than I should be."

"I guess that means you trust me."

That or he was a fool. He hadn't decided which yet.

She was silent a moment. "The fires, the phone call, Braden lying . . . None of this makes any sense to me."

"It will by the time we get to the bottom of it all."

"You sound so sure."

"I am."

She let out a low laugh. "Do you have any idea how it feels to hear you sound so confident? So assertive?"

Confident and assertive? Was she kidding? He had no idea what the hell he was doing.

"I'm just getting to know the man you've become," she said softly. "And you know what?"

He was almost afraid to ask. "What?"

"I like it. I like you."

He'd known she was attracted to his body, she'd made no secret of that. He'd also known that while she'd told herself it was purely physical, even she knew deep down it was more than that. Her words proved it.

But would she give them the time to take it where it might go?

"Oh! Before I forget why I called you, I've got a cab coming to get a ride to my car. I'm heading up Highway 8 to Cuyamaca Peak. A couple of customers came through the shop last week and said how they always get lost up there, and they asked me to lead them. You said you wanted to know what I was up to."

"I did. I do."

"I'm dressing right now. I'm wearing a bright red tank and black running shorts. Do you want to know what color my panties are?"

Yes. "Red."

"I'll call you later, and I'll give you a blow by blow of the rest of my day."

The image *that* put into his mind was not fit for mixed company. He pinched the bridge of his nose and wondered at his need for a doughnut. "Good-bye, Red."

"Bye. Oh, and they're black," she said. "Just plain cotton but string bikini cut. I say that because last night you seemed to enjoy—"

"Thank you." He wouldn't be able to concentrate on anything worth a damn now.

"You want to tell me about *your* underwear?" She laughed. "Or maybe you're going commando? I noticed you haven't done laundry. Not that I'm much better—"

He wasn't used to erections on the job. And damn it, he *was* commando. "I have to go."

"I know. But Joe? Thanks."

"For? . . ."

"For wanting me to stay with you. For caring. For . . . being there."

That she sounded surprised had his frustration with her fading away. "Just be careful on the mountain." He hung up and pocketed the cell before he realized he was smiling, for no reason at all.

Chapter 20

By that evening, Joe and Kenny had combed the Creative Interiors II fire site yet again. They'd cooperated with the insurance investigator, who was conducting a simultaneous investigation. They'd gone back for yet more interviews with all the players and witnesses, including Stella and Gregg, both of whom had been the second last to leave Creative Interiors II and had been in the warehouse several times in the months leading up to the fire.

Neither of them smoked or had a size eleven-and-a-half boot, or had been in the small bathroom of the store in the hours before the fire, but neither did they have an alibi for the hours after the fires.

The call Summer had received was traced to a pay phone in O.B., right by the pier, which made about as much sense as the rest of this whole thing did.

An hour ago Joe had put Ashes in her box in the corner of his office, where she'd fallen asleep. He'd pushed away from his too messy desk, bringing the papers he needed to the floor. They were scattered out before him, including the original warehouse fire investigation, but he'd found nothing there that stuck out at him. No size eleven boot with a diagonal tread. No traces of gasoline found. No cigarette butts. Not a single shred to suggest the old fire could be connected to two new fires.

So . . . a terrible coincidence?

Or clever arson? And yet if that was true, then half the possible suspects could be eliminated because they hadn't been around twelve years ago.

He heard footsteps coming down the hall, and knew by their light touch they were female. And still he was surprised when Summer appeared in his doorway. She hoisted a brown bag from which came a delicious scent, making his mouth water.

Or maybe that was just her.

"Hungry?" she asked, and waved the bag. "Low carb, no sugar or fat, I swear."

Her smile was warm, affectionate, and just unsure enough to have him tossing aside his pencil and notepad. "And here I was hoping for pizza."

Her light laugh filled him as she came into the room. She wore shorts tonight. Khaki cargo shorts with pockets everywhere, and a snug, thin scoop-neck T-shirt with a smiley face on it that said, *smile, it confuses people.*

"Did you just get back from your day hike?" he asked.

"Yep, I got them halfway to the summit, which was their goal. They want to try again later in the summer. They had a great time. Oh, and I got myself booked for more two hikes next week." Her smile faltered, and he knew that was because she hadn't planned on being here that long.

"You could have said no," he said gently.

"I could have. Didn't though." She sat on the floor next to him, hugged her knees close and smiled at him. "It gives me an excuse to stay."

"Do you need one?"

"Maybe I once thought I did. I know it doesn't make

much sense to you, but being so far from home for so long was . . . freeing."

"You think you'd lose freedom if you lived here, or used it as your home base?"

Reaching out, she stroked some hair from his forehead. The thick strands immediately fell back again, and she smiled. "I love your hair."

She sidetracked him like no one else ever had. "Red."

"Okay." She sighed. "I don't know about losing my freedom," she admitted. "I just know that I love being with you, in a way I'd never imagined. Can't that be enough for now? For the next few weeks, until I decide what the hell I'm doing?"

The way she looked at him, as if she expected him to push her away, pulled at him hard. She was struggling to find the path that was right for her, and he had no right, nor a desire, to stand in her way and direct her. She had a smudge of trail dirt on her jaw, a slight sunburn on her nose, and a wary light in her eyes while she waited for him to respond.

"I promised you one minute at a time," he said, and traced a finger over her jaw. "I'm trying here, Red."

She let out a tenuous smile, and as they stared at each other, time seemed to stop. It wasn't the first time that had happened, and a small part of him hesitated because he knew he was headed for a world of hurt.

"So." She glanced at all his paperwork scattered in front of them. "Getting anywhere?"

"No."

"Well, in that case." She scooted closer and kissed his chin. "Maybe we can get back to that one minute at a time thing."

Resisting was pointless when he wanted her bad enough

to take what he could get. He shoved all the paperwork away and pulled her into his lap.

Summer moved eagerly into Joe's arms, thinking he was just what she needed. He ran a finger down her throat, over her collarbone as she settled in his lap, and at the feel of him hard and muscled beneath her, she all but purred. "Is that a gun in your pocket, Fire Marshal Walker, or are you just happy to see me?"

"Guess," he said, and grabbing the hands she'd tried to dip into his Levi's, he pushed her to the floor, following her down, holding her wrists captive on either side of her head. "Now about that minute . . ."

"Yes?" she asked breathlessly, looking up into his face.

"I'm taking one right now. You're going to let me."

Her pulse leapt and she wrapped her legs around his hips, arching up, rubbing the hottest, neediest part of her to what she figured was the hottest, neediest part of him, dragging a groan from his throat. He released her hands to shove up her tank and unzip her sports bra.

She opened her mouth to tell him she hadn't showered, but all that came out was a garbled whimper because he took a breast in his mouth, sucking her nipple in deep, running his tongue over the tip as it hardened for him.

"Joe. I need to take a shower— Ohmigod," she gasped when he clamped his teeth down lightly and tugged.

"My minute isn't over." He surged up, slapped the lock on his office door, then tugged down her shorts and groaned. "You *are* wearing black panties."

"I told you—" She broke off when he put a big hand on the inside of her thigh and pushed her legs open.

"A minute wasn't enough. I'm taking another." He hooked the crotch of her panties with his thumb and slid it aside. "You're so wet. I have to—" He sank a finger in deep, and with a cry she couldn't contain, arched up for more. But even with the locked door, they couldn't. Shouldn't . . . "Joe." She had to lick her dry lips, her body quivering with his every touch. "We can't—"

He circled her nipple with his tongue again, and sank a second finger inside her. "Can't what?" he murmured in a low, thick voice as he brushed his thumb over her center.

"Can't . . . uh . . ." She couldn't remember.

Another glide of his thumb with the barest of pressures now, and she fisted her hands in his shirt with a helpless moan. *"Joe."*

"Look at you," he murmured as he drove her right to the edge and held her there with the steady pressure and rhythm she needed. Her head fell back while she panted for air. She was close, so terrifyingly close—

"Come for me," he whispered, his mouth brushing her jaw, beneath her ear. "I want you to."

She could no more have stopped a train on its tracks as she burst, exploding in a kaleidoscope of lights and sensations, eventually coming back to herself as Joe slowly stroked her down to earth. He brushed his lips over her damp temple. "Good?"

"Great. *More,*" she demanded.

"Greedy woman."

"I have a condom in my purse."

"Resourceful, too." He blew out a relieved breath. "I like that." He reached up for her purse just as his radio chirped on his desk. "Damn it."

"Don't listen." She arched her hips. "Inside me. *Now.*"

He opened her purse but his radio chirped again, and he sagged against her, pressing his forehead to hers. "I'm sorry. I'm so sorry, but I have to get that." His body was hard, quivering with it, but on his face was a resigned tension. And she didn't believe that tension was all for himself, but for her, too, and right then and there, something deep within her shifted. Softened. "Hey." She cupped his face, and smiled past the hunger flooding her. "It's okay, I can wait."

At that, something seemed to shift within him too, certainly a release of the tension that had gripped him at the sound of his radio, but something more. Something warm and deep, and maybe not all physical. He nuzzled close, gave her a quick, hard kiss on the lips and then pulled back with serious reluctance before answering the radio.

It was dispatch. There'd been a police call at Creative Interiors I, an intruder, though there was no one at the premises now. Given the arson issues, they'd contacted Joe as a courtesy.

With her stomach clenching, Summer adjusted her clothing and sat up. "I'm coming with you."

"Red—"

"Look, this is a nightmare, I know. But it's my nightmare." They left his office with Ashes coming along, and walked in silence to their cars. Summer followed Joe to Creative Interiors, trying not to think too hard. She'd always been able to clear her mind, through good music or breathing techniques, or her soothing crystals and teas, but it wasn't as easy with so many thoughts swirling in her head she felt as if they were coming out her ears.

In front of Creative Interiors, there was a police car. Joe talked to the cop for a moment, then came over to her. "The alarm went off. A witness said she saw a twenty-something-year-old guy in black from head to toe let himself in with keys, and then back out a moment later."

She blinked. "Braden?"

"They're looking for him now. They've called your mom and Tina."

This made even less sense now than it had yesterday. She went into the store to see if she could tell what might possibly be missing. Joe came in behind her. She flipped off the alarm and headed toward the back. The counter looked cleared off as usual. The cash register would be empty so she didn't bother to check there.

In the back she turned on the lights, surveyed the crowded storage area and sighed. Everything had been chaotic and unorganized since the warehouse fire, and after the other store's fire, things had only gotten worse. There were stacks of inventory haphazardly placed on shelves, on the floor, in and around the table and chairs used for employee breaks. On a shelving unit sat three of Bill's lighthouses, held up on either side with two of her father's travel books.

She ran a finger over a spine. "I was with him when he did his research for this one. We took a canoe down the Amazon. I'll never forget it."

"You shouldn't." He turned her to face him. "Maybe there's more you should never forget."

"I'm beginning to get that," she said softly, knowing how right he was. "It's just that I wanted to live in the here and now, you know?" She let out a sad smile. "Just wanted to hang out, see everyone, be happy, and then go on my merry way."

"Without looking back?"

"That was my plan. But . . ." She set her hand on his chest, slowly fisting it over his heart, staring at her fingers as she gripped him tight, binding him to her. "I don't seem to be able to manage it the way I thought I could."

He covered her hand with his. "Because it's all entwined. The past. The now. The future."

"I just want the now," she whispered.

He slowly shook his head. "That's not the way this works, Red. At least not for me."

Her heart sped up as she struggled to make sure he understood. "I've never really been a future sort of woman, you know that. And I sure as hell know you're not a past kind of guy. There's nothing there for you, you've said so yourself. When you look at it like that, all we have is now."

"*You* are my past. My entire past."

She set her forehead to his chest and took a moment to soak him in. Everything about him steadied her—his solid heartbeat, the scent of him, the way his hands felt on her, his voice, everything. "I'm so screwed up," she murmured. "I thought being here would help, but now I'm just feeling more confused."

He stroked a soothing hand up her spine, sinking his fingers into her hair. "That's because when your father died, when Camille closed herself off, all you saw was the pain from the loss. You're afraid you'll end up the same way if you ever love someone too much, so you close yourself off too," he said, brushing his lips against her temple. "Am I close?"

She was still staring at his chest, wondering how it was he saw so much, and understood her, maybe more than she did herself. "Let's just say you're warm."

"I'm more than warm, Red. I'm dead-on. Now you live your life in the present without looking back. It's easier to do that, easier to keep your heart intact and safe, but guess what? Shit happens and you had to come back here where the past and the present have collided like a plane crash, and there's no safety net."

"I know," she whispered.

"Look, you've lived good and well, but not deep. Maybe it's time to change things."

A moment ago he'd been forceful and sexy as hell with it. Now he was being so sweet and tender, and somehow it was even sexier. But that he saw her so clearly, so absolutely, stunningly clearly, terrified her.

How could he know her so well?

"I loved the girl you were," he said, and stroked a tear off her cheek that she hadn't even been aware she'd shed. "And I'm growing to love the woman you've become. Past and present, hopelessly entwined. So the future should be given a shot too."

"Joe." She squeezed her eyes shut.

"Look at me." He tipped up her chin. "You say that the past doesn't matter, but you stand there looking at that book of your father's and you ache. You say that what *we* had in the past doesn't matter, but you keep going back to it so that's yet another lie."

Into the silence her cell phone vibrated like an insect. She pulled it out of her pocket.

Joe moved away from her into the front room of the store and out of her view while she looked at the display. The phone vibrated again, shook and shimmied in her hand as she stared at it. By the time she followed Joe a minute later, he was talking to the police officer. She walked up to them and showed Joe the text message.

They won't stop looking for me until you're gone. Get gone.

He eyes slid over the digital read-out, then up to hers. He had his fire marshal face on, inscrutable. Only the corners of his mouth, turned slightly down, gave him away.

"I guess we're still bothering somebody," she said in a

surprisingly normal voice. "Or should I say me. I'm still bothering somebody. That's not really saying much though, since I've been bothering pretty much everybody I've come across since being home."

"Red—"

"Here." She thrust the phone at him. "Just . . . do what you do and figure it all out."

He grabbed her hand and squeezed until she looked at him again. "I will," he promised.

And though just about everything was going wrong, including them, she nodded because she believed him. She believed *in* him.

Chapter 21

Summer woke up alone in Joe's bed. She hadn't closed the curtains the night before and the early morning sun slanted in the high, narrow windows, warming her, making her squint as she looked around.

She was hugging Joe's pillow, lost in his warm comforter, and though the room faintly smelled like him, she was alone. As she had been all night.

Joe had sent her to his boat while he worked. Empathy and something else hit her, something that felt suspiciously close to neediness, and she tossed the covers aside. His bathroom was the size of a postage stamp, the shower even smaller. She pictured him in here, that tall, long body bumping into the walls as he soaped up. She used his shampoo, and then sighed dreamily over the scent of him lingering on her as she dressed and moved into the galley.

Her cell phone sat on his small wooden table, being used as a paperweight to hold down a note scribbled in Joe's handwriting.

Red,
Let me know where you'll be today.
Joe

Sparse, not a single extra word to it. Why hadn't he come to bed? Feeling out of sorts and frustrated with herself, she headed to the Gaslamp Quarter and the original Creative Interiors. The store wasn't open yet but Camille and Tina were there, sitting at the back table. They had a fresh pitcher of iced tea and a stack of catalogs, which they were poring over together.

"Hello darling," Tina said with a smile. "We're contemplating some of our fall stock."

"What's missing from last night? Anything?" Summer asked, her stomach tightening with nerves.

"Not a thing," Tina said.

Camille stood up and grabbed another glass, which she filled with iced tea. "Chamomile," she said, and handed it to Summer.

For its calming effect. "Thanks."

Camille stroked a finger over her cheek then turned away and sat back down.

Tina patted a chair. "Sit, darling Summer. It wasn't what the police thought. Braden had a key."

"He'd left his wallet," Camille said. "And forgot about the alarm."

"They took him in for questioning this morning, but let him go," Tina said. "Chloe's hot under the collar about it, says he's done nothing wrong."

"And what do you think?" Summer asked.

"I want to think the same. I *do* think the same. But Braden's pride is hurt and he's quit."

"How did Chloe take that?"

"Not well, as you can imagine. It's all such a mess. Gregg thinks he's being investigated for the fires, and Stella's going crazy. The twins . . . I found cigarettes in the outside trash this morning." Tina sighed and looked at

Camille. "Our group is losing it, but I just keep reminding myself we've never once made a wrong decision on any of the people in our lives, right?"

Camille looked at Tina for a long moment. "I'd like to think not," she said very softly, and began adding sugar to her tea.

Summer leaned in and hugged her mom. "You doing okay?"

"Always." But she let go of her teaspoon and hugged Summer back, hard. "Always." Then she pulled free and stroked Summer's hair from her forehead. "And because I am, it's time."

"Time?" Summer glanced at Tina, but her aunt lifted a shoulder. "Time for what?"

"For you to go back to your life."

"Mom." She pushed her tea away. "We've discussed this. I'm staying until it's all over." She thought of the text messages and knew she should tell them before they heard it from Joe. "And there's something else you both should know."

"Uh oh," Tina said.

Summer kept her hand on her mother's so she couldn't reach for the sugar. "I've received two text messages, anonymously, suggesting I need to leave."

Camille jerked, and spilled her tea. "Oh! I'm sorry." She jumped up and grabbed a towel.

Tina didn't move, just sat there in shock.

"I've told Joe about them," Summer said. "He and Kenny are on it."

"What do the messages say?" Camille asked, cleaning up the tea.

"The first one said 'Please, go away.' The second one

said, and I quote, 'they won't stop looking for me until you've gone.'"

Tina covered her mouth with a shaking hand.

Camille stood up. "That's it, you're done here, honey. I mean it. You're going back to your life. Your safe life." With that, she walked out front.

Tina pulled a flask from her purse and poured a healthy shot into her tea. "Our secret," she said and took a long sip.

"Aunt Tina—"

"It's not you. It's everything else. The fires, the rest of the family. It's all driving me to drink. Do me a favor, darling, and cover for the twins out front until they show up? I'm just going to finish my tea."

The twins were a full hour late, with no explanation. Stella and Gregg called in sick, which Summer took to mean they needed an attitude adjustment day.

When Madeline and Diana finally arrived, Madeline had a sneer on her face and Diana had her head buried in the latest *Teen People.* She peeked up long enough to look at Summer and shake her head mournfully. "Your horoscope was a doozy."

"Don't tell me."

"You're going to be extremely unlucky in love today specifically."

"As opposed to what?" Summer asked. "All the luck I've had?"

"Oh and also it said you probably shouldn't get out of bed."

"Great. Thanks," Summer muttered as she left. She got into the Bug and drove to Joe's work.

He wasn't there, though she found Kenny in the large common room on the ground floor, where the firefighters hung out when they weren't on a fire. He was sat sprawled in a faded orange corduroy couch that looked as soft and comfortable as it was old, eating soup out of a Styrofoam cup and watching a soap opera.

He winced when she caught him. "Don't tell Joe."

"Why would Joe care if you're eating Cup-O-Soup?"

He pushed up his glasses. "Not the soup, the soap opera."

Summer glanced at the TV screen. A beautiful young woman sat in a bubble bath, being attended to by an even more beautiful young man who sat shirtless at her side. He poured her wine and dropped rose petals over her body, flexing his muscles as he did.

"Let's face it," Kenny said. "Our Joe isn't much for flowers and wine."

Summer laughed. "No, he's not." She thought of their kiss on the beach, the way he'd painted her skin with his fingers when they'd made love. "But he can be romantic when he wants to be."

"That's because you're different from the other women he's been with," Kenny said. "I'm so glad you're different."

She wondered at the others.

Kenny grinned. "You've also got amazing restraint."

"I don't know what you're talking about."

"Go ahead, I'll give you a freebie. Ask me anything, I've known him for years. You want to know if he snores? Yes, when he's stressed. You want to know if he still thinks of himself as a fat loser? Yes, especially when he gets dumped by some silly woman who never understood him. You want to know if he's easily hurt? Double yes, way too easily."

There was something in Kenny's eyes now, some gentle reproaching warning not to hurt his close friend and partner, and the loyalty made Summer's throat thick. "How about I ask a question about you instead?"

"Okay," he said, surprised.

"What's going on between you and my mother?"

"Nothing." His eyes behind his glasses were right on hers, and as far as she could tell, honest. "Yet."

"What's *going* to go on between you and my mother?"

A small smile curved his lips. "Truth?"

"Please," she said.

"When this arson investigation is over, I'm going to date her. A lot. Is that a problem for you?"

"She's seven years older than you."

"Seven years is nothing. She's sweet, beautiful, kind, and she cares about me."

"Kenny." Torn between loyalties, she chewed on her lower lip. "She cares about men. That's never been the issue. She just never likes them for long."

"I'm a big boy, Summer. And anyway, have some faith in the power of love."

"Love?"

"Love," he said firmly. "Trust me."

Trust him. He hadn't been the first man to ask that of her. No, Joe had the distinction of that honor.

"Do you want to know where Joe is?" Kenny asked.

"Yes."

"Are you going to make him even grumpier, or turn the day around for him?"

Summer thought about that. She wanted to tell Joe how much she'd missed him last night. That she needed him. That she thought that maybe all those years ago she'd loved him as much as she'd been capable of, and it had scared her but she didn't know why, and she still didn't. "It might be a combination," she admitted.

Kenny nodded. "There was just a store bombing near the Amtrak station. A convenience store. Some punk tossed an M-80 through the windows to break in. They think it's the same punk who's robbed three other stores this year. Joe's working with the police, checking for evidence."

"Can you just tell him I came by, maybe ask him to call me?"

"You bet."

Summer turned to leave just as the soap opera went to a news bulletin. "We're on site at the convenience store bombing from earlier this morning," a newscaster said. "The third in this area this year. This time the suspect wasn't able to get the money from the cash register, and he vanished. The police think he's still in the immediate vicinity. We'll go to Tom now, on scene."

The camera cut to a young reporter holding a microphone, standing in front of the convenience store. The windows had been blown out and were blackened around the edges. Just inside a few officers moved around.

"Look." Summer pointed to Joe. He wore his usual uniform of jeans and his white button-down, half untucked and draped over the gun on his hip. He hadn't shaved and his hair was rumpled, and he looked so incredibly sexy she wanted to reach out and touch.

Kenny sighed as she sank next to him on the couch. "How many times have I told him when there's suits or cameras around, tuck the shirt all the way in and comb that mop masquerading as hair . . ."

The reporter began talking. "The police are confident that they have the suspect on camera—" A gun went off, and the reporter gasped, spinning around to take in the scene behind him.

A guy wearing a ski mask and holding a gun leapt out of

a large open tub of sodas. He waved the weapon, and as everyone else reached for theirs, the man closest to the perp dove forward.

Joe. He hit the suspect at midbelly and they both went down.

The gun went off again.

Four officers converged on them both, covering the view of the camera.

"Keep the camera on them, Ed!" yelled the reporter. "Keep rolling!"

But camera guy Ed couldn't get a clear shot, there were too many people yelling and talking, standing in front of the lens.

"Oh my God, did you see that?" Summer cried, leaping to her feet. "Joe just dove right at him. Was he shot? Could you see? I couldn't see!"

Face grim and tense, Kenny squeezed her hand then headed for the door. "I'll call you from the scene—"

"Oh, no, you won't. Because I'll be standing right next to you—"

They had to drive separately because Kenny was going in an official capacity, while Summer would be nothing more than one of the desperate crowd.

And she was desperate. Her heart was bouncing off her ribs like a Ping-Pong, the blood roaring in her ears as she played the scene in her head over and over.

Why had Joe tried to be a hero?

But she knew the answer to that. He'd been the closest, he'd had the best chance at taking the guy down before he'd shot someone. And yet the gun had gone off anyway.

She drove faster, cranking up her radio for news.

"One officer is down," a reporter droned in a nasally, impersonal voice as if reading the alphabet. "But the gunman is in custody—"

It took her four more long, agonizing minutes to get to the scene, the longest minutes of her life. She'd lost sight of Kenny's truck, and the entire block had been barricaded, but she moved in as close as she could. Unfortunately, she couldn't find a spot to park.

When an ambulance whipped past her, going the opposite direction, followed by a squad car, her heart kicked up a notch, if that was even possible. She was just about to abandon her car and say the hell with it when her cell phone rang.

It was Kenny. "Oh thank God," she said in lieu of a greeting. "Listen, I can't get in close, there's nowhere to park, I'm just going to—"

"Turn around." He sounded perfectly calm but Summer could hear the strain beneath the surface. "He just left in the ambulance, and is heading toward the hospital."

Now her poor heart stopped. "He was hit?"

"I don't have any details yet, but we both know Joe is far too stubborn to be anything but okay."

She heard Ashes let out a little bark, and knew she must be riding shotgun with Kenny. Summer let out a little sobbing laugh, and with the phone shoved against her hunched shoulder, tried to turn around. But traffic was a bitch and no one was moving and . . . and she was going to go postal here in a second. "Damn it!"

"Listen to me, Summer. You have time, so drive carefully. Summer? Are you there?"

Since she couldn't speak past the lump in her throat, she nodded as if Kenny could see her.

"Just get to the hospital," he said. "I'll meet you there."

Summer tossed the phone to the seat beside her and

weaved through traffic, snarling at anyone who got in her way. At the hospital, she parked crookedly and ran through the lot and into the emergency department, which was so packed there was standing room only. People lined the hall, sat against the walls, paced the floor. Summer made her way past all of them, skidding to a halt in front of the nurses station. The line there was long but no one seemed to be doing anything so she stood off to the side and caught the eye of a nurse. "Joe Walker," she gasped. "The fire marshal from the store bombing."

Miraculously, the nurse moved to the counter and consulted a clipboard. "Are you family?"

She debated with herself for less than a single heartbeat. She knew the rules. No family, no information. "Yes," she said because it was true. She was the closet thing to family he'd ever had.

"He's going into surgery." The nurse tossed a chin toward the waiting room. "Have a seat."

Chapter 22

He was five again, and had knocked a glass of milk over. He stood there quivering in his own skin staring up into his father's menacing face.

"Got to teach you a lesson, boy."

Joe knew the drill and bit his lip to keep his mouth shut because he wouldn't cry. But his father was all hands. Huge, hard, cruel hands—

"There, that'll help the pain. Joe? Joe, come on now, open your eyes."

Joe cracked open one eye and found himself surrounded by white and metal and a bright light that made him shut his eye again. His tongue felt swollen and his brain hazy.

"Do you remember what happened?" a female voice asked.

His nose was assaulted with a metallic scent, and a warm hand settled on his arm. Fixing an IV he realized, and his eyes flew open again.

The nurse smiled at him. "Hi there. Welcome back."

He remembered being in the convenience store, remembered the shouts, the punk lifting a gun, pointing it at an officer. He remembered thinking it was just a kid, a stupid kid, then the explosion of the gun near his ear and the fiery agony as the bullet had torn through his boot.

He'd been shot in the damn foot by a kid.

Jesus, he was getting old if he'd let that happen, and that sucked, too. He lifted his head and stared down at his foot, which was bandaged up like a mummy. "It's still there," he said with some relief, and lay back again.

"It most definitely is," the nurse said. "You have a nice hole in it though, and you won't be using it any time in the near future, but it's there. Your wife has been pacing the hallways waiting for you to wake up. Should I send her in?"

"My wife?" He lifted a hand to his head. No bandages.

"What's the matter?" the nurse asked.

"Did I hit my head?"

"No." The nurse frowned. "Does it hurt?"

The drugs had kicked in now, and things were nice and fuzzy. "I'm not sure." In the opened doorway he locked on to a set of jade green eyes, red rimmed with a smudge of mascara under each. They belonged to the one face that could both stop his heart and kick-start it with one look.

Summer sent him a tremulous smile. "Hi honey, I'm home."

"I just loaded him with morphine," the nurse warned her with a little pat on Joe's arm. "He'll be quite loopy, and it's possible he won't remember this at all."

"Christ, I hope I do," he murmured. "It's not every day I get to lay eyes on my *wife*."

Summer's cheeks glowed red but she moved to his bedside. "You okay?"

"I don't remember our honeymoon. Did you wear a pretty silky teddy thing?" He closed his eyes because his eyelids felt too heavy. At the same time, energy surged through him, making his skin feel too tight. "Because just naked is good, too."

"Joe."

"Summer," he answered obediently. "I can't feel a damn thing. That's a nice change. Even my heart doesn't hurt."

"Oh, Joe."

Because she sounded so sad, he blinked and tried to concentrate, but it wasn't easy. "My foot has a hole in it."

"I know." Staring down at his IV, she stroked his arm gently. "I was so scared."

She was so pretty with her sweet worry, with her fiery hair brushing her golden shoulders. She was wearing two tank tops layered together, one white, one sky blue, and a denim skirt that showed off her mile-long legs. He felt a grin split his face. "You married me. You must really looooove me."

A frown turned her mouth upside down. "You aren't that drugged, are you? You know we're not really married."

"I didn't take a bullet to the brain." Sighing, he lay back and closed his eyes. "I know where we are. You want to be friends, and occasionally fuck me." Suddenly the morphine wasn't enough. He realized his chest did hurt. His head hurt. His foot burned like a son of a bitch. And he was quickly sinking into the black pit where he'd run into his father's fists again. "Red?"

He felt her hand on his jaw, and he sighed, turning his face into her touch. "Don't go."

But he fell into the pit before he could hear her answer.

For three days the Creative Interiors case took a backseat to Joe's shooting. When he was discharged from the hospital, Summer drove him home and set him up in his bed, surrounded by the flowers and gifts people had sent, which looked almost obnoxiously cheerful when compared to his stubborn, set, irritated face.

"Where's Ashes?" he asked.

"Kenny's got her."

He frowned. "You should have taken me into work."

"The doctor said no."

He sent her a brooding glance.

"It's not the end of the world," she said, carefully propping his foot up on a pillow. "Taking some time off."

"Are you sure?"

In the act of smoothing his covers, she looked over at him, saw the irony in his expression. "Okay, maybe at first I thought it was, but I got used to it. I sure got used to seeing your face whenever I wanted."

He closed his eyes. "I've had just enough drugs to take that as a compliment." He lay on his bed very still, as if moving a single inch hurt.

The doctor had said no weight on the foot for one week, but after that he'd recover quickly. Summer wanted to believe that with all her might but he looked so haggard and hollow and pale. His mouth was tight, as if the pain meds weren't working, or maybe that was just because she was hovering.

Not wanting to leave him alone, she sat on the edge of the bed.

"Hey, wife," he said, eyes still closed, not moving a single muscle.

"Do you need anything?"

"Nah. Just checking to see if you'd answer to the title."

"Funny."

One side of his mouth quirked, and she caught a flash of his dimple. "Gotta get your kicks where you can when you're down," he murmured.

"You won't be down for long. Are you hungry?"

"Yeah. I want a Big Mac and a Supersized order of fries, extra carbs and cholesterol please."

He'd lost weight in the past few days. And since he was still so carefully not moving, she figured the order was more wishful thinking than anything else. "How about some soup and tea?"

He made a very soft noise of aversion and then was quiet.

So was she. For days she'd been living with the nightmare of what could have happened. How much worse this could have been. He could have taken the bullet in his chest, or in the head, in which case, she might be sitting by his grave—

She put her fingers over her mouth.

"You going to stare at me until I'm better? Because that might be a while."

"Yes," she said a little shakily. "Until you're better, I'm not going to take my eyes off you."

"Even when I'm in the shower?"

"Why not? I've seen it all before."

"Not on a regular basis. Only when you're needing a distraction."

She stared down at him, horrified that that's what he thought he was. She had nobody but herself to blame for that, because she'd started this whole thing with him for exactly that. A distraction. "Joe." Her throat went tight. "You know how I feel about you, right? You know I—"

He opened his eyes for this.

But it wasn't as easy when he was looking at her, she discovered. Not that there was anything remotely easy about speaking of her feelings at all. "Um . . ."

He arched a brow.

"I . . ."

He snorted and shut his eyes again. "Don't hurt yourself."

God, she felt like a fool. Why couldn't she just say it? He made her laugh, he made her feel good, he made her happy. And if that meant she'd deepened her feelings to . . . love . . . then that's what it was.

"I'm hot," he said.

Pathetically grateful for the break, Summer leapt up and pulled off his blanket.

"Still hot."

"You're only in a sheet." But she removed that too, dragging it aside in a way that he could easily pull it back over him if he wanted. He wore only low slung faded gray sweat bottoms. His chest was bare except for the light dusting of hair that ran from pec to pec. His belly rose and fell with his breathing, hard and ridged with muscle, but also nearly concave from not eating for days.

He hadn't shaved, and she looked at the shadow on his jaw. At the shadows beneath his eyes. And everything within her softened, melted. "Can I get you anything?"

"A hammer to the head."

"You need more pain meds?"

"No."

He'd been stubborn about those, and she knew why. He hated to be out of control, hated to feel weak. She shifted a little closer and put her hand on his chest, and then frowned at how hot he really was. "You *are* too warm."

His fingers came up to cover hers. She would have softened some more, melted some more, but he shoved her hand off him. "You don't have to stay," he said. "Kenny's coming later. I'll be fine until then."

"You think I don't want to be here?"

He didn't answer, and that made her mad. Leaning over him, she put her hand back on his chest and waited until she felt each of his muscles tense in reaction at her touch. "You of all people should know I don't do anything I don't want to do."

"I'm not in the mood for this, Summer."

Summer. "Well, isn't that fine and dandy, because I'm not in the mood to watch you go through all this pain, through being laid flat and helpless when I know damn well how much you love that."

A long moment passed. Joe was still in his own zone.

"Stop staring at me," he finally said. "Your thoughts are so loud they're penetrating the pleasant buzz of the drugs."

"You haven't taken any drugs."

"Then you're penetrating the pain, an admirable feat. Why don't you go for a run?"

"I don't want to leave."

"Odd, since before I was shot, you didn't want to stay."

"Maybe watching you be so stupid changed things."

"Changed what?"

It'd made her realize how fragile a balance life could be. That maybe living for the moment wasn't quite enough. That maybe there needed to be sustenance, too. Up until now, the men in her life had all been like junk food. Fun, but not necessary good for her. Joe was sustenance. Very good for her. She ran a finger down the center of his chest to low on his belly, then swirled it around his belly button.

"Red."

The word, uttered with soft warning, gave her a shiver. "You should let me get you something to eat."

"Stop changing the subject. *What changed?*"

"Shh." Her gaze held his as she ran her finger down a little further, to the edge of his sweats.

His eyes went opaque. It might have been pain but she was willing to bet not. She began to slowly pull the tie on his sweats. "You're grumpy," she murmured. "I know you have good reason but I feel obligated to cheer you up."

"Nothing could do that."

Kenny had told Summer that Joe thought getting shot had been all his own fault, that if he'd only been quicker, faster, it wouldn't have happened. No one believed it but Joe himself, and in fact, the doctor had said that his regretful, self-pitying thoughts might even slow down the healing process.

That wasn't going to happen on her watch.

The bow gave way. Her eyes locked with his as she slowly slid her fingers just beneath the waistband of his sweats. "Commando?" she whispered when she didn't come across anything but smooth, hot, hard flesh.

His eyes were closed again. Sweat had broken out on his skin. "This is not going to work."

"Really?" She wrapped her fingers around more hot, hard flesh. "Because everything appears to be in perfectly fine working order."

"I can't— I won't be able to return the favor—"

"But that's the beauty of this." She tugged his sweats down his hips, springing him free, smiling at the evidence that no matter what he said, he was in need. "I owe you one."

"Red—"

She fanned her breath over him.

He moaned, his fingers sliding into her hair as his hips arched helplessly.

"See?" She licked him like a lollipop. "It's kinda nice to lean on someone once in a while, isn't it?"

His answer was unintelligible.

*   *   *

"I'm going to go make you soup and tea," Summer said much later, when Joe was sprawled out flat on his back like a boneless fish. "Wait here."

"As opposed to leaping up and helping you?" he asked deprecatingly.

"Hey, I worked hard to make you not grumpy. Don't ruin it."

There was nothing but a thoughtful silence from him as she moved into the galley. Then, "maybe I need more work," he called out.

Her mouth twitched into a smile as she took out a can of soup and a pot. She hoped the fact that he had any humor left at all meant he wasn't in too much pain. For days he'd been in agony, and so stubborn about the painkillers. Seeing him suffer had nearly killed her. She eyed the pill container on the small counter. She could lace his soup. It would get him through the night.

"Don't even think about it," he said. He stood in the doorway, gripping it with one hand, a crutch shoved under the armpit of his other arm. He was pale. No, make that green.

She rushed over to him, backed him up to the bed. "Lie down."

"I'm tired of lying down."

"Don't make me get rough." She helped him stretch out, but when she would have left him alone, he reached for her hand.

"Stay."

"All right, I'll just clean up—"

"Stay," he murmured stubbornly with a grip of steel on her wrist, tugging her down until she was sprawled out besides him. "And don't think I've forgotten that you owe me a bedtime story. You were going to tell me what things have changed between us. It sounds fascinating."

"Joe . . ." She danced her fingers over his chest, and he let out a shuddery sigh.

"Feels good." He hadn't let go of her other hand, but his fingers relaxed in hers. "Really good. What changed?"

Jesus, he had a one-track mind. "Okay, maybe I like you more than I thought I did."

Eyes closed, he smiled.

"Don't smile. I don't *like* liking you more than I thought."

"It's not your fault, I'm irresistible." He seemed to be drifting off in spite of himself. "Don't go."

"I won't," she promised as he let out another exhausted sigh and went still. "I won't."

Chapter 23

Everyone took turns watching over him. Tina, Camille, Kenny, some of his other coworkers, and Summer, until two days after he'd been released from the hospital, he kicked them all out.

He was fine on his own. Totally and completely fine. To prove it, he wrapped his bound foot in a garbage bag, secured it with duct tape, and got into the shower. Shaky but determined, he made it all the way through soaping up before having to sit down to breathe through the pain, the water pounding down on him.

He had to crawl out and air dry right there on the floor. When he could talk, he called Kenny. "Bring me into the office. I need to see the files."

"You've seen them a hundred times. You lived and breathed them. Nothing's changed."

"I've been thinking about that old warehouse fire. There was never any evidence found. The area of origin was ground level, beneath the loft."

"So?"

"So I was there," Joe said. "I know I was a kid, but I remember everything. That fire burned hot and damned fast.

And yet the area of origin was nothing more than stacks of cardboard boxes."

"Flammable enough."

"Flammable, definitely. But not enough. There was an accelerant there, there had to have been. It just wasn't detected."

"Okay, so let's say there was an accelerant," Kenny said reasonably. "Let's assume gasoline, like the subsequent two fires."

"Right."

"But we've been through this. That would clear just about everyone except . . ." Kenny's voice trailed off. *"Shit."*

With Braden not working, Creative Interiors needed accounting help. Summer'd had some training at the expedition company, as sometimes in the off-season she worked in the San Francisco office. She figured she could at least handle the payables and receivables.

Camille was a self-proclaimed computer illiterate, so all help was welcome. Oddly enough, for the past two days her mother had been extremely quiet, wearing an expression of misery that suspiciously matched Kenny's. When Summer asked about it, she hit a brick wall, and finally, she gave up.

Every day at lunch she checked on Joe. He'd remained frustrated, grumpy, and mostly uncommunicative. She was willing to give him all three for the time being because she figured he'd earned them. She spent her afternoons on guided hikes or kayak rides. Word was spreading quickly, and she already had more calls than she could take. She loved it.

At night, she went back to Joe's. She'd pet a sleepy

Ashes, then slip into bed with Joe, breathing in his scent, his warmth, wondering how in the world she was going to ever get used to sleeping alone again.

"Maybe you could get a blow-up doll and paint my face on it," Joe said.

She went still. "What?"

"You were wondering how to sleep without me."

"I said it out loud?"

"Sure did. You said 'how in the world am I going to ever get used to sleeping alone again?' I'm just offering suggestions. You could tape my picture to your pillow."

"You're teasing me."

"And you're killing me." He rolled them over—he was clearly feeling better—and pinning her to the mattress, kissed her hard. "The answer is simple, Red. Don't go. Damn it, don't go."

Simple . . . Had he said *simple*?

She lay there surrounded by him, her heart and soul terrifyingly connected to his and she just knew if she kept this up, she'd lose herself, she'd . . . end up like Camille.

Joe's fingers traced her hairline with a sweet tenderness. "Relax, Red. This isn't supposed to hurt."

Summer wasn't sure what it was about him, but even when she was feeling sharp as a tack, he cut right through her crap, through her neurosis, through everything to see the real her. Unlike any other human being on earth, he could piss her off, turn her on, make her question everything she believed in, and in general provoke the most uncomfortable feelings.

He wanted answers. He wasn't going to push her for them, but his need was there, the third person in the room. Eventually she was going to have to face it, but for now, she hugged him close and didn't say anything at all.

Joe let out a quiet sigh and hugged her back, resting his cheek against the top of her head, brushing his lips to her temple as he fell asleep.

But she didn't fall for a long, long time.

A few days later, Summer sat behind the counter of Creative Interiors on the computer. She'd finally entered in everything since Braden had left, and had managed to figure out how to download the receivables and payables to the general ledger.

Camille came in and offered her iced tea. It was delicious, as always. "Kava?"

"Hmmm," Camille said.

Summer narrowed her eyes. "Isn't that a fix for a broken heart?"

"It's for a lot of things."

"Mom, if you want Kenny, why don't you just go out with him?"

"Honey, some things are just complicated."

Tell me about it. "He's a good man."

Camille pretended not to hear as she glanced at her watch. "Oh, would you look at the time," she murmured.

Summer sighed, and drank her tea for broken hearts. Eventually the fire would be solved and she'd be long gone. In fact, she could have left by now. Most of the fire-related paperwork had been done, the rest was now up to the ongoing investigation by MAST and the insurance company.

The truth was she wasn't ready to go. She wasn't ready to give up this burgeoning relationship with her family.

And she sure as hell wasn't ready to give up whatever it was she was doing every night with Joe.

She hit ENTER and sent the receivables and payables on

their way to the general ledger. The receivables were immediately kicked back with a blinking warning message. They couldn't be sent until they were in balance.

Huh?

She checked her work, but everything looked right. She'd entered the deposits from the cash register's receipt report. She knew that Braden had entered the receivables after the fact, from the receipt brought back from the bank deposit. He'd gotten that routine from Camille and/or Tina, who'd done the same before Braden's hire. But it shouldn't have made a difference, the numbers should be the same.

She checked her work and hit ENTER again, and again was rejected. Damn it, she missed Braden. He'd always made this look so effortless. She glanced at Chloe, who was sweeping the wood floors. She still had her green-tipped hair and matching vivid green eye shadow, but she wore a rather sedate cargo skirt in khaki with a white T-shirt, and for two weeks hadn't said a single sarcastic thing.

"You miss Braden too," Summer said.

Chloe kept on sweeping, not missing a beat.

"Or . . . you're not missing him at all because you're still seeing him." She caught the flash of guilt in Chloe's expression. "On the sly. Oh my God, you are."

"I don't do anything on the sly." Chloe stopped sweeping and leaned on the broom. "Okay, fine, Sherlock. I'm seeing him. It's not that difficult. He's working at Ally's."

"Ally the Loon Ally?"

"Who pays twice what we paid. Apparently her business has tripled since our troubles. And a good bookkeeper is hard to find."

"Chloe . . ."

"I love him, Summer."

Summer swallowed. "You fling that word around awfully easily."

"It's the way it is."

"He's a suspect in a crime."

"We're all suspects. When they discover the truth, he can come back here."

"Is that what he wants? To come back here?"

"Well, no. But for me, he'd do it."

"So he loves you too?"

Chloe's gaze slid away.

"Oh, Chloe."

"Okay, maybe he won't *say* he loves me, but I know he does." Chloe sank to a love seat behind her. "He's just embarrassed about his past, and what we all think of him."

Summer sat next to Chloe, tucking a leg beneath her. "I know I haven't been around all that long, but—"

"Uh oh, is this the mushy speech? Where you say you care about me and don't want to see me hurt?"

Summer laughed. "I was thinking about it."

"Save it. Your side of the family gets hives using the L-word."

"Do not." Summer braced herself. "I love *you*."

"Hmm. Soon as you can tell the rest of the family and Joe, I'll really be impressed."

Summer found herself crossing her arms defensively. "We were talking about you."

Chloe patted her arm. "Whatever makes you feel better." She rose. "I've got work."

And so did she. Summer went back to the annoying computer and told herself to concentrate. She wasn't lifting her butt off the stool until she made serious headway into the receivables issue.

It took another hour to figure out it wasn't her fault that

the receivables really didn't match. They didn't match because someone had messed with the books.

Specifically, with the money going into the books.

Summer sat everyone down at the table in the back room. Camille, Chloe, and Tina. Bill was there too, he'd stopped by with lunch. She put the pitcher of tea in front of her mother and moved the sugar to safety in front of her aunt, then opened the laptop. "We have a problem, a big one."

"Sounds serious." Tina eyeballed the computer as if it had wings.

"It is serious." Summer took a deep breath. "Someone's been messing with the receivables. The totals from the bank don't always match what's on the cash register receipts."

Tina frowned.

Camille began pouring tea.

Chloe blinked in confusion.

Bill, a man who'd given a perfect stranger the shirt off his back, shook his head. *"What?"*

"I know. It's crazy. But we're missing money." Summer put her hands on her hips and surveyed the group. "So. Who makes the deposit?"

"Whoever's going past the bank," Tina said with a baffled shrug. "You've been here a while now. You've seen how it works."

Yeah. Everyone had access to the register, and no one watched over it that carefully. Absolutely anyone could have stuck their hands in the bank deposit envelope, pulled a fistful of cash, adjusted the deposit slip for a new total, and no one would have blinked. "Who empties the register at the end of the day?"

"Same answer," Tina said. "Whoever's working. The

register spits out a report telling us how much there is. As a backup, the checks are added up. The cash is added up. The numbers are compared to make sure."

"And that gets done for certain?"

"It's supposed to," Chloe said. "Or we get in trouble."

But then she and Tina and Camille all exchanged a long look. A long *guilty* look.

Bill groaned. "Oh, ladies."

"Okay, so we don't always check," Tina admitted. "I trust the printout. I mean, a computer can't add things up wrong, everyone knows that."

"Me too," Camille said softly. "I trusted the printout."

Chloe winced. "And I guess this is where I admit I've never added it up, I just say I do."

Bill put his heads into his hands. *"Christ."*

Summer sighed. "So there's no check and balance system?" She got a bunch of blank looks. "Okay, we'll get back to how stupid *that* is in a minute. You fill out a deposit slip, right? Listing both the cash and the checks? So it'd be hard for someone to actually change the cash *and* the total, right?"

Another look between sisters.

Chloe studied the ceiling.

"Hello?" Summer said. "Anyone home?"

"I don't always separate the numbers," Tina admitted. "Sometimes I just put down the total, no breakdown of checks and cash."

"Me too," Camille said.

Chloe added a guilty shrug.

Bill just shook his head.

Summer sighed. "So the deposit is taken to the bank, by whoever's available, without a breakdown of cash and checks, and then credited to the account. You all realize there's only about four different places where it can go wrong, where the cash can be separated from the checks without a system in place to stop that from happening."

"How many discrepancies did you find?" Bill asked quietly.

"Three hundred and fifty dollars for this first half of the month alone," Summer said. "And I'd be willing to bet this problem goes back a while, so three hundred and fifty bucks minimum a month for all the years in business . . . We need to check it out."

Tina's frowned deepened. "On the computer?"

"I can try to do it, but I'll need help."

Tina bit her lower lip. "I wouldn't know where to start."

Camille shocked Summer by squeezing her hand. "I'll help."

Joe spent a long, seriously frustrating day spinning his wheels. He'd tried to go into work against the wishes of his doctor and therapist, and before he'd even left the boat, he'd managed to trip over Ashes on the upper deck, lose a crutch into the water, and nearly himself while he was at it, and by the end of the day was so damned sick and tired of being sick and tired.

He went to bed, frustrated and edgy.

Hours later Summer came to him, appearing in the doorway between the galley and his bedroom. The moon was high, the water quiet. Wordlessly she moved closer and stood at the foot of the bed, slowly letting the straps of one of those gauzy sundresses he loved so much fall off her shoulders.

"Any more text messages?" he asked, just for something to do with his mouth rather than drool.

"No," she said to the same question he'd asked her every

single day, and began working on the long row of tiny little buttons down the front of her dress. One, two.

She exposed a strip of smooth flesh.

"Uh . . ." His brain skipped. "Anyone with a size eleven-and-a-half shoe and a gallon of gasoline present himself recently?"

"Not exactly."

"What exactly?"

"I'll get to that in a minute." Three buttons. Four. She wasn't wearing a bra. The material slipped but clung stubbornly to her nipples.

His thoughts slipped as well.

Five buttons. Six. Their eyes met. In hers was a need, a hunger, and a deep, unwavering affection that turned his heart on its side. Her belly button ring gleamed in the moonlight, and he groaned as the material finally fell to her waist. She was the most beautiful thing he'd ever seen, and as her own hands lifted to cup her bared breasts, he stopped breathing.

Seven buttons. Eight. The material dropped to her hips, full and curvy and perfect for holding on to.

"Red." His voice was rough and serrated to his own ears. "You're not wearing anything beneath that dress."

She lifted her gaze and unerringly met his in the dark. "Not a damned thing."

And she let it fall.

She moved then, putting a knee on the bed, crawling slowly up his body until she sat astride his hips. "How was your day?" she asked as if they were having tea.

His hands came up and cupped her breasts. Her nipples beaded in his palms. "Sucked until now."

Her head fell back. "Mine, too. We found some discrepancies in Creative Interiors's accounting." Then she scooted aside to tug the sheet off him.

"What do you mean, discrepancies?" He wore only a pair of running shorts. Tented running shorts. She toyed with the elastic waist banding.

"There's some issues with the receivables," she finally said, her fingers making him twitch.

"Issues?" It was getting to be a struggle to keep track of this conversation.

"The amount of money deposited into the bank doesn't always match what was put in the register." She tugged his shorts down. With a little hum low in her throat, she wrapped her fingers around him.

"Red." He groaned, arching his hips helplessly. "I'm try-ing to concentrate here."

"So am I." She stroked long and slow, the way she'd learned he liked it, then reached into the drawer of his nightstand for a condom.

"How much money is missing?" he asked.

"Don't know yet."

"Who—" He broke off as she tore the packet open with her teeth and protected them both, taking her time about it too, dawdling with her fingers. "*Jesus.* Who had access to the account?"

"Everyone." She surged up and sank down on him, drawing him into her body to the hilt.

He swore, gripping her hips, gritting his teeth not to lose it at the feel of her, hot and wet, surrounding him. "Don't move," he begged, holding her still. "God, don't move."

"I can't help it." She wriggled, then ran her hands up his arms until their fingers were entwined on either side of his head. Leaning down, she kissed him softly, deeply, and his heart tumbled. "You feel so good, Joe. So damned good."

He pulled his hands free and rolled them, tucking her beneath him, flexing his hips, pressing her into the mattress, thrusting in deep. "And how do you feel?"

Arching into him, she wrapped her legs around his hips. "When I'm with you? Like I could walk on air."

As far as declarations of feelings went, it was a doozy. And it took him right over the edge. He made sure he took her with him.

An hour later he lay sprawled on his back, Summer snuggled up to his side, the cool night air drifting over their nude, still sweaty bodies.

Ashes had joined them and lay at their feet.

Summer was lazily trailing a finger over Joe's chest, occasionally tweaking his chest hair. He loved the way she touched him. He loved the way she panted his name when he was buried deep within her. He loved the way her smile lit up his life. And he loved how he felt when he was with her.

She shifted a little closer, cruising her mouth up his throat. Life didn't get better than this, he thought.

"Your foot is doing good," she murmured. "Isn't it?"

Sure, unless he stood on it for more than sixty seconds. "If you're worried, you can pamper me anytime. All the time." He lifted his head and propped it up with a hand. "Move in with me."

Her fingers went still on him. It was dark but he sensed the rest of her going just as still. "Or is that too involved with the future, which you don't do."

"You know I'm leaving." She pulled away from him. "You've known all along."

He reached out and flicked on the bedside lamp. "You said you'd come back this time."

She blinked like an owl and sat up, curling her arms around her legs. A defensive, closed-off pose. "Here and there."

Here and there. *Christ.* "I thought maybe, given all we've come to mean to each other, you could use San Diego as your base. Instead of San Francisco."

"That doesn't change the fact that I'm still gone more than I'm around."

"I'm not asking you to change your job, Red."

"No, you're only asking me to change my life."

"I love you. And goddamnit, I think you love me back."

She said nothing, just stared at him.

And though his heart cracked and separated into a million pieces within his chest, he let out a low laugh. "Okay, maybe you don't."

"Can't."

"Won't."

She tightened her mouth and looked at Ashes asleep at the foot of the bed. "I don't know what you want from me."

"Something you apparently can't give me," he said softly, feeling destroyed. He grabbed his shorts. "I'm sorry."

"Why are you sorry?"

"Because I let you think I could pull this off. That I could have a casual relationship with you and then let you walk away."

"No." Her voice was thick. "Remember in the beginning? You told me you couldn't handle me walking away again. You wanted to stay away from me, but I wouldn't let that happen. This is my fault, not yours."

"Yeah, well, whoever's fault it is doesn't matter." He felt raw. "I've gotta go."

At the word "go", Ashes leapt down, at the ready to follow him to the ends of the earth.

Joe stepped into his one shoe, grabbed his crutches.

"Joe, stop," Summer protested. "This is your place. *I'll* go." She slipped into her sundress and sandals, and then had to walk by him on her way to the door. She stopped to press her mouth to his.

He tasted lost dreams, broken hearts and tears, and he couldn't do it, he couldn't let her go. He snagged her hand, holding her to him.

She hesitated, then without looking back, pulled free.

"I don't want you to be alone," he said to her back.

"I'll stay with Chloe." And then she was gone.

Ashes sat on his good foot and whined softly.

"Yeah," he murmured, and stroked her head. "I know just how you feel."

Chapter 24

Summer spent the next few days trying not to think about anything other than numbers, because if she did, she just might realize that she'd walked away from the best thing that had ever happened to her. Her days seemed longer without Joe in them, the nights eternal.

It was as if a piece of her, the best piece, was gone. It was a huge gaping hole in her heart, and the biggest problem she'd ever faced. Needing to keep up some semblance of normalcy, she walked into Creative Interiors, the second biggest problem in her life.

Everyone agreed the fires were arson, but they remained unsolved. Now someone had stolen money from her mom and aunt right beneath their noses, probably someone she knew, and in all likelihood loved. Maybe even her own mother—which maybe made it not stealing at all.

Hell, she was so confused.

Everyone was at the store, and Summer attempted a broad smile. Attempted but did not achieve.

Tina put down a box and moved closer. "Darling?"

Camille was right behind her. "Summer, what is it?"

Be strong. Be sure.

Instead, she burst into tears.

Everyone shoved close—Camille, Tina, Chloe, the twins, even Stella and Gregg, who'd been bolstered by Camille and Tina's adamance of their innocence and had been working harder than ever.

Summer sniffed and looked around at the kind, friendly faces. "I screwed up."

"What? Honey, no you didn't. You're helping us, remember? You're doing a great job."

"With Joe. I screwed up a great thing with Joe, just because I was scared."

"Oh." Camille let out a long breath, going typically silent in the face of deep emotion.

"I once walked away from a great thing," Tina said, stroking Summer's hair. "I was too afraid to go for it."

"Who?" Chloe wanted to know.

Tina looked at her daughter. "Your dad."

Chloe gasped. "I thought he walked away from you! He was an artist. He left you and went to France."

"He wanted me to go with him." Tina sighed. "My biggest regret."

"I too walked away from a great thing once."

Everyone stared in shock at Camille, who'd spoken.

Her smile was a little shaky. "Actually, twice."

"Twice?" Summer asked.

"Your dad had to chase me."

"Once," Tina said. "He chased you once. You were fifteen."

"The second time wasn't Tim. It was more recent." At that, Camille's eyes locked on Summer's.

And she realized who. Kenny. She'd walked away from Kenny.

"And I regret it greatly," Camille admitted, gently

stroking Summer's hair. "Don't live with regrets, honey. It's just not worth it."

"Madeline and I warned you about your horoscope," Diana said. "Remember?"

Madeline nodded with her twin. Yes, they'd warned Summer.

"The only warning you gave me was to not get out of bed."

"Or something bad would happen. Which it did."

There was no arguing with Diana.

"I don't have a regret." Chloe flashed them the tiny braid of gold on her finger. "It's a promise ring. Braden's going to go back to school to become an accountant. We're going to make a real life, no matter what happens."

Gregg grabbed Stella's hand. "It's not about the regrets. It's how you deal with them."

"And how you learn from them," Stella said softly, squeezing Gregg's hand, smiling into his face. "We've made lots of mistakes, and have hopefully learned a lot."

"I have cookies," Madeline said, and everyone stared at her in surprise because she never talked. "Oatmeal raisin. I made them myself. Nothing heals a heart faster than oatmeal raisin."

So they sat around and ate cookies and drank herbal iced tea. Summer didn't feel any better afterward but she felt far less alone. That afternoon, Madeline and Diana took her out. Not to a college party or the mall, but on a bike ride along the beach. They culminated that with lying on the sand, soaking up some sun, eating ice cream, and talking about the male species. Diana confessed to having a thing for a guy who worked at the art gallery next to Creative Interiors, and Madeline for the frat boy who worked at the sandwich shop on the other side of the gallery.

"That's because he smokes with you," Diana said in disgust.

Summer went from relaxed to tense in zero point four. "You smoke?"

"I'm almost eighteen," Madeline said defensively. "And besides, it's my body."

Diana rolled her eyes. "And *my* lungs."

Summer kept her silence but her eyes cut to Madeline's feet, relieved to see she had nowhere near a size men's eleven and a half.

That evening after closing, Bill went with Summer to the bank. They'd been making the deposit in twos since the discrepancies had been discovered. Summer had barely begun to scratch the surface of figuring out how much money was missing, never mind who'd taken it. She had a lot of people interested in the outcome: Camille and Tina obviously, also the arson team, the police, and the rest of the staff. It was a big, black cloud hanging over all of them. A new nightmare.

"Are you getting anywhere with the records?" Bill asked her.

Summer lifted a shoulder. "Slowly."

They stared at each other somberly, knowing no one was going to like what they found.

"It's scary," she admitted.

"No one would blame you if you left now," he said very gently. "Your future isn't here."

"Really? So where is it?"

"None of us really know."

"But most of us at least know what we want."

He looked at her blandly.

"You don't?" she asked in surprise.

"What, just because I'm old, I'm supposed to know what I want to be when I grow up?"

"You're an artist."

"Yes, and by the very definition of that, I'm eccentric, addicted to antidepressant meds, and unreliable. I wouldn't recognize my future if it bit me on the ass. Look, Summer, all I'm saying is that it's okay not to know what you want to be. There's no need to settle."

"I'm not settling. And I know what I want to be. I'm an expedition leader." She out a long breath at his patient silence. "I know it's not rocket science. It's more like . . . brain candy. But that's what I am. Who I am. I like it. I just don't know *where* to be it."

"Of course you do." He ruffled her hair. "You just haven't admitted it yet. Look, it's simple. You want to head out of here, go. You want to stay, then stay."

"What would you do?"

"Ah, now that's even simpler," he said with a real smile. "I'd run far and long and never look back."

"Really?"

"Really."

But that's what she'd been doing. She'd been running for so long she thought maybe she was tired of it. It was easy to go. Even easier to stay gone.

And yet the alternative shook her to the core.

Joe had to take a taxi into work. This was because no one would pick him up and drive him there. It didn't matter that they'd claimed to desert him out of love. "That's bullshit anyway," he told Ashes on the ride. "If they loved me, they'd get their ass over here."

The cab deposited them at the fire station, where he paid a small fortune for the honor. By the time he'd maneuvered himself up the front stairs, with Ashes patiently sticking to his side, he had a line of sweat trickling down his back and was shaking like a baby.

Oh, yeah, he was in great shape. Just great.

He barged into Kenny's office and locked his legs into place so he wouldn't fall down. "Where are we with the Creative Interiors case?"

Kenny stroked Ashes, who'd leapt into his lap. "You look like hell."

"The case, Kenny."

"Nice to see you too."

"You just saw me," Joe pointed out. "Last night. You brought me Chinese."

"When you admitted your doctor told you to stay off work for another three weeks."

"Yeah, yeah. Listen, I've been going over the notes." Screw it, he was still shaking like a leaf, so he admitted defeat and sank into a chair. "But I'd like to see what else we've got."

"The only 'we' here is me and whoever the chief can spare to help me." Kenny's eyes flashed regret. "You know that."

"Don't block me out."

Kenny swore at that.

Joe rolled his eyes.

And Ashes, already aware of who was hers, jumped down from Kenny's lap and headed to Joe's.

"Please, Kenny. I need to *do* something. I'm losing it."

"*Christ.* Fine." Kenny tossed him a huge file. "We're still watching the regulars."

Joe read through everything carefully. "You and I both know that approximately eighty percent of the time, the owners turn out to be the culprits."

"Yeah," Kenny said miserably.

"Tina has an alibi. She was with her husband during both fires. The twins corroborated this, which gives all four of them an alibi."

"Right." Kenny's mouth went grim. "Which leads us to the second owner."

"Camille."

"She didn't do this," Kenny said firmly.

"There's no evidence against her," Joe agreed. "But we know she was holding back in the interviews. It was also out of character for her to call Summer that night of the second fire."

"You think she started the fire, then realized Summer was in there, and panicked?"

"She has insurance motive."

"She has plenty of money."

"Look, I know how you feel about her, Kenny."

Kenny just looked at him.

"I know because I'm there," Joe said quietly. "I'm in hell over her daughter, all right?"

"No, not all right. I'll give you that there's some circumstantial evidence against her. There's also the fact that the fires accomplished something nothing else had."

"They brought Summer home," Joe said grimly.

They both looked at each other for a long moment.

"Let's widen the scope," Kenny finally said. "Back to all the players for a minute."

"Okay." Joe flipped a few pages. "Braden told the truth about quitting smoking. His doctor confirmed."

"Yes."

"And Ally. She's never smoked, nor does she wear a man's shoe. She also, thanks to the art gallery owner next to her, the one who has a crush on her, has a rock solid alibi.

He was watching her through the windows. He saw her doing her books the night of the store fire."

"Creepy but correct."

"The twins."

"Too young for the first fire."

"Stella and Gregg," Joe said. "Neither of them smoke or have a size eleven-and-a-half shoe, though they have no alibi for either fire. Plus there's the fact they lost a store of their own, and kept that quiet. Revenge."

"Gee, Joe, you're good at this. Maybe you should get a job here."

"Ha ha. We need a real motive, Kenny."

"And a real suspect."

Joe leaned back in the chair, his head against the wall, his legs spread out in front of him. The exhaustion had set in. "My brain is so tired I could crash right here."

"You shouldn't even be here," Kenny said. "Where's your watch woman? I told Summer to keep you in bed."

"That's not really working out for us."

Kenny looked disgusted with him. "You kept your mouth shut again, didn't you?"

"Ironically, no. This time I opened up, all the way. And this time, unlike any of the others, I actually did the dumping."

"Well, that was stupid," Kenny said.

Joe had to agree.

That evening the phone rang while Joe was sharing a can of SpaghettiOs with Ashes.

"Summer needs you," Chloe said without a greeting.

"What?"

"Just get here. Oh, and don't tell her I called you."

He paid yet another cab driver yet another ridiculous

amount of money, and twenty minutes later got out in front of Chloe's condo. "Where is she?" he asked when Chloe opened the door.

"In the kitchen. I burned dinner and the smoke alarm went off. She sort of freaked."

He found Summer sitting on the counter, hugging her knees, staring out at the ocean. At the sight of him, she let out a long breath and shook her head at her cousin. "Damn it, Chloe."

Chloe chewed her fingernail. "I'm so not sorry."

"Well, I am." Summer turned to Joe. "You didn't have to come."

"Tell me what happened," he said.

"Nothing."

Chloe snorted. "You had a damn panic attack."

"Did not."

"Right." Chloe rolled her eyes at Joe. "I think I'll leave her to you."

When she was gone, Summer sighed. "I really am sorry. It's just that the alarm triggered some stupid response in me and in a heartbeat, I was back at that warehouse fire."

"There weren't any alarms at that fire."

Her eyes were clouded. "No, but when I woke up in the hospital, Tina was there, holding my hand. It was a few days later, and I was so groggy. I was awake for a few minutes before she realized, and she was talking to someone about the fire, and the lack of an alarm. I guess that stuck with me."

"Was she talking to your mom?"

She squeezed her eyes shut. "I can't remember. My head hurt. God, it hurt so bad."

"You took a good hit," he said quietly.

"Yeah." She rubbed her chest as if that hurt too. "I was pinned on the floor of the warehouse. Couldn't breathe."

Joe blinked. This wasn't a hospital memory, but from the actual fire. It was coming back to her?

"I can still hear my dad." Her voice broke. "I tried to get to him but the beam held me down."

Small tremors wracked her body and he limped closer, knowing she'd never remembered past this point. "Red, don't. It's okay—"

"I screamed. I wanted help. And through the smoke I saw someone, only they didn't come help me." She clapped her hand over her mouth and stared at him. "Oh my God."

He set down the crutches and put both hands on her arms, gently squeezing. "It was me. You saw me. I came up those stairs after you and was there right after you got hit."

"Yes, I could hear you calling my name behind me. I could hear you pounding your way up the stairs." She fisted her hands in his shirt and clung. "But in front of me, I saw someone else."

"Who?"

"I don't know." She closed her eyes tight and shook her head. "I don't know. But someone else was there, Joe. I know it."

"Your mother?"

"No. No, she couldn't have been."

"She's covering for something."

"Someone." Summer dropped her head to his chest and drew a shuddery breath. "I think she's covering for some-one."

"Tina?" Joe asked.

"Well, look at my timing," Tina said, and came into the room. "Chloe called your mom, darling, but she's not home, so you get me. I'm sorry it took me so long to get here. There's a jackknifed semi on I-5." She looked from Joe's face to Summer's, then back to Joe's. "Tell me what's happening."

"We're talking about the first warehouse fire," Joe said.

Tina's smile faded. "Oh."

"Someone else was at the fire that day," Summer said.

"Are you sure?" Tina's face was all concern as she hugged a clearly shaken Summer. "Darling, are you sure? Or are you wishful thinking?"

"There's nothing wishful about it. Someone else was there." Summer stared at Joe as the implications sank in. She was now a witness to a crime. To a possible murder. "Do you believe me?"

He looked into her eyes. "Yes."

"Thank you," she whispered.

"How about a hot bubble bath?" Tina asked. "That'll soothe your mind enough to help you sleep later, at least."

She nodded, and let Tina lead her out toward the hallway.

Joe knew she'd want to be alone. *And wasn't that half the problem.* He had no choice but to watch her walk away, and he had to wonder. When the hell would he get used to it?

They spent long hours working on the accounting discrepancies, not an easy process. Summer, Camille, and Tina started by figuring out which dates had cash missing from the deposit. This in itself was a huge chore, as the original deposit slips had not been kept with the daily records, but in a filing cabinet. Actually they'd been literally thrown into the bottom drawer and never looked at again. All the hundreds and hundreds of little white strips were in there like a tossed salad.

Summer had taken the job of pulling them out and putting them in order to compare with the bank statements. After that, she'd go back and figure out who had been working on each day, who had closed, and who had gone to the bank with the day's deposit. She didn't know what she'd find, but she knew she wasn't going to like it.

At the moment, Summer and Camille sat on the floor of the back office, alone. Tina had gone to pick up lunch. Chloe was working the front of the store with the twins. Summer was doing her best not to think about Joe. "This is shocking," she said flipping through receipts that dated back fifteen years. "You're both such smart, modern women. How did you get so completely record challenged? I mean, *fifteen* years, Mom."

"I know it looks bad, but the truth is, once a year we bring our accountant the general ledger from the computer printouts. He's never asked for paper backup. We never needed these little slips, you're lucky we even kept them."

"We could call the accountant for help now."

"Sure, but he'd cost a fortune, not to mention think we were the biggest idiots in town."

Summer's stomach rolled as she listened to her mother's reasoning. Was embarrassment the real issue here, or was there something else?

God, she hated this doubt, this never-ending fear.

Camille was sitting on the floor. "What I don't get is why you haven't run screaming for the hills." She wore a peasant blouse and a full denim skirt that was splayed around her, and four beaded bracelets up her right arm that jingled together with her every movement. "I'm beginning to think you're enjoying yourself here."

Summer looked into Camille's smiling but baffled expression. "I am, actually."

"You weren't at first."

"I know, but that was my fault. I kept you all at a distance. I'm good at that."

"What changed?"

"I don't think it's a what." Summer set down a fistful of deposit slips. "I think it's a who."

"Joe?"

Summer held her suddenly butterfly-ridden stomach. "Yes," she said in a hushed whisper as if giving away a soul-deep secret. It felt like one.

"Oh, honey. He's just what I would have wanted for you. Caring and compassionate, strong and kind. Like you."

Summer was so stunned that for a moment she couldn't speak. "You think I'm all those things?"

"I know it. Your dad used to say it all the time."

"Mom." Summer shook her head. "How come we never talk about him?"

Camille closed her eyes. "Too painful."

"It'd be less painful to let it out. I want to let it out. I've been thinking about everything for so long now: Dad, life, love. How to make the motions of going through it all."

"Having any luck?"

"No, and I'm going to lose Joe forever if I don't figure this out."

"I don't know, maybe it's a matter of getting past the fear."

Summer laughed. "You have a book for that?"

Her mom remained serious. "Maybe you just do it. Maybe you just leap. Without looking."

"That sounds painful."

"Not as painful as *not* living," Camille said. "Right?"

Just when Summer thought her mom not quite in touch,

she went ahead and said something so profound it set everything in its place.

"Of course," her mom added. "It's one thing to say leap. Another entirely to do it."

There came a soft knock on the door. They looked up to see Kenny standing in jeans and a polo shirt, looking tall and extremely GQish. No clipboard in sight. "Hi," he said, eyes on Camille. "Busy?"

"Uh, yes, actually," Camille said.

"No." Summer snagged the towering stack of deposit slips from in front of her mom and gathered them into her own pile.

Camille snatched them back.

"Mom." Summer leaned in and whispered, "Do it. *Leap.*"

Camille stared at her, then bit her lip as she tipped her head to Kenny. "I guess maybe I'm suddenly not so busy after all."

Kenny crouched next to her. "I'm off today. Thought maybe we could go have lunch."

"Lunch?"

"Sure, you remember, where we sit across from each other over food and talk. Smile. Even laugh."

Camille stared at him in indecision.

Kenny just waited with that endless patience of his.

"This is such a bad idea," Camille finally said. "It'll just lead to one thing or another . . ." She broke off, leaving Summer to wonder what exactly those "things" were, and had her mother and Kenny already done them?

Oh boy. Summer began to get up but Camille put her hand on Summer's arm. "I thought we agreed not to see each other any more."

"No," Kenny said. "We agreed to let you think about it.

Me, I'm done thinking. I want to see you after this investigation, no matter the outcome. I want to see you a lot."

"When I'm sixty, you're going to be fifty-three."

"And when I'm one hundred you're going to be one hundred and seven. Looks like we both know our math."

"Oh my God." Camille looked at Summer, just a little scared and a lot lost.

Leap, Summer mouthed.

Camille looked disconcerted at having her own advice flung back at her. "You should go out with a woman who will marry you and give you children," she said to Kenny.

"Camille," he answered with a low laugh. "I'm looking for a sandwich and some conversation. Not a white dress and a white cake and a new set of china."

Camille hesitated. "Well, I guess under those conditions, I could use a little nutrition."

He stood and held out his hand for hers.

"Hang on a minute." Camille pulled Summer aside. "Thanks for lending me some of your endless courage."

Courage? Is that what her mother thought she had?

"You're so full of life." Camille smiled, even as her eyes went misty. "So like your dad."

Summer's heart filled. "Mom."

"It's true. He'd never have done as I did, shutting myself off. Especially not from you. Promise you won't take after me and shut yourself off," Camille whispered fiercely.

Summer leaned in and kissed her mom, on first one cheek, and then the other. "I love you."

Camille gathered Summer in for a powerful hug, then pulled back, cupping her daughter's face. "We're going to be okay."

"Yes. Now go take your leap."

When Camille and Kenny left, Summer looked around

at the messy room. Now it was her turn to leap. Without looking. Without a safety net. Without a damn thing but her so-called courage.

That night, Summer went to her cottage instead of to Chloe's. She needed some clothes, and some alone time. It was dark and quiet, and feeling mentally and physically exhausted, she lay down on the couch and closed her eyes, telling herself she just needed a moment.

She woke up in the middle of the night to her cell beeping, signifying a new text message.

In the ensuing silence, her stomach clenched. It was never good to get a message in the middle of the night. It meant someone was hurt, sick, or dead.

Or it was Chloe, wondering where the hell she was.

She reached for the cell phone on the coffee table, retrieving the message with shaking fingers.

I've asked you nice. Now I'm not asking, I'm telling. LEAVE.

Chapter 25

Her heart pumped hard as Summer punched in Joe's number.

"Walker," he said, bringing her out of her mindless panic like no one else's ever had.

He sounded sleepy. He sounded . . . warm and rumpled, and damn, she'd missed him. She'd missed him so much. "It's just me."

"A bad dream?"

She didn't question how he knew something was wrong, it was the middle of the night. But even if it hadn't been, he'd have known because he'd pretty much always been that tuned in to her. "I have a problem."

"Define problem."

No longer sounding sleepy, he spoke in his fire marshal–calm, alert voice. She knew his eyes would be flat and unreadable. "I received a new text message." She read it to him.

"Where are you?"

Damn, she'd known he'd ask. "Don't get mad."

"Red—"

"I'm at the cottage."

"I'll be right there."

"Oh, no. Don't drive. I'm sorry, I didn't think— I should have called Kenny. I just got spooked. Anyway, it can wait until morning—"

"Red."

She gulped in a breath. "Yeah?"

"Lock your doors."

"I did."

"Keep your blinds shut."

Oh, God. "They are."

"Keep breathing, I'm already in my car."

"But you shouldn't drive."

"Too late."

"You have a clutch."

"Yeah." His voice was tight now, probably with pain. "I'll be fine." Indeed she could hear the engine roar to life. She realized she was rubbing her chest where it had pulled tight like a fist. "I'm sure I'm just fine," she said.

"I'm sure you are, too, though we're going to talk about why you're there alone." There was a slight edge to his fire marshal cool now. Temper, though not aimed at her. Okay, maybe some aimed at her.

"Where are you with the books?" he asked.

He was trying to keep her calm. Distracted. "Not far enough. I brought the stuff with me."

"How long until you have a list of everyone who made a deposit with missing cash?"

"Maybe never," she admitted. "I'm discovering that there's often no way to tell who made what deposit, and on the days everyone was at work . . ."

"You can't even guess."

"No. Because *everyone* goes to the bank, it just depends on who feels like it."

He was silent a long moment. Thinking. God knew about what.

She voiced her fear. "I'm thinking I'm hitting a nerve with someone."

"You certainly have a knack for it. Were you sleeping when the call came in tonight?"

"Dreaming," she said. "Joe—"

"Yeah?"

I missed you. I miss you so damn much. "Nothing."

"Jesus, Red. Just say what you're thinking. It can't be *that* hard to level with me."

It never had been, but now there were new and fairly terrifying feelings on the line, and she hadn't exactly dealt with them.

"Let me cut you a break since I figured you could use one," he said quietly. "I miss you. Is that anywhere in the ballpark of what you wanted to say?"

"You always could read my mind," she said shakily.

"I miss your smile," he said quietly. "I miss your laugh. I miss the way you make me laugh. I miss you teasing me, making sure I don't take myself too seriously. And I miss having you touch me at night. I really miss that."

"You have all the words," she whispered, her throat tight. "I don't know how you come up with such things."

"Just open your mouth and let it roll out."

"I'm not sure where to start."

"You could have called the police. You could have called Kenny. Or anyone. But you called me. There's a reason for that, Red."

"I wanted you." The words were on her tongue and out her mouth before she realized it. "I got scared and you were the only person I wanted. I miss you, too. Thanks for doing this, coming out here in the middle of the night."

"Don't thank me, I haven't yelled at you for being alone yet. There's a bunch of no-parking signs posted on your street."

"They're going to repave or something."

"I'm walking in from around the corner. Or hopping rather."

She hurried to let him in from the night. He wore a black T-shirt draped over his gun and faded soft Levi's that were molded to his long, tough form, hunched slightly these days as he used the crutches to walk. There was a Lakers cap on his head and a deceptively relaxed air to him as he moved toward her.

He held out his hand. She put the cell phone in it. Wordlessly he shifted gears and looked at the display. His jaw was scruffy, unshaven, and she stared at it while he read the text message. She remembered all the nights he'd rubbed that sexy stubble against her body, remembering the things he'd said to her, done to her, the way he'd made her feel. "I really did miss you," she whispered softly.

He looked at her for a beat. "I'm going to call this in." He hobbled into the kitchen, murmured into the phone for a few minutes, then hung up and faced her. "We'll go to the station in the morning to make a report. Do you have the accounting stuff you've been working through?"

"On the table."

"Let's look."

"It's two in the morning."

"Let's look," he repeated stubbornly.

They spent an hour at it, Summer showing him how she'd put the deposit slips in date order, and had painstakingly matched each to the bank statements. They typically made a deposit every day, sometimes every other. In the past twelve months, cash had gone missing out of approxi-

mately one deposit a week, the amounts varying from three
hundred and fifty dollars to two thousand dollars, for a total
of thirty-six thousand four hundred dollars.

Just for the past year.

"Multiply that by all the years they've been in business ... ." Joe let out a low whistle. "Someone's been getting a nice bonus. Let me see the employee schedule."

She handed it over, but that was a problem too. There
wasn't, and never had been, a regular schedule. Tina and
Camille kept it in their head, changing plans on a whim to
accommodate all of them. And even if a schedule had been
kept, it couldn't be relied on because of how often it would
have been adjusted at the last minute. So they went through
the payroll records, through each individual time sheet, and
began a new list, writing down the employees that had
worked each day there'd been cash missing. It took a few
hours, and when they were done, they had a new problem.

"Not a single person worked each of these dates," Summer said.

"Except . . ." Joe looked at her, his face impassive. His
fire marshal expression.

"My mother and Tina." She picked up the phone and dialed her mom, then listened to the phone ring and ring. "It's
five in the morning, and she's not home. She's probably
having another hot tub episode."

"Hot tub episode?"

"Yeah, her and Tina— Never mind." She dialed her
aunt's place and got a sleepy sounding Bill.

"I'm sorry," Summer said. "I know it's late. Or early, de-
pending on how you look at it. But these accounting books
have been calling my name all night. Are my mom and your
wife boozing in the hot tub again?"

"No, sorry, Camille's not here."

Summer had forgotten. Her mother had taken the leap. "How about Tina? Can I talk to her?"

"What's up, Cookie? Because I hate to wake her. She's been having such trouble sleeping."

"I know." Summer chewed on her thumbnail. "Listen, I wish I already knew this because it makes me sound like a horrible niece and daughter for having to ask, but . . ."

"What?"

"Neither of them are in financial trouble, are they?"

Bill laughed. "Those two penny-pinchers? Are you kidding?"

When Summer didn't laugh, he got serious. "Okay, what's the matter? What did you find?"

"Nothing concrete," she said, suddenly deciding this would be better done in person. "Tell Tina I'll meet her at the store in a few hours." She clicked off and sighed.

Joe was still sifting through the papers. "Let's keep going."

Half an hour later, with the sun coming up, Summer's cell beeped. Startled, she stared at Joe for a long breath, then looked at the message.

Stop remembering. Leave. *This is your final warning.*

Joe stared down at the digital display. "How spooked are you?"

"Uh . . ." On a scale of one to ten, make that a twelve, please. "Not too much."

"Truth."

"Truth?" She dropped her head to the table with a thunk. "I think my mother is covering for Tina. I think Tina is covering for my mother. And that it could be either one of them is making me want to throw up."

He put his hand on her back and stroked. "Your polite but terrifying stalker is trying to scare you out of here because you know something."

"I don't remember any more than what I've said."

"They're not sure of that."

"I'm not afraid of anyone here." She wasn't. Her terror was bigger than that. Such as the reality of seeing someone she cared about go to prison. "Much."

Joe sighed, then gathered her close. "Do you want me to stay?"

Being held by him was like coming home again. Shockingly good, shockingly right. "Yes, but it has nothing to do with being scared." She pressed her face to his throat and inhaled his scent.

"Red." This was a low groan. He let out another when she licked him. "Don't." His arms tightened on her in direct opposition to his words. "God, don't. I can't resist you. It's like every bad diet out there, I'm good for a day or two and then I have this terrible, clawing craving that I can't escape from."

"So let's satisfy the craving."

"I can't do this, Red. I can't make love to you and then get out of your bed and go home to my cold one. I hate connecting with you like I do, and then waking alone."

"Then don't go home. Wake up here, with me."

He fisted his hand in her hair and pulled her head back so he could see her face. His eyes were dark, his body tense.

"Don't go home tonight," she said again. "This morning. Whatever it is. Stay with me."

He cupped her jaw, ran his thumb over her lower lip. "Why?"

Leap. If her mother had done it, she sure as hell could at least try. "Maybe I want to try it on for size."

"Try what?"

"You." She smiled shakily. "Look, probably you've already realized, I'm a little slow at this stuff."

"No," he said wryly. "Really?"

She rolled her eyes. "I want you to be happy. I want to be the one to make you happy, but I have to go at my own pace, I just do. I can't speed that up, Joe. Not even for you."

He closed his eyes, then opened them again, and they were filled with things that caught her breath. He grabbed a crutch and stood up, reaching for her. "A bed this time," he said. "Your bed."

"Yes." Turning, she put her shoulder beneath his, acting as his crutch for that side, and led him to her bedroom. The sky had just barely begun to change, lighten. A new day.

Sunbeams slanted in through the shades, creating bands of light over her bed and the soft sheets and blanket there. He sat on them and drew her between his legs. "I like your pj's."

They consisted of an oversized white T-shirt and boxers. He wrapped his arms around her and hugged his face to her middle, rubbing his jaw against her belly in a sweet, loving gesture that had her throat tightening.

She tossed his cap aside and sank her fingers into his hair. He took his hands on a leisurely cruise down her spine, over the backs of her thighs, then her calves. Given how hot and explosive their past encounters had all been, she'd have expected him to dive in. Wanted him to dive in.

He didn't. He kept nuzzling her belly button, slowly bunching up her shirt until he could stick his tongue in her belly ring, then pressed a kiss to the curve of the abdomen she could never get quite flat, making her squirm.

He looked up. "What?"

"Maybe you could concentrate on a more flattering spot."

"Are you kidding me?" He palmed her belly, his fingers just barely dipping beneath the elastic of the boxers. "I love this spot. It's one of my favorites." He pushed her shirt up further, exposing her breasts, which hardened just because he looked at them. "Here are two of my other favorites." Leaning forward, he put his mouth on one nipple and his fingers on the other, tugging lightly.

She felt her eyes roll back. Then her T-shirt vanished over her head and sailed across the room. Joe kissed his way over to her other breast, his fingers hooking into the elastic banding of her boxers. "I do have a couple of other favorite spots," he murmured, and tugged. "Want to guess where?"

Her body was both humming and throbbing. She couldn't talk. She was halfway to orgasmic bliss from nothing more than his mouth and fingers stripping her naked.

"Mmmm," he murmured, dipping his fingers between her thighs. She was already wet. "Here's one."

She managed to pull at his shirt. "Lose this."

For a guy who was handicapped, he stripped down to his birthday suit so fast she got dizzy. Suddenly she was grateful for the bright slats of light because she loved looking at his amazing body. In fact, she could almost just look and be happy.

Almost.

She pushed him back on the bed and sat on him, bending low to brush kisses over his chest. With a groan, he tunneled his fingers into her hair and pulled her head to his for a long, hot, wet kiss that her panting for more. Then in one fluid movement he rolled, tucking her beneath him. "There," he said, and slid his hands up her arms, linking their fingers on either side of her head. "Now you won't be able to rush me."

"Rush you?"

"You have a tendency to race for the big bang." He kissed her shoulder, her throat.

"I like the big bang."

"You'll get it." He bit her jaw lightly. "Eventually."

He wasn't kidding. It took him forever. First he skimmed his hands over her, then replaced his fingers with his tongue, by which time she was writhing, begging, panting. He pulled her over the top of him, gripped her hips, and thrust into her with one stroke.

He held her like no other ever had, and when it was over, when she'd collapsed on his chest, gasping for air, sated and replete, he gathered her close and pressed his lips to her damp temple. They lay there for a long, relaxed moment.

"I can go home," he eventually said. "If that's what you want."

Her arms instinctively tightened on him. She wasn't frightened. She wasn't lonely either, or under the influence. She just wanted him to stay. An entirely new and not entirely unwelcome feeling. "I want you to stay," she said, and pressed closer.

Joe woke up with the sun fully risen, the smell of smoke stinging his nostrils and burning his lungs. He sat straight up, the remnants of an old nightmare claiming his senses.

He was alone in Summer's bed, surrounded by thick, clinging, choking smoke, so dark he couldn't see past his own nose. "Summer!"

He heard nothing but the ominous sound of flames fueling itself up, crackling, growing in strength.

Diving out of the bed, he hit the floor, sparing a moment

to writhe in agony because he'd forgotten about his foot. As that pain sang up his leg, stabbing into his brain, he lay low trying to get air for his already taxed lungs. "Summer!" he yelled again.

Still nothing but the popping of the flames. He crawled around the foot of the bed and saw the fire had overtaken the hallway and was biting at the bedroom door. He whipped around, back toward the bed, crawling over a shoe, which jabbed into his knee, reminding him that he was naked. Grabbing his jeans from the floor, he wrestled them on and then headed for the window. Up on his knees, he tried to push open the glass but the heat had stressed the wood, and it wouldn't budge. Whipping around he snatched the blanket off the bed, wrapped his arm in it and punched the window. The fire was so loud behind him as it ate its way into the bedroom, he couldn't even hear the tinkle of the glass as it fell to the ground outside.

He climbed out of the window and stood barefoot in the planter, surrounded by jagged glass and a burning cottage. "Summer!"

In the early morning light, fire trucks came careening up the street, lights and sirens flashing. Fast as he could, heart in his throat, Joe limped around to the front door. It was engulfed with flames, so he kept going, hopping on his one good foot until he got to the back door. He had to find Summer, but just as he reached for the handle, the door blew out, and he flew backward, knocked flat on his ass by pieces of glass and wood.

Before he could get to his hands and knees, there were three firemen there, holding him back. "She's still in there!" he yelled. His head was spinning, and something trickled down his temple. "I don't think she got out!"

"Joe!"

He whipped around and nearly sank to his knees with relief. Summer was racing up the beach. She wore running shorts and a tank, and was breathing as if she'd run miles. She probably had. He tugged free of the hands trying to hold him back from the fire and staggered down the steps, meeting her halfway.

"What happened?" she gasped, staring up at the cottage going up in flames behind him.

"I woke up surrounded by smoke." He hauled her into his arms and buried his face in her hair. She felt like warm, soft woman, and he didn't think he could let her go. If he did, he was going to fall down. Way down.

She pulled back to see his face and touched his forehead. "You're cut."

Now he knew how disconcerting a panic attack could be. He couldn't breath. "I thought you were—" He couldn't even say it. Spots danced in his vision, and he had to squint to see through them. He was still shaking from just thinking about what could have happened to her. Or maybe that was from being hit by the exploding front door, but his world began to spin. *"Christ."*

"We've got to get you to the paramedics."

He was a little surprised to still be upright because his vision had narrowed to a tunnel. "It's nothing. Jesus, Red, I thought you were—"

With a soft sound, she wrapped her arms around his neck and burrowed close. "I couldn't sleep. I didn't want to wake you—I'm so sorry. I'm so sorry." Again she pulled back and gently touched his face. "I think you singed off an eyebrow."

He also had a few burns on his bare chest, which had begun to send waves of pain to his brain. Each knee was fairly screwed up as well, but it was his foot that was killing him.

And those damn spots. Ah, hell. They were mingling together, so now his entire view was blurry—

She backed him to the curb. "Sit." She whipped around to get help.

He opened his mouth to reassure her, but she threw her arms around him and hugged him so tight he couldn't breathe. Could hardly hear—

"I love you," she whispered in his ear as his head began to buzz. "God, Joe, I love you so much."

He opened his mouth but everything was spinning wildly. His vision faded. Oh, no. Hell, no. Not now. He wasn't going to pass out *now*.

She was still talking to him. He knew this because her lips were moving, her eyes lined with concern and fear, but he couldn't hear.

And then everything went to black.

"Scared the hell out of me," Kenny said, and sat on Joe's hospital bed. "Don't do that again." He pushed up his glasses. "Not ever again."

Joe blew out a breath and slowly, carefully sat up. "How long have I been here?"

"You don't remember?"

The last thing he remembered was passing out in Summer's arms. Had she really said she loved him? Or had that been just another fantasy? "Fill me in."

"The cottage is gone. A complete loss."

"Damn." Joe shook his head, then groaned and held it on his shoulders. "Note to self, don't move."

"Not with your concussion, I wouldn't."

"We've got our work cut out for us."

"We? I've already started, on the way over here. Did you know the cottage was Tina's? Not a business property either, but personal."

Joe went very still, mostly out of necessity, but some out of shock. "Summer told me the place was Chloe's roommate's. I assumed it was owned by the roommate's family."

"Nope."

"Shit." It all clicked into place with a ferocity that made his head spin. His heart began to pound. "Where's Summer?"

"Camille and Tina showed up just as you were being forced into the ambulance kicking and screaming."

"Very funny."

"Well you didn't exactly go graciously. They were going to bring her here. They haven't shown up yet."

"How long ago?"

"Twenty minutes."

Joe shoved his sheet aside.

Kenny leaned forward and put a hand on him, holding him down. "What are you doing?"

"Gotta go."

"Whoa. The doctor said—"

"I've figured this thing out." Joe put his good foot to the floor. "Crutches."

"Your ass is hanging out—"

"Jesus! Get me some clothes then. Just hurry."

To Kenny's credit he did just that. "We're going to have to break you out of here, you know that, right?"

"Did you hear me say I figured this thing out?"

Kenny handed him his crutches, his face impassive. "Yes."

"It's not Camille."

Kenny stared at him, then let out a slow breath. "I knew that."

"Get me out of here and I'll tell you on the way."

"On the way where?"

"To save Red's life."

Chapter 26

How ironic was it that she'd finally told Joe she loved him and he'd passed out before he could hear it? Summer couldn't believe it. She had to see him, but she looked out the window of her aunt's car and frowned. They were pulling into the burned-out warehouse instead of heading toward the hospital. "Where are we going?"

Tina got off her cell phone with Bill, turned off the engine, looked somberly at her sister riding shotgun, and then at her niece in the backseat. "I want to finish this first."

"Finish what?"

"Bill suggested I do it here, and I think he's right. Everyone out." Tina shut the door and walked toward the burned warehouse. As they hadn't yet decided whether to rebuild or lease something else, no work had been done yet.

Camille looked at Summer as she got out of the car. She shrugged and followed Tina.

"Damn it," Summer said to no one, and got out, too, just as her cell phone rang. It was Joe. "God, Joe, are you okay?"

"Yes. Red, listen to me." He sounded so urgent. "Tell me exactly where you are."

"At the warehouse, if you can believe it. We were coming to see you when Tina decided to stop and have a fight with my mom."

"I'm on my way," came his terse reply. His fire marshal voice.

"But I thought—"

"Where are Tina and your mom?"

"Inside, I think. Mom?" she called out as she entered the damaged open hull where the front door had once been. Everything was blackened and grimy, and she forgot about the earlier fire, forgot about Joe as she was hit with a terrible sense of déjà vu.

That long ago day she'd been choking with smoke as she'd run through, desperate to get to her father. She'd made it to the very spot where she stood, and now her feet felt rooted as her breathing quickened. Oh, God, not now. "M-mom?"

"Up here."

Tipping her head up she looked at the loft. All around her were burned-out walls and soot. The railing on the stairs was gone completely, though the stairs seemed intact.

If she closed her eyes she could hear the flames. Could feel the heat searing her. Could taste the smoke. Her chest tightened. "I don't like this," she said to herself, and phone still in her hand at her side, trailed after her mom and aunt.

The north and east walls of the loft were scorched. The south and west walls were down to the wood studs, allowing a view below to the main floor. In some places, where parts of the floor had collapsed, they could see all the way through to the basement.

Camille and Tina stood in the middle of the room, right where Tim's desk used to stand. Uneasy with the height, Summer didn't look down. "What's going on?"

Camille looked at Tina.

Tina reached for her sister's hand. "It's time to find out."

Camille looked worried. "Tina—"

"I love you, Camille."

Camille's eyes filled. "I love you, too. I figured you had a good reason for taking the cash. And if you needed it, I wanted you to have it."

Tina's eyes widened. "What?"

"But now I'm afraid that you taking the money is somehow related to these fires, and that's killing me."

Tina shook her head. "No, I—"

"I never believed you started any of the fires," Camille told her. "It never even occurred to me. But then Summer came back and began digging around—"

"Hey," Summer said. "I wasn't digging—"

"And you changed," Camille told Tina in a shaky voice. "You got scared, and so did I. If you had anything to do with this fire, Tina . . . my God. I don't know how to deal with that."

"Camille—"

"You didn't want to rebuild, you wanted the cash from the insurance. I never understood that back then. But then we eventually rebuilt anyway and life went on. Then it burned again, and then the store, where Summer nearly died—" Camille's put her fingers to her mouth. "And then she started getting those text messages. You were trying to scare her away. I was so terrified for the both of you, I didn't know what to do. I tried to talk her into going, but she wouldn't. I just wanted her safe."

"I thought you didn't want me here at all," Summer said softly.

"Oh honey, no," Camille whispered. "I was just scared."

Tina looked sick. "You think I'd hurt Summer?"

"I think you're in trouble with money somehow, and not thinking clearly."

"Camille, I thought *you* were taking the money! *I* was covering for *you*! That's why I brought you here. Bill said I should just get it all out with you."

The sisters blinked at each other.

Summer divided a gaze between them. "Are you telling me neither of you took the money? Or had anything to do with the fires?"

Camille shook her head.

So did Tina.

"But if it wasn't either of you," Summer said slowly. "Then . . . who?"

Tina and Camille stared at each other for a long beat. "No," Tina whispered, then staggered back a few steps to sit on a box.

Camille just gaped at her. "You really think—"

"Who else? Oh my God, who else?"

"But you said he was with you during the fires. You said you were both sleeping."

"I know, but I sleep like the dead. He could have . . ."

"And you didn't know," Camille breathed softly. "You really didn't know."

Tina put her hands over her mouth and shook her head.

Camille dropped to her knees in front of Tina. "Oh, sweetie. Oh, God. I'm so sorry."

There was a creak on the stairs behind them, and the scent of a lit cigarette. Summer whipped around and saw black boots. Painter's pants. An old T-shirt with ceramic stains across the chest. An apron over hips carrying an assortment of tools for working with clay that clinked when he walked.

Bill.

She closed her eyes, and lost the twelve years in a flash. That day, when she'd run up the basement stairs and into the fire, crying for her father, she'd seen black boots and painter's pants, just before her world had gone black. "You," she whispered, her grip tightening on the cell phone at her side. *Joe.* She hoped he was still there, listening. "It was you." Fear took a backseat to rage. Pure, unadulterated rage. "You killed my dad—"

"No," he said, with real regret in his eyes. "I didn't kill him."

"You did."

"No, damn it. He was supposed to get out of here. I called him to make sure of it. He was supposed to meet me for a drink, but he didn't listen, he never fucking listened, that's all."

"That's all?" Tina yelled. "*That's all?* What about what you nearly did to Summer?"

His eyes were tortured. "She got out. She wasn't killed."

Tina let out a growl. Eyes wet and wild, she lunged at him.

Bill whipped out one of his tools, a nasty-looking sculpting tool with a jagged edge, and wielded it like a knife. "God, Tina, don't. Please don't make me use this, not on you."

Camille caught Tina around her middle and held fast.

Tina was staring at her husband as if he'd grown a second head. *"Who are you?"*

Bill's eyes were damp. "I'm so sorry. I just wanted the money, I swear. None of this other stuff was supposed to happen."

"You wanted the money for the racetrack."

"Yes."

Tina looked sucker punched. "You should have told me, why didn't you tell me?"

"You said you'd leave me if I got into trouble gambling again." He shifted on his feet, looked down at the weapon in his fingers as if surprised to find it there.

"Again?" Camille asked, confused.

"He was an addict," Tina admitted, struggling against her sister's hold. "But I thought he'd recovered years ago, and had it under control. My God, Bill—" She let out an anguished moan and covered her face.

"I'm not a bad guy," he whispered. "I'm not. I just kept having this unlucky streak, see." He was blocking their exit, breathing erratically as he looked at Tina with tears in his eyes. "All I wanted was for you to come into the insurance money. I just needed the extra cash, that's all. The warehouse paid off nicely, remember? You lent me money for my old debts."

"Oh, Bill."

"I had some nice winning streaks after that. Lasted a good long time. I didn't think it'd be necessary to do it again, but then I ran into another bad row." He looked so baffled at that, that Summer couldn't reconcile the two different Bills—the sweet artist . . . and the murderer.

"You killed Tim." Tina shook her head and clung to her sister. "And you nearly killed Summer and Joe!"

Bill was shaking. "No. It was never about Tim." His gaze landed on Summer. "Or you. I thought you couldn't remember the fire, but that changed. I'm so sorry. And it certainly wasn't about Joe. I didn't even know he was there that night, I didn't see his car." He shook his head, looking more than a little crazy with his wild shock of gray hair waving around his face. "I'm sorry, I'm so sorry. But I just kept thinking that insurance is just one big huge scam anyway. No one was supposed to get hurt."

"It's too late for that." Tina turned in Camille's arms to bury her face and burst into tears.

"So what now, Bill?" Camille asked, holding her sobbing sister. "What are you going to do?"

Bill's eyes shone with a tortured regret. "I don't have a choice. There's going to be one more fire." He backed down a step. "One more terribly tragic fire." He looked at the burning tip of his cigarette. Reaching into his pocket he pulled out some sort of remote. "I've learned a few things along the way. This time no one's going to find any accelerant, or Tim's old size eleven-and-a-half boot print." He lifted his foot. "I've had these since the day he lent them to me fourteen years ago." He let out a low grief-stricken sigh. "Don't worry, this'll be quick." He held up the remote.

"Bill," Tina choked out. "Don't."

"I have to," he whispered.

"You won't get away with this," Summer said, and took a step toward him.

He lifted his lethal looking gouging tool. "I don't want to use this, damn it. Just stay right there, and it will all be over soon, I promise." He began to back down the stairs.

Go after him, a voice screamed inside Summer's head. *Don't let him do this.* She took a furtive step, and saw a long, lean shadow flattened on the lower stairs. *Joe.* Seeing him gave her courage, and she took another step.

"Summer, no," her mother breathed.

Bill began to turn away, toward the shadow, and afraid for Joe, Summer made a split second decision. She leapt at Bill—and landed on the top few steps, arms empty, air flattened right out of her lungs. Joe had surged up, wrapped his arms around Bill's lower legs, and pulled.

Bill went down hard, but so did Joe, the two of them entangled on the narrow, steep stairs. Wrestling, they grappled for space at the very edge, dangerously close to where the railing had collapsed.

Summer shoved upright to her knees. "Joe! Careful—"

But they rolled right off.

And fell into the dark, open chasm.

Chapter 27

Summer staggered to her feet. Tina and Camille flew to the side, all braced for the impending explosion from Bill's rigged device.

Nothing.

Summer flew down the stairs, then stopped in horrified shock at the gaping hole in the main floor.

The two men had fallen straight through to the basement below. Heart in her throat, she dropped to her knees at the torn, splintery edge. "Joe!" she cried.

From the terrifying black silence came a beam of light. Kenny was down there, on his knees, speaking into his radio, calling for an ambulance. His glasses were crooked, his face filthy when he looked up.

"Kenny," she cried urgently. "There's some sort of a device—"

"I got it."

"Joe—"

"I've got him, too. Listen to me, Summer. All of you. Back up away from the edge."

He didn't want her to see, which meant it was bad. Camille had dropped down next to Summer, gripping Tina with one hand, her daughter in the other. Summer looked into Tina's blank and shocked eyes, and then back at Camille. "I love you both," Summer said fiercely, knowing she'd never hold back those words again. Not ever. And then she ran for the stairs that would lead her down to Joe.

Kenny quickly moved to block her way. "Summer—"

She shoved around him. Joe lay on his side, covered in dust and debris, eyes closed. "Oh my God."

"Don't move him."

"I won't." His big, long, beautiful body was far too still. Whipping around, she searched out Bill. He was there sitting up, his back to a wall, his leg bent at a funny angle, cradling his arm, his face pale and clammy, eyes closed. Summer didn't waste another second on him and turned back to Joe, dropping to her knees at his side.

In the distance came the sirens, and she nearly cried in relief. "Hang on," she told Joe. "You hang on." She covered one of his hands in hers. It was warm with life, and she bowed her body over his, as if she could protect him, but it was too late for that. He'd put it all on the line.

For her.

"I love you." She stroked a light finger over his jaw. "Joe. I love you so much. Please hear me."

Pounding footsteps hit the stairs, and then there were more lights, and she was gently shoved out of the way. The paramedics moved Joe onto a stretcher with a c-collar and a firm backboard, immobilizing him, and then began an IV.

Surrounded by Tina and Camille, Summer watched him being loaded into the ambulance, then Bill into another one, with a police escort.

"I'll take all of you to the hospital," Kenny said.

Camille hugged him hard, then cupped his face and kissed him right on the lips. "Yes, take us to the hospital. And then you can take me. Anywhere. I'm yours."

Kenny let out a rough sound and hauled her close for a tight, hard hug.

At the hospital, the doctor came out and looked at Summer. "Mrs. Walker."

"Yes," she said without qualm. "Tell me."

"He's in ICU. Stab wound to the thigh, broken sternum, three cracked ribs, and we're watching his O2 stats to make sure his lungs are okay. He's also got a severely bruised spinal cord and a concussion. No elevation of intracranial pressure so far, which is promising."

Summer covered her mouth, nodded her head. "Can I see him?"

"One at a time for brief periods of time."

He lay so still in the bed, one arm and shoulder in a sling, the rest of him covered in sheets and bandages, and connected to all sorts of machines that bleeped and blipped. But his chest rose and fell, and keeping her eyes on that, she sat next to his bed and stroked his fingers. "That was a damn stupid thing to do," she told him. "I had things under control. You didn't have to be the hero. You didn't have to try to save me." She stared at his far-too-still face. "I've been so stupid, Joe, so slow, and all along, the truth was there." She leaned in, close to his ear. "You are my whole life. I don't know how I ever lived it without you." A tear escaped and she sniffed, wishing she had a tissue but not wanting to leave his side for a second. "Are you listening to me, Joe Walker?"

"Hard not to." Eyes still closed, he grimaced, and licked his dry lips. "You're shouting."

"Oh my God. Joe! I love you so much."

"Well look at that," he said slowly, eyes still closed. "You didn't . . . choke over it."

She let out a laughing sob. "No, I didn't choke on it."

"How bad is Bill?" He spoke very softly, as if it hurt to talk.

No doubt, it did. It must hurt to even breathe. "Just a few bumps and bruises. He's going to jail."

"Tina?"

"Joe, please," she begged. "Don't worry about any of us. Just rest."

Opening his eyes, he took in her face, then blanched. "You're crying." He closed his eyes again. "Oh, Christ. I finally get you to say you love me and I'm dying."

"You're not—"

"My head's going to fall off. And I have this pain in my chest—"

"That's the concussion and the broken ribs."

"No. I see a bright white light. You'd better devote yourself to me for the few minutes I have left. Let me die a happy man. Just say you'll marry me. Then I can let go."

"Joe." She had to laugh. "I'd promise you the moon, but—"

"Red." His pupils weren't the same size and there was a world of pain swimming in those whiskey orbs. "Just say 'yes, Joe.'"

Her heart stopped. "Are—are you serious?"

"As serious as falling thirty feet."

Her heart kicked back into gear, slamming against her ribs. "But we can't—you can't just—"

"I'm dying," he reminded her.

"You're not—"

"Humor me."

"Okay, but my job—"

"I don't care. I don't care if you come and go daily. Just mostly come, and be mine while you're at it."

She bit her lower lip. "I don't want to go at all. I want to stay here in San Diego and run day trips. I want to be home every night. I want to be with *you* every night—"

"Excuse me, Mrs. Walker." His nurse rushed in to the cubicle, followed by the doctor. Both shooed her out of their way and began asking Joe questions. Did he know where he was? Did he know what year it was? Could he see clearly?

"All I know is that I hurt like hell and you're blocking my way," he said. "I'm trying to talk to my almost fiancée."

The nurse frowned. "You're already married. You don't remember?"

A slow smile broke out over Joe's face as he studied Summer. "Oh, yes. It's all coming back to me."

"Excuse me," the nurse said to Summer. "You're going to have to leave now."

"Don't go far," Joe said. *"Wife."*

Summer looked back at him. Though his eyes were closed again, his mouth was shooting her a crooked smile that flashed his dimple. "I love you, Joe."

"Hold that thought. You're good at that."

Unbelievably she laughed through her tears. "Maybe I was, but no more. Life is too damn short. I'm not holding back on anything, not ever again."

"I'll take that in writing," he said, just as the nurse pushed her out and slid the curtain shut in her face.

"I love that woman ridiculously," she heard him say to the doctor, and her entire heart just tipped on its side. She turned and saw her mother waiting, her hand in Kenny's. Next to her stood Tina. Chloe and the twins had shown up, too, and they had their arms around their mom, Chloe chomping on a big wad of bubble gum, Diana clutching a magazine, Madeline with her head on her mom's shoulder.

The whole gang. The whole family.

Rallying for one of their own.

As she moved toward them, Summer realized they'd all stiffened, their faces drawn with fright and concern. And she realized she had tears streaming down her face and that she must look like a complete wreck. "It's okay," she said. "He woke up."

They let out a collective sigh. Everyone hugged, and then Summer took her mom's hands. "I'm going to stick around for a while. What do you think?"

Camille cupped her face. "I think I could get used to that."

"Me too," Summer said, and turned when the nurse stuck her head out of Joe's cubicle.

"Mrs. Walker? We need you back in here. He won't co-operate unless he can see you."

Indeed Joe was arguing with another nurse over something, and just the sound of his voice made her heart sigh. She could get used to that too, she decided. Very used to that, and moved to stand at his side. "Problem?"

"Tell me again," he demanded and gripped her hand tight. "I want to make sure I wasn't dreaming."

Her heart melted. "I love you."

He sighed and relaxed, and let out a smile. "So it was real."

"As real as it gets," she promised and sat at his side.

EPILOGUE

Six Months Later . . .

Summer sat on the beach not too far from the pier, sipping from a strawberry shake. Her diamond ring twinkled in the sun. She'd had it for months and she still couldn't stop looking at it. "Trade," she said, and took back her frozen yogurt from Joe.

Ashes sat at their feet, perfectly alert, watching every "trade" with careful, hopeful eyes.

Joe shook his head. "She's worse than having a kid. Can you imagine?"

Though she knew he truly couldn't imagine having a child, their child, *she* could. The past six months had been heaven on earth for her. She'd begun her own expedition company, all of her treks right here in Southern California, and it fulfilled her like nothing else had.

Except this man. He fulfilled her. He fulfilled her heart and soul, and she was ready to do as she'd promised him six months ago in the hospital. She wanted to be his wife. She wanted him in her bed every night, and her biggest secret . . . she wanted his children.

"Red?" With a finger to her chin, he tipped her face up,

concern creasing those eyes she loved so much. "What are you thinking about?"

"I can imagine having a kid," she whispered. "*Your* kid, with your beautiful eyes, and kind, huge heart, with your passion and strength and love of life. I can imagine it, Joe, because you'd make the best dad in the world."

His eyes slid to her belly, which while not exactly flat, did not have a baby in it. "I'm not pregnant," she said quickly. "I'm just saying."

He stared at her, his shake forgotten. "Red—"

"I know." She managed to smile past the lump in her throat. "You aren't interested. It's okay."

"It is? Are you sure?"

She took his hand. "Kids I can live without. What I can't live without, Joe, is you."

His eyes went suspiciously bright and he brought her hand to his mouth, kissing her palm. "You humble me right to the core. You know that? And the truth is, kids might be a part of this adventure I shouldn't miss."

Her heart was going to burst right out of her chest. "Joe."

Leaning in, he nipped at her jaw, her ear. "In fact . . ." he murmured.

Her pulse raced, her eyes drifted closed. "Let's begin practicing?"

"I thought you'd never ask . . ."

National bestselling author
JILL SHALVIS
is turning up the heat.

BLUE FLAME
0-451-41168-4

When San Diego firefighter Jake Rawlins is injured in a fire, he retreats to the Blue Flame, the Arizona guesthouse he inherited from his father. He wants solitude, but finds Callie Hayes, the ranch's tempestuous manager. Neither Jake nor Callie can forget their stormy past. But Jake has changed, and soon he's setting off sparks hot enough to change Callie's life forever.

WHITE HEAT
0-451-41142-0

Bush pilot Lyndie Anderson lives only for her plane and the open sky, and she'd like to keep it that way. Firefighter Griffin Moore hasn't been himself since an Idaho wildfire claimed his entire crew. But when Lyndie is hired to fly Griffin into the heart of a raging inferno, the sparks of desire begin to fly...

Available wherever books are sold or at
www.penguin.com

o861

All your favorite romance writers are
coming together.

SIGNET ECLIPSE

COMING JUNE 2005:
Beyond the Pale by Savannah Russe
My Hero by Marianna Jameson
The Chase by Cheryl Sawyer

COMING JULY 2005:
Much Ado About Magic
by Patricia Rice
Love Underground: Persephone's Tale
by Alicia Fields
Private Pleasures by Bertice Small
Lost in Temptation by Lauren Royal